PRAISE FOR DEAD LETTERS

A fiery family drama unfolds in this compulsively readable mystery. *Dead Letters* has it all—priceless stolen artifacts from an archeological dig, kidnapping, murder, handwriting analysis, and terrorism. Tension mounts as Lowe holds readers captive with her latest international adrenaline rush.

— Laurie Buchanan, author of the Sean McPherson Novels

Dead Letters is an entertaining thriller set in Egypt, Gibraltar, Arizona and London, starring two heroines, an expert handwriting analyst and her intrepid niece. This novel will get your heart racing and also give you a fun education on ancient Egypt history at the same time.

— Matt Witten, bestselling author of *The Necklace*

Dead Letters is a delicious romp through exotic locales with relatable characters and fascinating tidbits about archeology and handwriting analysis sprinkled throughout. Lowe's recipe for tension had me at the first paragraph, and I feasted on the twists and turns until the very last page. If you want to treat yourself to a fun read, this is *it*!

— Saralyn Richard, award-winning author of the Detective Parrott mystery series and *A Murder of Principal*

Whether hunting a terrorist cell across Europe or suffering through a young woman's first whirlwind romance, Sheila Lowe's *Dead Letters* knows how to keep a reader turning the pages until the heart-pounding finish.

— August Norman, author of the Caitlin Bergman Thrillers

BOOKS BY SHEILA LOWE

FORENSIC HANDWRITING SERIES

POISON PEN

WRITTEN IN BLOOD

DEAD WRITE

LAST WRITES

INKSLINGERS BALL

OUTSIDE THE LINES

WRITTEN OFF

DEAD LETTERS

BEYOND THE VEIL MYSTERIES

WHAT SHE SAW (PREQUEL)

PROOF OF LIFE

NONFICTION

READING BETWEEN THE LINES: Decoding Handwriting

ADVANCED STUDIES IN HANDWRITING PSYCHOLOGY

PERSONALITY & ANXIETY DISORDERS: How They May Be Reflected in Handwriting, And Other Important Topics

THE COMPLETE IDIOT'S GUIDE TO HANDWRITING ANALYSIS

HANDWRITING OF THE FAMOUS & INFAMOUS

to [illegible]
with all good wishes
[illegible]

DEAD LETTERS

A CLAUDIA ROSE NOVEL

SHEILA LOWE

ISBN-13: 978-1-970181-15-9 (Paperback)
ISBN-13: 978-1-970181-16-6 (EPUB)

Library of Congress Control Number: 2021908994

Cover Design: Terry Rydberg, Fine Print Design
Book Design and Project Coordination: Victoria Rydberg-Nania

Write Choice Ink
Ventura, California
www.sheilalowebooks.com

ACKNOWLEDGMENTS

Long before psychics told me I was a scribe in a past life—since I was six years old—I was fascinated by Ancient Egypt. I never made the trip myself, but more than a year ago, I was lucky enough to find renowned archaeologist Dr. Pierce Paul Creasman, whose generosity with his time and information gave that part of the book far greater veracity than it otherwise would have had. I deeply appreciate his patience with my many emails and all questions answered.

Likewise, thanks are due to Arizona attorney and author Chris de Rose, and Tucson-specific attorney Janet Altschuler, who helped me navigate the differences between the California and Arizona legal systems. Also, to Derek Pacifico, who, as a former detective and police chief, knows how prisons work. Always, thanks to my friend and fellow author and former FBI Special Agent dude, George Fong, for everything I need to know about that stuff.

The fabulous cover is the work of Terry Rydberg. Everything else in getting the book out into the world can be attributed to her stunning, amazing (there are not enough superlatives) daughter, Victoria Rydberg-Nania. Thanks too, to Ruth Castleberry, who lent her long expertise in marketing, and to David Ivester for all he's done for me, above and beyond.

More gratitude goes to the usual suspects: Bob Joseph, always my first reader and critiquer; to Gwen Freeman of the original SCVW group. To Ellen Larson, who has been my editor since the first edition of Poison Pen. To author friends, Peg Brantley and Chassie West for having the forbearance to read an early draft, and to my street team, the Write Choice Inkers, who read the final one. And certainly not least, thanks to my longtime friend, Nina Nelson, and devoted reader, Linda Hall, for their eagle eyes in spotting my many typos.

England was my original home, and the last trip I took there was made extra-special by knowing I was going to write about it in *Dead Letters.* Thanks to my cousin Lisa's husband, Elliott Field—I didn't ask if it was okay to use him as Claudia's reporter friend again, but I used him anyway. And though he won't see this, thanks to Romulus my Uber driver, with whom I shared a fascinating conversation between Heathrow and Tower Hill in London.

Gibraltar was the birthplace of my great-great-grandmother, Carolina Maria de Perera Garcia Clarke. After wanting all my life to see it firsthand, that dream coming true was due in no small part to the efforts of cousins, Moira and Roger Potten. And, she didn't know it, but cousin Carol Gates' flight from Italy and the long bus ride from Malaga helped, too. Besides that, they all put up with me being unable to hear much of anything after getting an ear infection on the plane over from UK. The Rock Hotel is as classy as Claudia experiences it, and inability to hear notwithstanding, staying there was a thrill.

I hope you enjoy reading *Dead Letters* as much as I enjoyed writing it.

1

MONICA

SOMETIMES, THERE IS A MOMENT WHEN EVERYTHING THAT COMES afterward—the excitement that fizzes up and bubbles over, the fear that threatens to overwhelm, even the pain—when every decision, every act feels as though it were pre-ordained.

The journey officially began at the Mortuary Temple, but looking back, Monica realized the magic had been in the air at the Crocodile the previous evening—the thrill of celebrating dig season's opening day. The lively chatter of people having a good time. Traditional Egyptian folk music, passed down two thousand years, sounding alien and exotic to young American ears.

And across the restaurant, Colin Vine.

Colin must have felt it, too—the *moment*. As if divining her thoughts, his eyes strayed from the group of female grad students hovering around him—giggly satellites orbiting a bright planet—and turned in Monica's direction, his gaze locking on hers. Considering all that happened later, it seemed trite to think of it that way—'their gazes locked across the room'—and yet, there was something undeniably magnetic and unsettling in the glance that passed between them.

For the space of a breath, Monica was as dizzy as if she teetered on the edge of a ravine. What was it about him that had drawn her attention? On any other man, that wild burgundy topknot might have drawn her scorn. Maybe it was the easy self-confidence he radiated. In his open-neck shirt worn loose over jeans, sleeves rolled to the elbow, showing tanned, ropy forearms, there was no disputing Colin's hotitude.

Archaeologists were not the creaky old fossils they used to be.

Monica's hands were itching for her sketchbook. Would anyone notice if she took it out of her bag and—

Her roommate chose that moment to slide into the chair next to her. "Don't bother," McKenna Ryan said with more than a touch of acid. "He's a man ho."

Monica nearly choked on the *karkade* she was drinking. "Seriously, McK? *Man ho?"*

McKenna leaned in, the tang of beer sharp on her breath. "Colin Vine is a dude who 'lays women like bricks.'"

"I got that from 'man ho.' Are you speaking from experience?"

With her long black hair and blue eyes, McKenna Ryan might easily attract Colin Vine, or any man, but she left the question unanswered.

"He's hot and he's super-talented, *and* he's a screwup."

That doesn't make him a man—what you called him."

Lowering her voice so Monica had to listen hard to hear her over the din around them, McKenna leaned even closer. "Ask me why he nearly got kicked off the dig last season."

A furtive glance at the object of this scandalous piece of gossip showed Colin throwing back his head, laughing at something one of the women had said. Could he really have jeopardized his place on a team that required such a lot of study and dedication to get accepted? Not that Monica had earned her way in as the others had. But she was infinitely grateful to be there, and willing to work day and night to show her appreciation.

While she was telling herself that it was not cool to be disappointed in someone she hadn't even met, curiosity pushed her to take the bait. "Okay, why?"

"He was hanging out with a gang of tomb robbers." McKenna's

mouth tightened into a smug moue. "It's not exactly a secret. Supposedly, they 'found' some artifacts and got caught selling them on the black market. What kind of archaeologist does that?"

"He admitted it?"

"Pfft. Swore he didn't know a thing about what they were doing. Professor Hawkins-Whyte let the whole thing go with a warning because he's such a fan. Pretty obvious to me, he didn't want to know the truth." McKenna flicked a glance at the women talking to Colin. "Look at them, drooling over him."

Monica sipped at the traditional hibiscus tea as a cover to avoid following her gaze. "Not a problem for me. I'm here to work, not party."

And yet, when she noticed that Colin Vine had abandoned his fan club and was wending his way through the crowd toward them, her Spidey senses started tingling. As he closed in on their table, McKenna got up. "You should listen to the voice of wisdom. I'd hate to see you get hurt." Brushing past Colin without speaking, she disappeared in the direction of the Ladies' room.

The tingling didn't stop when Colin dropped into the newly-vacated chair and stuck out his hand with a warm smile. "We haven't met. Colin Vine with the Hawkins-Whyte project."

The firm pressure of his hand closing around Monica's softened her resolve to be cautious, but her smile was brightened more by her reply than any ability of Colin Vine's to charm. "I'm with Frank Booth's dig."

"Do you have a name?" he asked with a good-natured grin. "Or is it 'Ms. Frank Booth's dig?'"

She grinned back. "It's Monica. Monica Bennett."

"From your accent, I'd say you're a long way from home, Monica Bennett. The States, is it?"

They were all a long way from home. The dig teams were an international community made up mainly of graduate students years older than Monica. As uncommon as it was for someone recently out of high school to be accepted to a dig like this one, the Booth group had welcomed her as kindly if she were the team mascot.

"I live in Los Angeles," she said. "I've wanted to see Egypt forever."

"Then I'm happy to say, you're in the right place. The last time I checked, Luxor was in Egypt. And look, here we are in Luxor."

Monica couldn't help noticing that Colin's smile went all the way to his eyes. And she couldn't stop beaming. "Yes, we are."

She could say it a hundred times and it wouldn't feel any more real. Perhaps by the end of her stay it would grow old, but she doubted it. Everywhere she turned was both foreign and wonderful. Spice shops and bazaars. Enticing dishes named *koshari, kofta* and *balah el sham.* She couldn't wait to try them all. Everything looked and smelled incredible—well, except for the camels. But that was part of the adventure, too, and she intended to ride one while she was here.

Even the noisy streets were different from home, with the honking horns of a marriage caravan late at night, and people always out in the streets having a good time.

"I had to twist my dad's arm to let me come," Monica added, immediately kicking herself for sounding like an eight-year-old who had to ask permission, rather than an adult who could plan her own trip across the world.

Colin appeared not to notice her chagrin. "Good dads want to protect their daughters."

She smiled. "I have a *very* good dad."

The fact was, by the time she had convinced Pete Bennett that she was going to Egypt one way or another, Monica had begun to feel as much a captive as Rapunzel, locked away in her ivory tower. It had taken all of her persuasive skills for him to squash his dad fears.

"Well, now that you are in Egypt, what are you going to do first?" Colin asked, giving the impression that he was genuinely interested in her answer.

"That's easy. Hatshepsut's Mortuary Temple."

"Ah, the queen who ruled Egypt as king. Good choice."

"My Aunt Claudia gave me a book about Egyptian queens when I was a little kid. I always thought Hatshepsut was the most awesome."

"Well done, Aunty." Colin contemplated her with a teasing smile.

"Did you know that your eyes are all shiny? I'm dead chuffed that you're in love with archaeology."

Monica, who had a terrible habit of blushing as bright red as a tomato at the most inconvenient times, felt the hot blood rush to her cheeks. "I know, I'm a dork."

"But such a lovely dork."

An amused giggle escaped her. "It sounds funny when you say it with your British accent. '*Dawk*.'"

"Now you're making fun of me. I'm mortally wounded."

"Oh, too bad; I think you'll get over it."

"Never!" His faux remorse lasted all of two seconds, replaced by an approving nod. "I must say, Monica Bennett, you're really fit."

"I'm fit?"

"Fit. You know: pretty. Sexy. Pretty sexy. Must be a British thing."

She couldn't find a response that didn't sound even dorkier. McKenna wasn't kidding about him being a flirt.

"When are you thinking of going to the Mortuary Temple, then?" Colin went on as though he hadn't flustered her.

"First thing tomorrow. After that, we'll be working all the time."

"Has anyone warned you about all the guides who'll be running after you for a fee, and the children begging for *baksheesh?* They're relentless."

"I've heard you're supposed to ignore them." The prospect of dismissing beggars and others who might badger her for money had been bothering her a lot—the girl who her aunt said had the kindest heart in the world. She couldn't imagine turning away children.

Colin was reaching for his phone. "Your team is at Petrie House, isn't it?" Giving her no time to nod, he said, "I've been to Hatshepsut's Temple dozens of times. Give me your mobile number; I'll fetch you in the morning and show you 'round."

And just like that, McKenna's warning was forgotten.

Monica's first view of the soaring cliffs of Deir el-Bahri stole her breath.

Hatshepsut's Mortuary Temple, more imposing than any modern building, was tucked protectively into a natural bay at the base of the cliffs. Each of its three levels boasted a grand colonnaded terrace, where magnificent statues had stood in ancient times. They walked along the vast avenue that led up to the temple complex.

"Most of the statues were stolen or destroyed," Colin said, stepping smoothly into the role of tour guide and painting a vivid portrait of the edifice as it had been in 1470 BC. "In the nineteen-sixties, they reinstalled the nine statues of Hatshepsut as the god Osiris, but only the top tier is close to being completely restored."

"It must have been incredibly beautiful. You make it easy to imagine—the pools and the gardens."

Colin looked pleased by the praise. "They were once surrounded by frankincense trees for medicine, and myrrh for incense."

Enthralled by everything she saw, Monica wanted details. "Hatshepsut was such a great queen. Or should that be king because she was a pharaoh? Which is weird since she was a woman dressing as a man, though that's no big deal anymore." She couldn't stop prattling, but Colin seemed amused by it.

"Hatshepsut was a brilliant pharaoh for twenty years. She commissioned the most fantastic monuments and temples ever built. *And,* she famously sent an expedition to the land of Punt, where her granny was from."

"*'The mysterious land of Punt,'*" Monica quoted.

"You've done your homework, I see. Do you know where Punt is thought to be now?"

"It's Somalia, right?"

He rewarded her with two thumbs up. "Monica Bennett wins the grand prize. As a woman, she wasn't able to lead her troops into battle, so that expedition really boosted her rep. They brought back all sorts of exotic animals and gold and—"

"Oh!" Monica came to a halt with a gasp, no longer listening. They had arrived at the foot of the first flight of temple steps. Impossible not to gape open-mouthed at the structure towering above them.

"A bit much to take in, isn't it?" said Colin softly.

"*The Djeser Djeseru*. Did I say it right?"

"You did, indeed; the name Hatshepsut gave her temple. It translates to '*Holy of Holies*.'"

They climbed the steps and he showed her the Night Sun Chapel, the Solar Altar Court and the Anubis Shrine, explaining the significance of the scenes on the walls and ceilings.

She knew the names and noses had been chiseled away on the great pharaoh's statues, but seeing it in person saddened Monica. "Was it because female pharaohs were looked down on?" she asked.

"Hatshepsut's stepson, Thutmose the third, had it done after she died, most likely to cement his right to the throne and let everyone know what a mighty ruler *he* was."

"Why the nose?"

Colin tapped her nose gently, sending a delicious secret shiver coursing through her. "You need your nose to breathe," he said. "Removing it symbolically killed the person for all eternity."

SHE HADN'T EXPECTED to need a break, but after four hours of walking through the vast temple complex, Monica's senses were on overload and she was starved. Colin, as nonchalant about treading the ancient stones and peering thousands of years into the past as if it were an everyday occurrence, suggested lunch. Oh. For him, she reminded herself, it *was* an everyday occurrence.

He took her to the Sunflower, a charming restaurant situated next to the Nile, where they could watch the lazy progress of feluccas and launches on the river. They ordered chicken shawarma and Moroccan fish tagine, and shared pieces of flatbread and tidbits about their lives as they ate.

Between bites of pita-wrapped chicken, Colin asked questions.

"Last night, you said it was your aunt who got you going on Ancient Egypt?"

"She's a graphologist, so she's interested in hieroglyphics."

His head tilted to one side like a curious bird. "She's a what?"

"A graphologist—she's famous."

"You'll have to explain that one."

"She studies handwriting. It tells your personality traits."

"Bloody hell, I wouldn't want her to see *my* scrawl." The look of dismay on Colin's face made him look like a little boy caught stealing.

Monica laughed. "That's what everyone says."

"What's graph—what did you say—graphology? got to do with hieroglyphics?"

"She can analyze the *hieratic* texts." He would know that she was referring to the ancient cursive form of writing.

"Does it not matter that it's not in English?"

"She analyzes handwriting in lots of languages she doesn't speak."

More food arrived and they dug in. She gave Colin time to swallow a mouthful, then asked where he was from, and wondered what caused the shadow that crossed his face as he answered.

"Born on the Isle of Wight—it's off the South of England. Between Uni and digging, I don't get home much."

"Where do you go to university?"

"Oxford," he said, then deftly switched the topic back to her. "You're from L.A.?"

"Born next to the Pacific Ocean, which makes me a native daughter of the Golden West."

He reached over to stroke her arm with his index finger, tracing a shivery trail down her skin. "No wonder you have such a lovely tan."

The blush blazed on her cheeks, and it was all she could do not to fidget. "You must get your tan from working in the desert."

When he smiled, his eyes crinkled at the edges. "As much as I can. Now, tell me about this marvelous aunty of yours."

"Claudia? She's my dad's sister. She's been kind of a second mother since my mom died."

He winced as if he had made a faux pas. "Ouch. I'm sorry, luv, I didn't mean to—"

"It's totally fine. Claudia's great. I'm so happy she got me interested in all of this—" Monica waved her arms, encompassing the Nile and everything it stood for.

"I'm happy about that, too." He hesitated. "Do you mind if I ask what happened to your mum?"

Six years later, the dull ache lurked, ready to engulf her. She took a deep, steadying breath. "She went to buy some ice cream for me. On the way home, she got broadsided by a drunk driver." For an instant, the great river, the launches and feluccas, the dense city on the other side, fell away and she was twelve years old again, trying to comfort her grief-stricken father. Colin's voice brought her back.

"God, that's horrible."

Monica could feel him searching for something to say, the way people did when there was nothing adequate. She had learned that it was easier to talk about anything other than her own pain.

"What about you? Are you close to your parents?"

His answer, when it came, reminded Monica of Harry Potter's invisibility cloak—a shield to protect himself from being seen. "My mum is—well, she's got her own problems. My father buggered off to South America when I was scarcely three. I never knew him particularly well and he died two years ago. He was an archaeologist." The twist of his lips said, 'now you know where I get it from.'

She reached her hand across the table, compassion flaring in her chest. "That's so sad. I guess it's my turn to say I'm sorry."

Colin gave her hand a squeeze and let go. "No worries, little Mo—all right if I call you that, yeah?"

"Yeah, it's fine." At five-seven she was hardly 'little,' but if he wanted to give her a nickname, she wasn't going to argue. She wanted to look away from the intensity of his grey-eyed gaze; whatever magnet had pulled them together wouldn't let her.

"The one good thing my dad did was pay my school fees," Colin went on as if nothing had happened—and maybe for him, it hadn't. "Mum burned through the insurance money in the first year. The thing is, if I can't finish my PhD, I'm not sure old Hawkins-Whyte will keep me on here."

He rubbed his hands over his face with a long sigh and shook his head like a wet dog. "Bloody hell, listen to me, pouring out my troubles to a girl I've just met. You must think I'm a right prat."

Monica was not sure what a prat was, except it must be an insult. "I do *not* think that; I'm happy to listen."

"You're far too easy to talk to," Colin said, self-mocking. "The thing is, I've got to find a way to stay at Uni; that's all there is to it."

"You'll find a way; I know you will."

"'Course I will." He pushed away from the table. "Now, that's enough of my rubbish; let's make the afternoon count. Tomorrow, we'll be up at the crack of dawn, working ourselves to death."

Monica made no attempt to hide her excitement at the prospect. "I know; I can't wait."

IN THE VALLEY OF THE KINGS, they bought tickets to three tombs. Colin had warned her there would be a lot of walking in the Theban Necropolis. The down-slanted corridors were cut hundreds of feet into the limestone hills, making Monica glad she had listened and worn comfortable walking shoes.

Colin shifted back into tour guide mode as easily as putting on a pair of comfy slippers. "Sixty-three tombs have been excavated, but they never open more than eighteen at a time."

"I read that people kept using them after the burial," said Monica.

"That's right. They brought offerings of food and beer; sometimes jewelry." They entered tomb KV8. "This one belonged to Merenptah, the son of Ramesses the second; only when they opened the tomb, his mummy wasn't here. They found it in Amenhotep the second's tomb in 1898, along with eighteen other mummies. They'd all been relocated in antiquity."

"Eighteen? Who moved them?"

"The priests, wanting to keep tomb robbers from destroying them. The robbers would rip them apart, looking for valuables. Did you know that, until Tutankhamun, the *only* pharaoh found in his original tomb was Amenhotep the second?"

"Wow; no, I didn't. I went to the Tutankhamun exhibit at USC in 2018 with my aunt." She smiled at the favorite memory. Her interest in Ancient Egypt had taken off like a rocket after that visit.

"What did you like best?" Colin asked. "The golden throne? The death mask?"

She could see he was teasing her and she liked it. "Not the fancy things. It was the small sculptures. You know the one of the boy standing on a raft? Like that. A wooden box with carvings of Anubis and Horus. Oh, and a pair of Tutankhamun's sandals. I couldn't stop thinking of him actually wearing those sandals I was looking at, thousands of years later."

"There are more than five thousand of his artifacts at the Cairo museum now." Colin's eyes gleamed with fervor for a topic he clearly loved. "Wouldn't it be incredible to own one of those pieces?"

Monica shot him a look, remembering what McKenna had said about him 'hanging out with modern tomb robbers.' What he had said was innocuous enough; yet, as they took the path down the steep shaft to the burial chamber, his arm linked through hers, an uneasy feeling crept in and settled on her like a too-hot coat.

"They designed various traps to keep tomb robbers out," said Colin. "That didn't always work, though."

"Why not?"

"Because their grandfathers and great-grandfathers were the tomb *builders* and would give them a map."

The uneasy frisson tugged at her again. She wanted to ask him what had happened last season, but there was no tactful way to bring it up. Anyway, if Professor Hawkins-Whyte had believed in his innocence, why shouldn't she? And she had a lot of other questions to ask:

How had the ancient builders created these astounding pillared chambers with their lofty ceilings, using the tools they had?? How did they make the nested sarcophagi that held the pharaoh's remains? How had the artists and scribes decorated the hundreds of feet of walls and ceilings with so much beautiful artwork, having no floodlights to work by? The oil lamps they used couldn't have provided all that much illumination, could they?

Colin grinned at her. "I'd love to stay here all day, answering every question you have. But we still have KV9 to see."

Monica heaved a sigh. "There's so much to see. KV9 is Rameses' tomb, isn't it?"

"Two Rameses—fifth and sixth—uncle and nephew."

Colorful celestial scenes covered the ceiling, hieroglyphics on the walls of the burial chamber. Far into the tomb, standing in its own niche, was an immense green sarcophagus that had been badly damaged and pieced back together—a 3-D puzzle. "It's like a surreal sculpture." Monica said, marveling at the empty spaces on the sides where huge chunks of stone should have been. "What happened to it?"

"Smashed in ancient times. Tomb robbers again."

"It's awful what they did. I can't stand it."

Colin backed away from the niche and moved on to the next area. Did his lack of response to her remark have anything to do with his modern 'tomb robber' friends? Monica couldn't read his expression and he changed the subject too quickly to be sure of what she thought she detected.

"There's a face mask of Rameses the sixth," he said as they continued through the tomb. "You'd have to go all the way to England to see it. It's kept in the British Museum."

"England? Maybe someday. I wish Claudia could see all this; she'd love it as much as I do."

"You'll have to bring her back for a visit next season."

"I'm definitely going to come back if they'll let me."

Colin chuckled. "Let's see if you feel the same after a few weeks of hard, grubby work."

Monica made a face. "Don't worry, I will."

"I hope you do," he said as they exited the tomb into bright sunshine. "Now, we'll end with KV14, the deepest tomb in the Valley."

Monica didn't think she could have been any more excited about Egyptian history, but as they entered the tomb of Tawosret, she caught herself gawking at the colors of the wall decorations, which were as fresh and bright as if they had been painted last week.

"There's so much to learn. I want to know *everything.*"

"I can teach you a little while we're here, if you like."

She could see from Colin's pleased smile that he was enjoying her newbie enthusiasm. "Are you serious? That would be fantastic."

He started walking backwards, talking to her as they went. "All right, then, first lesson; Tawosret was another queen who ruled as Pharaoh for a short while—not famous like Hatshepsut, of course. This tomb was meant for her and husband, Seti the second. But after they died, Pharaoh Setnakht came along and had Seti re-buried in another tomb. He took over this one and made it look like everything in it was his."

They walked and talked for hours, Monica soaking up the scenes of Ancient Egyptian life, wishing every minute could stretch into days. She wanted to see it all, but the few weeks of volunteering at Frank Booth's excavation was nowhere near long enough to slake her growing thirst for learning the secrets hidden under the desert sand.

When at last they climbed into a taxi, dusk was beginning to fall. Monica, who had been too excited to sleep for more than a few hours the night before, rested her head against the seatback with a long sigh of contentment. When Colin's hand closed over hers, she let their fingers intertwine and curl together. Imagining the lulling movement of the vehicle as a cradle, her eyes drifted shut.

One second, she was half-dozing; the next, Colin was shouting, his arm a steel rod across her chest.

2

The shriek of brakes, the squeal of tires. Monica's upper body shot forward, caught by the seat restraint and Colin's arm. The taxi slammed into the trunk of a sporty BMW in front of them. The Beemer's trunk crumpled right up to the rear window and hit the car ahead of him, an accordion between the two vehicles.

The taxi driver, yelling in Arabic, stumbled out of his ruined vehicle holding his head.

Monica's heart was hammering her chest wall, her pulse pounding her ears in the shocked silence that followed the metallic crunch of the collision. People running from all directions were pointing at the road in front of the lead car. She strained to see what they were looking at. "Was somebody hit?"

Colin gently turned her face toward him. "Look at me, Mo. Are you all right?"

She stared at him, trying grasp what had just happened. "Just shaken up. Are *you* all right?"

"Yeah, I'm good." He looked through the windshield at the other car. "Not sure about him, though."

Monica unbuckled her seatbelt and was reaching for the latch when Colin put a restraining hand on her arm. "We have to go see—" she protested.

"You stay here; I'll have a look."

As trembly as she was, that was fine with her. He hopped out and went to rap on the Beemer's driver window, tried to open the buckled door. Going around to the other side, he leaned in to check on the driver. Monica heard him shout to their taxi driver, first in English that the Beemer guy was unconscious and his seatbelt was stuck shut, and when the taxi driver turned away, his phone stuck to his ear, Colin spoke louder, in Arabic.

When they'd hired him, the driver had plenty to chat about in reasonably good English. Now, he ignored his passenger.

With a sharp jab of anxiety, Monica saw that wisps of smoke had begun to rise from the seams of the Beemer's hood. Broken glass and fragments of red and orange taillights littered the road, and the crowd around the car in front of the Beemer was growing. Only Colin was paying attention to the unconscious driver, kneeling in the passenger seat, trying to get his seatbelt unstuck. Still rattled, she climbed out of the taxi and went to see if she could help.

Colin glanced over at the rubberneckers and then at her. "Do you speak any Arabic? I need a knife for the bloody seatbelt."

Feeling the worst kind of useless, she shook her head. "Hardly any."

"No worries, luv." Backing out of the car, Colin bellowed at the crowd: "*Iddini sakin?* Anyone got a knife?" Then returned to trying to free the driver.

A middle-aged man talking speed-Arabic came out of the crowd and thrust a rusty old pocket knife at Monica. It wasn't the best, but nobody was offering anything better, and with no sporting goods store in sight on the desert road, Monica summoned up the all-purpose word, "*Shukraan.*" 'Thank you,' and accepted it. Too late to regret having spent most of her time reading up on Ancient Egypt and next to none learning the modern language,

Colin took the knife, darting a glance at the crumpled front end of the vehicle. "Christ, look at the smoke. You'd best move away, Mo. The engine's going to blow." He ducked back inside the cabin and was sawing at the seatbelt's polyester webbing when a bang came from the engine compartment, loud enough to provoke shrieks from the retreating crowd and to drown Monica's frightened yelp.

The acrid odor of melting rubber stabbed the dusk. Tongues of orange flame licked out from under the dashboard, a hungry dragon, probing for prey.

As if he couldn't feel the heat for himself, Monica screamed at Colin to get out. That the driver would burn to death was something she could not allow to enter her mind.

Whether he didn't hear her plea, or was ignoring her, Colin kept sawing until billowing smoke drove him from the cabin. He stumbled a few feet from the car and coughed and spat, wiped his eyes. Then, filling his lungs with air, he pulled his shirt up to cover his nose. The instant he plunged back into the car, the upper half of his body disappeared in the smoke.

Monica stood on the roadside, panic rising like a cyclone. How much time did he have? The car was going to explode any second and Colin was going to die along with the driver he was trying heroically to save. There was nothing she could do, and she felt as alone as she ever had in her life.

She was just about ready to drag him away by the seat of his pants when suddenly, the seatbelt gave way. In one great lurch, Colin dragged the unconscious driver across the seats and out of the burning car. As the driver's Courtside Sneaker-clad feet hit the tarmac to the cheers of the crowd, a louder blast than the first sent the onlookers scurrying. Two seconds later, the BMW was the fiery pit of hell.

Colin got hold of the driver's shoulders. Trying not to think about the heat, Monica grabbed his ankles. Together, they hauled him away from the blast furnace that had been his very expensive sports car. The instant they laid him down at the verge of the road, Colin started laughing. And when he stopped laughing, he let out a tremendous *whoop*. Sheer relief, Monica guessed, while all she wanted to do was curl up in a squishy ball and sob her eyes out. It was when she sank down beside the driver that she saw he was scarcely more than a kid no older than she was.

DARKNESS WAS COMPLETE; the bystanders had lost interest and gone their separate ways. Colin was checked over by EMTs and given oxygen. The hair was scorched off his right forearm, but he waved off any further treatment. The fire engine and two ambulances drove away, leaving only the headlights of the police cars to illuminate the scene. One ambulance carried the young driver, who had suffered a concussion and burn injuries. The other took the pedestrians he had hit and seriously injured.

"These people, they not value their life," the taxi driver railed, having miraculously regained his English-speaking skills. His contempt was for the injured family, not the driver of the car that hit them.

"They run across the motorway like that; don't want to walk the extra four or five miles to the bridge crossing. They run in front of the cars; they get hit." He spun on his heel and marched over to the policemen.

Watching the rescue vehicles disappear down the road, the taxi driver's disparaging sneer torpedoed Monica's hopes. "Do you think they'll be okay?" she asked.

"It looked pretty bad." Colin reached up to re-tie his topknot, which had come free in the commotion and was hanging loose in burgundy strands around his sooty face. "I'd bet anything he's trying to dodge the blame."

Handing him a tissue to wipe off the soot, Monica's outraged reply was cut off by the arrival of a policeman speaking in rapid-fire Arabic. Colin answered in the same language. All she understood was 'Hawkins-Whyte' and 'Frank Booth.' The two dig projects where tomorrow, they were set start to work. When the policeman barked an order, Colin handed over his crimson British passport and told Monica to do the same.

Flipping through her royal blue US one and noting the sole stamp for Egypt, the policeman handed it back. He called to a colleague and as he dropped the British passport into his shirt pocket, the second policeman whipped Colin around and handcuffed him, not bothering to be gentle with his singed arm.

"What the fuck—" Colin shouted in very plain English.

"What are you doing?" Monica cried out. "He saved that kid's life."

The taxi driver sidled over, all sanctimony now, and pointed at Colin. "The passenger, this man, he distract me. He pull on my shoulder, cause accident. Look my taxi broken."

Colin's face drained of color. "You know that's a lie. I was asleep. I didn't—"

One of the officers snapped something that shut him up. Another opened the rear door of one of the big black SUV police vehicles and ordered them in English to get in.

Monica slid into the seat, her heart thudding all over again. "What's going on? Why—"

Colin climbed in after her. "Well, we're not being given a ride home, luv." He shifted around, trying to find a position that would allow him to sit comfortably with his hands behind his back.

"Don't make fun of me, Colin, I'm serious."

"Yeah, I'm feckin' serious, too. Obviously, they've gone and arrested me."

"Why? What are the charges?"

"They haven't said. That lying taxi driver—it's a load of bollocks." In other circumstances his grimace, coming through his soot-streaked face, might have been comical. There was nothing funny about this situation. He grimaced. "They'll expect to be paid off."

"Paid off?" Monica's aunt was married to a homicide detective and though she was vaguely aware that such things happened in other countries, police bribes were not part of her cozy world.

"The police have a reputation for corruption. They won't ask for it straight out, but they'll expect me to pay up if I'm to be let go."

Monica went for her purse. "I have some cash; not a lot, but—"

"No, luv, you're not to worry about that. They aren't holding you." The policeman, who had been conferring with the taxi driver, was heading back towards them. Colin started talking fast.

"Look, here's what I need you to do, all right? When they take me away, phone *Farouk Badr.* Can you remember that? Farouk Badr. He's a friend. He'll know what to do."

"Shouldn't I call the British Embassy?"

"Don't worry about that now. Call Farouk—please, Monica."

"Farouk Badr. How do I find him?"

Colin cursed under his breath. "They've taken my bloody phone with his number in it." He went silent, thinking. "McKenna can get hold of him. Tell her to have him phone you. And don't tell *anyone* what happened except Farouk. I don't want the professor hearing about it right on the first day of work."

AT THE POLICE STATION, they cooled their heels for an hour until the policeman who made the arrest returned. The taxi driver had been there for a while, then he wasn't. Had he come up with bribe money and been released? Officials came and went, pointing at them and shouting in Arabic. Why did they always have to shout? Monica wanted to ask Colin what they were saying, but a morose silence had settled on him and she didn't think she should break it.

She couldn't stop thinking of his bravery at the accident scene. Without him, that boy would have been toast. *Literally.* And for his pains, Colin was under arrest.

Eventually, they took him away to a cell. Monica didn't wait for anyone to ask where she was going. She hurried away from the police station and phoned her roommate from around the corner.

"What happened?" McKenna demanded, sounding thoroughly put out at the request to call Farouk Badr. "Oh, never mind, I get it. Colin's gotten himself into trouble and he's dragged you into it. Didn't I warn you?"

"He didn't do anything wrong," Monica protested. "Absolutely nothing, I swear it."

"What*ever*." Her roommate's derision came across loud and clear. "You do know we have to get up at four-thirty and start work tomorrow, right?"

"Yes, I know. This is really, really urgent or I wouldn't bother you. *Please* call Farouk?"

"Fine."

Monica ended the call slightly shamefaced. She didn't want to be on the outs with her roommate. It was true, she hadn't listened to McKenna's warning. But this wasn't Colin's doing and it was nothing like dealing in the antiquities black market.

FAROUK BADR ARRIVED WEARING a blue *galabeya,* the traditional Egyptian garment for men, and a turban over his curly black hair, which peeped out. The worry in his dark eyes ratcheted up Monica's own as he told her to wait in his car with the doors locked while he did what he could to free Colin.

She wanted to talk to her best friend, Annabelle, but it was four o'clock in the morning in California. She couldn't call her Aunt Claudia, either, and definitely not her dad, who would want her to come right back home, when she'd only just arrived. So she fretted alone, her eyes riveted on the police station.

It wasn't until two hours later, when she was positive something had gone wrong and didn't know what to do about it, that the two men walked through the front door of the police station and Monica let out the breath it felt like she had been holding the whole time.

They stood a few feet away from Farouk's car, speaking together for a few minutes. After his long ordeal, Colin looked the worse for wear, and smelled it, too. He climbed into the backseat of Farouk's car apologizing for the rancid odor of urine on his clothes.

"Sorry about the pong, luv. They put me in an open cell with three Egyptian guys and a stinking toilet in the corner."

Monica, overjoyed as she was to see Colin safe and free, couldn't care less about the smell. In her opinion, he deserved a medal for saving the young driver.

He shuddered. "I was sat on the floor, asking myself if I was ever going to get out of there. I knew that taxi driver would try to put the blame on me, the tosser. I was never so pleased in my life when they called my name and I saw my friend, Farouk."

The Egyptian bowed his head in acknowledgment. "I am honored to help my friend."

Colin reached over and clapped him on the shoulder. "If it wasn't for you, they would have put me in jail for vehicular manslaughter and forgotten me. That bloody kid who was driving the car—"

"His family will not allow him to be charged." Farouk's eyes went to the rearview mirror. "Somebody must be faulted for the accident."

"Wouldn't you know, it turns out the lad's got relatives high up in the government."

Monica twisted in the front seat to face him. "They'll get him off, you mean."

The look on Colin's face said he knew he was flogging a dead horse. "The family has wasted no time involving themselves. Did you see that car he was driving? Worth at least a hundred-thousand quid. He'll never be charged with anything."

"If our taxi hadn't been too close, we wouldn't have rear-ended that boy when he hit the other car that hit those poor people," Monica exclaimed. "It was obviously *his* fault. All you did was save the boy."

"The police, they seeing that now." Farouk rubbed his thumb with his index and middle fingers to indicate the exchange of money. Monica could only speculate on what it had cost to convince them.

"It was incredible, the way you went into that burning car," she declared. "I was afraid you were going to die."

Colin's amused eyes met hers. "I couldn't have the lad getting barbecued now, could I?"

"You were the only one who cared enough to save him."

"And you," he said with a wink. "If you hadn't got hold of that knife and helped me get him away from the car afterward, he would have been a goner, and probably me, too." He laughed. "You might say I owe you my life."

Monica blushed with pleasure. This time when McKenna's warning not to trust him nipped at the edges of her mind, she refused to hear it at all.

3

THREE WEEKS LATER - CLAUDIA

CLAUDIA ROSE REACHED UP TO TOUCH THE DIAMOND PENDANT HER husband had fastened around her neck, his fingers lingering on the bare skin, making her shiver with pleasure as his touch always did.

"Welcome home," he murmured, pressing a kiss behind her ear and making her shiver again.

Romantic gestures didn't come naturally to Joel Jovanic. As a homicide detective, he was trained to be practical and realistic, a problem solver. But Claudia had been out of town for close to two weeks and it was Valentine's Day. She turned from the mirror, reaching for him.

"I love it. And I love you."

How could she have forgotten how soft and welcoming his lips were? Wrapping his hands around her back, he pulled her close enough to feel his heartbeat. The last eleven days swept away as if they had never been.

"We have dinner reservations on the patio at Whiskey Red's," he said, still holding her.

Claudia leaned back to look into the slate-grey eyes. "Wait a minute—a beautiful necklace *and* dinner? Did you do something bad while I was gone?"

He grinned and let go of her. "I'm just glad you're home. That bed was damn cold without you in it."

"Same. And not because I'm thrilled to be away from my mom. I missed you so much."

When her father had called with the news that her mother had a broken ankle, he had asked Claudia to help out until he could find a home care aide with skin thick enough to deal with her.

When Claudia balked, Robert Bennett had switched to cajoling. "You and your mother will get along fine. Remember Christmas? Everything went smoothly and we were all together then."

"That was for a weekend, Dad, and Joel was there as a buffer. You know Mom likes him better than me. Hell, she likes everyone better than me."

"Aw, come on, cupcake; it's a couple of days. I'll book your flight, business class."

"Dad! Don't try to guilt me with comfortable travel."

But even as she said it, Claudia knew she had been bested. After all the years her father had done his best to shield her from the worst of Sylvia Bennett's judgments, she owed him. So, she had flown to Seattle and endured her mother's never-ending complaints and criticisms until the agency had located the right person. The next day, Claudia had waved goodbye with a clear conscience, and Joel had picked her up from LAX two hours ago.

WHISKEY RED'S had changed its name over the years, but the food and enchanting waterfront view remained the same. Across the marina, lights from the blocks of condos and hotels shimmered on the water like a Monet. Flames danced in the fire pit near their table, keeping them comfy on the February evening.

Joel signaled the waiter to refill their glasses, and when the champagne was poured, raised a toast. "Here's to the next three days: no demands, no hassles, no problems."

Claudia touched her glass to his. "You're off rotation. Annabelle is busy with school and work. Pete is at his reunion. Monica is in Egypt. We're as free as birds."

His mouth curved upward. "I didn't know Monica had it in her. She twisted Pete's arm so hard I thought for sure she'd snap it off."

"My niece is stronger than we give her credit for," said Claudia, enjoying the pleasant fizz of amber liquid in her mouth. "She's been planning this trip for a long time."

"Yeah, but *Egypt?* Why not, oh, I don't know, Italy, France—"

"My fault. Years ago, I gave her a book about the Egyptian queens. She's been determined to go there ever since." She remembered her young niece's excitement over that book. "Other kids build forts; Monica wanted a pyramid. She can tell you most of the Pharaohs *and* their dynasties. She even taught herself to read basic hieroglyphics."

Joel drained his glass. "After you took her to that King Tut exhibit at USC, it was all she talked about for weeks."

"That's where she got that figurine of Bastet, the cat goddess she gave me. She's truly the sweetest girl ever."

"Which is why I'm surprised Pete would let her go to the Middle East," Joel said. "The violence against foreigners—"

"Dude," Claudia interrupted with a straight face. "The Arab Spring happened over ten years ago. Foreign archaeologists are back, digging again. *And* they're making incredible finds. We checked."

Joel's eyebrow quirked upward, the way it did when he was skeptical. "It's a big solo trip for a kid her age."

"Not solo, she's with a team of undergrads and the professor in charge is a friend of a friend of Pete's. And she's eighteen."

He pretended to be shocked. "Good God, I thought she was fifteen or sixteen. Are you *trying* to make me feel old?"

"If you're old, that means I am, too."

"Good point. Now, who is this professor, brave enough to take a bunch of undergrads to Egypt?"

Claudia contemplated her husband across the table. She loved how his eyes crinkled when he smiled, which she thought he didn't do often enough. Being a homicide cop didn't give him a lot to smile about.

"My computer genius brother saved his buddy's company millions of bucks when his business got hacked. Later, a friend of his friend—a professor of archaeology—happened to mention that he was leading an excavation project in Egypt. Pete called in the favor."

"And Monica got to go on a real dig. I remember now."

"She's volunteering; clerical work, data entry, gofer stuff. Pete made a nice donation to the project. My parents kicked in spending money on top of what you and I gave her—she *is* their only grandchild. She can go shopping and have fun."

Joel nodded approval. "Is she loving it?"

"Every time I hear from her, she's having a blast."

"I bet your brother isn't thinking about Monica right now," said Joel with a knowing chuckle.

"Not while he's partying with his old college buddies." Claudia was glad Pete had decided to go to his reunion. Since his wife's death he had been extra-protective of their only child and Claudia knew it weighed heavy on him to see her cross the world by herself, even if she was joining a team. His decision to drive to Tucson for his reunion was, she decided, a sign of growth and healing at long last. "Dig season is over at the end of next week and Monica will be coming home," she said. "Pete will be so relieved."

"Everyone is taken care of and all we have to think about is us."

Claudia gave him a slow smile. "We can stay in bed the whole weekend if we want to."

The smoldering look he sent her held the promise of a very enjoyable weekend. "Babe, you've been gone almost two weeks. We *definitely* want to. Starting tonight."

"Starting tonight." Her sigh was pure happiness. "My idea of heaven. Nobody to bug—"

She hadn't finished her sentence when her phone's generic ring sounded in her purse. The people she cared about had special ringtones. She silenced the phone without looking at it.

"Whoever it is, I'll get back to them. In a day or two. After a lot of snuggling. Or whatever you want to call hot sex."

"Call it anything you want," said Joel. "And the sooner the better."

The waiter came by to top off their glasses and remove their plates. Claudia could not remember the last time she had felt so content.

Then Joel's phone rang.

"I'll turn it off," he said, taking it out of his pocket.

He sneaked a glimpse of the screen and his expression changed. The sinking feeling Claudia got when she saw how serious he looked was a premonition that made her want to whimper.

Joel turned the phone so she could read the screen: *Pima County Detention Center.*

Good news never came from an address like that. It wasn't unusual for Joel to get a call from a county lockup, even in another state, but her brother's reunion was taking place in Tucson, Arizona, which was in Pima County.

"Answer it," she said, and as he did, checked the missed call she had blithely ignored.

The charm of the marina faded; the happiness ebbed away. The call had originated from the same location.

The longer Joel listened to the caller, the tighter the muscles got around his mouth. At length, he said, "Of course, buddy. We'll take care of it. Hang tight, bro." He dropped the phone back into his jacket pocket and signaled for the check.

It was a point of pride for Joel to keep his emotions to himself, which made it all the more remarkable for him to show how much the one-sided conversation had troubled him. When he dropped the bomb, Claudia understood why.

"Pete's been arrested for murder."

4

THE CHAMPAGNE, WHICH HAD BEEN SWEET AND LIGHT, SUDDENLY tasted like sawdust. Claudia set her glass on the table, her mind refusing to accept what she had just heard.

"That can't be right. Pete would never kill anyone. What—how—"

"He says it's some kind of a mix-up."

She second-guessed what Joel, the cop, was thinking: everyone in jail says that. They're never guilty. "Of course it's a mix-up. What happened? What evidence do they have?" She didn't want to ask the ultimate question, but there was nowhere else to go. "Who do they think he killed?"

"Those calls are recorded. He was smart enough not to give any details. He wants us to get him a private attorney in Tucson. You can do that, right?"

"Yes, but—"

Joel pushed back his chair and rose. "Let's go find your brother an attorney."

THE FIRST THING Claudia did when they got home was to book a nonstop flight to Tucson, departing at noon the next day. The second was to scroll through her contact database, searching for good defense lawyers in Tucson.

Joel, being in law enforcement, had no allies on what he called the Dark Side—criminal defense. Claudia's forensic handwriting examination practice, on the other hand, was split between civil and criminal cases. She had worked with hundreds of attorneys around the country and in other parts of the world.

"How about Kelly?" Joel suggested, looking over her shoulder, referring to Claudia's best friend, Kelly Brennan, who was a family law attorney. "Could she give you a referral?"

"I can't call her. She's having a tough time right now. She doesn't even know her own name half the time."

"What about the Cunninghammer?" Ann Cunningham was a tough attorney friend who had helped Claudia out in the past.

"I wish. She passed away last year. Liver disease—and she wasn't a big drinker."

He tossed in a couple of other names he had heard her mention, all of whom she vetoed. This was her brother's life. She had every intention of being as picky as she needed to be and she was ready to scrutinize every attorney in her database to find the very best person to help Pete out of the jam he had landed in.

She leafed through the long list of names. "Attorneys are like cops, honey; not all created equal. And I have to find exactly the right one in Arizona."

Her husband gave her shoulders a light squeeze and leaned down to kiss her cheek. "I'll fire up my laptop and see if I can pull up anything on the arrest. Glass of wine?"

Claudia gave him a grateful nod. "I'm sorry about our weekend."

There was something philosophical in his shrug. "Family takes priority. Raincheck."

"Yeah, raincheck."

She didn't need to hear Pete's side of the story to know he had to be innocent. He was the mildest guy she knew. She could recall only once when she had witnessed him going full on mad dog, and that had been in defense of his wife, Nancy.

But murder? It was beyond comprehension.

It wouldn't be a DUI. After Nancy's death was caused by a drunk driver, Pete became rabid about not drinking and driving, so she was positive it wasn't that. Something had obviously gone horribly wrong.

A name jumped out from the list of Arizona attorneys: Robin Cross.

She read the notation she had made in the contact window: *Pitbull. Super-aggressive.*

Robin Cross had once retained Claudia in a murder case where a handwritten threat letter came into play. In her early thirties, the diminutive attorney had the kind of youthful presence that put people off guard—surely, she couldn't be old enough to take the bar exam, they would think—until she opened her mouth and went on the offensive. When Robin knocked them off their feet, they didn't get up again.

Sitting at the defense table as a trial consultant, Claudia had been thankful it was not she who was on the receiving end of the questions and challenges Robin hurled at the opposing document examiner. Unlike many defense attorneys who didn't care whether their client was guilty, Robin believed in hers and was hungry to fight the system. The opposition hadn't stood a chance.

At this time of year, Tucson's time zone was an hour ahead of California, which made it close to nine-thirty there. Claudia dialed her number anyway, holding her breath until the attorney answered.

"Claudia. What a surprise."

"I'm sorry to call so late—"

"Hey, it's an exciting Friday night of bingeing Netflix. What's up? I can hear in your voice that you're not calling for a cookie recipe."

Now that she had Robin's ear, Claudia couldn't control the wobble. She tried to blink back the tears that spilled out, leaving a wet trail on her face. "My brother has been arrested—for—for murder—"

"Whoa," Robin broke in. "Hold up. Take a minute to breathe, then you can tell me everything."

Claudia grabbed a tissue from the box on her desk and blotted her face. Steadying herself, she repeated what Pete had told Joel, which was next to nothing. At the end of her short dissertation, having handed the burden over to someone who knew what to do with it, she let out a deep breath and the tension began to ease a little.

"Since he was calling this evening from the jail," Robin said, "we have to assume he'll have his initial appearance tomorrow."

"On a Saturday?" Claudia's hopes rose. "I thought he would have to wait until next week. In California, if you get arrested on a Friday, you're screwed until the next Monday or Tuesday." This was something she had learned from criminal cases she had worked on.

"In Arizona, we don't make someone spend more time in jail than that without an IA. Here's how it will go: until he retains private counsel, he'll get a public defender to represent him and request bond. If there's probable cause and he's charged with murder, I can promise the bail amount will be high. It could be as much as a half-million."

Claudia gulped inwardly. "Is the bond fee the same? Ten percent—fifty grand for that amount?"

"That's right. Now, what I've just told you is all done via video. A group of defendants gets lined up at the jail; they go in front of the camera one at a time and plead. The judge is at the courthouse in another location, which makes better financial sense than hauling a load of prisoners on a bus to the courthouse and back to the jail afterwards."

Prisoners. Jail buses. Claudia's head was spinning. How could they be talking about her brother? She made an effort to keep her focus on what Robin was saying. "What happens after that?"

"The case will go to the grand jury on Monday and we'll find out the bond amount. The bondsman gets hired and paid, gets the money together, and your brother will be lucky if he gets bonded out on Tuesday afternoon."

"My husband and I are flying out there tomorrow. Will we be able to see him?"

"These days, you can do virtual jail visits with an appointment. The inmate gets to use an iPad."

"I want to see him in person. My husband is an LAPD homicide detective. Will that do anything for us?"

"You can bet I'll try it. They might show him a little more courtesy and make special arrangements for out-of-town visitors. If your brother wants me to take the case, I'll go see him at the jail, and I'll be there for the arraignment."

"Pete asked me to find him a good attorney. If you're willing to take it on, we want you."

"Fine. I'll go ahead and call the jail and make sure you guys get in to see him tomorrow afternoon. Remember, Pete will have to produce 10 percent of the bond, which he won't get back. As long as Pete shows up for the prelim, the bondsman keeps that money. If he doesn't show up, he'll owe the whole amount. I'll talk to him myself about my retainer. For a murder rap, it's substantial. I have to hire an investigator."

"It doesn't matter what it costs. Pete's a really sensitive guy. He can't stay there."

Robin's tone brooked no nonsense. "It's not a hotel, Claudia, he doesn't get a choice; he'll have to stay, at least until the arraignment. It'll be too soon for any lab results. There won't be a police report at this point. I'm sure I don't have to tell you a defendant has the right to a speedy trial, and everyone wants that. The problem is, speedy doesn't allow enough time to provide the best defense. I'll strongly recommend Pete waive time. That way we can wait and get all the discovery from the D.A. when it comes in. I'll need to review it and look for any holes in their investigation. That sort of thing."

"If he waives time, a trial could take months to schedule."

"You're right."

"It's Pete's choice, but I'd be surprised if he decided to go that route."

"We'll see. I'll make the call first thing tomorrow to get you in. Get back to me after you see him."

"I will. Thank you, Robin, thank you so much."

"Hey, thanks for thinking of me. And, Claudia–? It's gonna be okay."

As much as Claudia trusted Robin to do whatever could be done in Pete's defense, it didn't feel like it was going to be okay.

. . .

JOEL WAS IN BED, laptop on his knees, a glass of Chardonnay on each nightstand. He set the computer on the floor by the bed as Claudia undressed and crawled in beside him. "What did the attorney say?"

She summarized the conversation.

"Sounds like she knows what she's doing".

"Well, duh. That's why I called her."

Joel gave her leg a playful flick. "What if Monica calls you, looking for her dad?"

"Crap, I didn't think about that. What am I gonna tell her?"

"It's a lot for a kid. I'd wait until we see Pete and get a better picture of the situation. He can tell you what he wants her to know."

"It's a lot for anyone." Claudia slid down on her pillow, pulling him with her. "Let's think about something nicer."

They started to make love, but thoughts of Pete kept intruding. What must he be feeling, locked up in the Pima County Jail? Her heart wasn't in it and they kissed goodnight with apologies and promises.

Thanks to countless late-night calls to crime scenes, Joel's detective skills included the learned ability to crash whenever and wherever he had an opportunity. Unless he was on an airplane—he hated flying—he would be asleep the instant his head touched the pillow.

Long after they had switched off the light and he was snoring, Claudia glared at the clock on the nightstand, which had slowed to a crawl. Memories of her brother streamed like an old-time movie reel. When her parents brought him home from the hospital, she had adored him at first sight. The squalling infant with his wrinkled pink face was her new doll. She didn't mind when it became clear that 'baby Petey' was the light of their mother's life, while everything Claudia did annoyed her.

When he was big enough to hold without her getting yelled at, his big sister would dress him in her cast-off baby clothes and push him around the house in her doll carriage. When he was two and she was five, she taught him to read.

There came a time when she became a teenager and they'd

detested each other on the basic principle that they were siblings. As soon as she moved away from home, the love miraculously returned.

Thinking of the times when they hadn't gotten along but had stood up for each other, she willed the red LED numbers on the clock to change faster…

CLAUDIA WOKE WITH A START, her heart racing. As she lay there, telling herself it was only a nightmare, the dream sequence came creeping back.

Constrained in a punishing squat, she had been trapped in a small, dank, airless box. She was wide awake now, her limbs as stiff and sore as if the torture box had been real. Taking care not to disturb Joel, she slipped out of bed and started doing yoga stretches to remind herself that she could move her arms and legs as freely as she pleased.

The sky that poked through the gap in the window shade was still inky black. Claudia had a feeling that five hundred miles away, Pete was lying awake, too, as confined in reality as she had been in the box of her nightmare.

5

SATURDAY - CLAUDIA

THEIR SOUTHWEST FLIGHT, A RAPID HOUR AND TWENTY MINUTES FROM LAX, arrived on time at Tucson International. Joel reclaimed his service weapon, which he had been required to check for the flight, while Claudia ordered an Uber.

Google Maps put the Pima County Adult Detention Complex at ten miles from the airport. They sped along the desert road, for a time flanked on their right by homes scattered across the sandy terrain. Soon, whole communities surrounded by block walls materialized on one side of the road. The jail, which had all the charm of a high school gymnasium, rose on the other.

"It looks like the Getty Museum," said Claudia at her first glimpse of the unforgiving stone walls and fourteen-foot-high chain link fences topped by rolls of razor wire.

Joel snorted. "If you think the Getty looks like a prison."

"Well, yeah, I kind of do."

The driver turned onto a long, tree-lined driveway with a roundabout at the building, braking to a stop outside the front doors. Having arrived, Claudia didn't want to leave the car and enter the innocuous-looking glass facade.

"It's a lot nicer looking than the last facility I visited," she said.

"Last time I went to a prison was when I went to Maine to see Roxanne Becker. This is minimum security, no serial killers here. Anyway, it's a jail. Serial killers are in prison."

With a gentle nudge, Joel opened the car door. "Quit stalling. Are you ready?"

She threw him the stink eye. "No, but let's do it."

THE JAIL'S website instructed scheduled visitors to arrive four hours in advance of the visit. Regular visitors were required to visit their loved ones via an electronic screen in a room lined with small booths. Jail in the twenty-first century.

Thanks to Robin Cross' intercession and Joel's credentials, they were asked to deposit their belongings in a locker and were able to bypass the insanely long check-in mechanism. They were escorted to a private room, where they would hold their meeting in-person, a privilege normally accorded to attorneys visiting a client.

The room, surface clean, had absorbed an underlying reek of desperation and old sweat. They sat on molded plastic chairs, waiting for Pete to be brought in. Panic fluttered in Claudia's chest. Knowing she could get up and leave after the visit didn't help when her brother couldn't leave with her. The walls of the small room closed in as they had in her nightmare. Her hands wanted to fidget, to touch her face, her hair, to do *something*.

Joel reached over and covered her hands with one of his, reminding her that she was not alone in this nightmare. She was about to say something grateful when the door opened.

A burly guard escorted Pete into the room, slapping Claudia in the face with the reality of her brother's plight. Pete had a black eye and the shell-shocked thousand-yard stare of someone who could not quite believe the circumstances they had landed in.

It was only a week since she had last seen him. It must be her imagination that he looked thinner in the baggy orange jumpsuit. His hands were cuffed in front of him and she noticed that the knuckles on his right hand were scraped raw.

The guard put him at the metal table, withdrawing as silently as he had arrived. As the door clicked shut, Pete leaned forward. "Thanks for coming, you guys. Did you find an attorney?"

"Someone right here in Tucson," said Claudia. "I've worked with her and she's excellent."

Pete blew out a deep exhale as if he'd been holding it for a long time. "Thanks, Sis."

"What the hell happened, Pete?"

Joel, long accustomed to dealing with the newly arrested who were trying to come to terms with their situation, broke in with a caution. "Be careful what you say, Pete. They record everything."

"Even in an attorney room?" said Claudia, startled.

Joel shot her a quelling look. "For right now, tell us what will be in the police report."

Pete nodded. "Thursday night, I was at this bar. We went there to kick off the reunion—most of the old gang."

"What's the name of the bar?" Joel asked.

"Dirtbags."

"*Dirtbags?*" Claudia repeated with a look of incredulity.

Pete's faint smile came with a shrug. "It's a dive bar, been there since the 80s. You know how it is—study all week, go pound alcohol on the weekend. It's always been packed with frats. It's right across the highway from the U."

Claudia noticed a fine sheen of sweat had broken out on his forehead and cheeks as he spoke. Joel must have noticed it, too. "Take your time, Pete," he said.

"We were having a good time, catching up on twenty years. We'd been there a while, had a few drinks when this asshole, Mitch Graham, showed up."

Hearing that name prompted an unpleasant memory bump. Claudia put it away for later. Right now, she concerned about the flames she was seeing behind Pete's narrowed eyes.

Joel held up his hand. "We get the picture. This Mitch Graham was someone you knew in school?"

Pete nodded gloomily. "Yeah. He was—we had some history. Claudia can fill you in."

"So, sticking to what I'd find in the police report—"

"He starts hounding me. I told him to fuck off, but he kept going and we got into it. The cops came and told me to leave. I did. That's all there was to it. Next day, when I went back to get my truck, the parking lot was blocked off and there were cops all around."

"You didn't drive your truck that night?" Joel asked.

Pete shook his head. "Too wasted."

"Where'd you go?"

"My hotel was too far to hoof it and it was too late for Uber. I slept it off in a doorway." Pete huffed a sound of self-contempt. "I'm such a dumbshit. I should've slept in my damn truck. It was right there in back of the bar by the dumpster."

Joel nodded, letting him know he was paying close attention. "Where was the doorway? Can you describe it?"

Pete's brow furrowed as if conjuring an image. "There's an alley right behind Dirtbags' back parking lot. There's a building across the way. Go right and then left at the corner; you come to steps that lead up to an alcove. There's a doorway there. That's where I ended up."

"Okay. So, going back to yesterday morning—Friday? You went back for your truck and the lot was cordoned off?"

"Yeah, Friday. I asked one of the cops if I could go get my ride. He asked for my ID. When I showed it to him, he arrested me." Pete's face was the picture of stunned disbelief. "They said Mitch was dead and I killed him."

"How'd the fight start?" Joel asked. "Tell me what you told the cops."

"Mitch threw the first punch. Like I said, I tried to walk away. What the hell was I supposed to do with this asshole hitting me? Look, man, when the cops showed up and told me to leave, I did. Mitch was fine. I never saw him again." Desperation glazed the green eyes that were so much like Claudia's. "You can't tell Mom and Dad about this, Claud. Or Monica."

"You'll have to tell them sometime."

"Not today, okay? I need to get this fixed first."

"Fine, but what am I supposed to tell your daughter when she wants to know why you aren't calling her or answering her calls?"

Pete raked his hands through his hair, leaving it standing on end. "Tell her—tell her I'm camping with the guys and there's no cell service."

Claudia sighed. "If that's what you want. I hate lying to her."

"Me, too, but it's better than 'your dad's in jail for murder.'"

He was right, and there was no point in spoiling Monica's trip when there was nothing she could do to improve the situation.

"Let's talk about your attorney." Claudia said, and told him about Robin Cross and bail and finances.

"Whatever it takes," said Pete. "I have to get out of this place. If I have to mortgage my house, so be it."

"Yeah, about that—" Joel interrupted.

They both looked at him as he outlined what would happen with the grand jury and bond hearing to take place on Monday. When it dawned on Pete that he would not be going anywhere for the next three days, the air went out of him. He sank in his chair like a deflated balloon.

"You can't imagine what it's like in here. Guys screaming and yelling all night long. Some of these people are mentally ill. They don't belong in jail; they should be in a mental health facility."

"You're right," Joel concurred. "And you're stuck until Tuesday, bud. Your attorney will find out what the charges are and see you on Monday. In the meantime, you can talk to her on the phone. Just remember, they record the calls."

Pete looked bewildered. "I don't understand. They said I was being arrested for murder. Isn't that the charge?"

"There's a code difference between Murder One, which is premeditated, and Murder Two, which isn't."

The guard rapped on the door to let them know time was up. Pete's head whipped around. "I *swear* to you, I didn't do it. I'd tell you if I did."

Touching inmates was against regulations or Claudia would have reached out and hugged her brother. "I'll be right here in Tucson," she said. "I love you."

The door opened and the guard leaned in. "All right, guy, let's go."

With a dispirited nod, Pete stood, and the guard, holding the door open with his back, waited in silence for his detainee to pass by.

Claudia and Joel watched from the doorway as the two men disappeared down the endless corridor.

6

Another Uber dropped them at the Arizona Inn. The boutique hotel Joel had booked was less than two miles from Dirtbags.

The hotel website described the place as 'uniquely charming,' with 'antique accents,' and 'family owned and run since 1930.' Had their reason for being in town not been grim, the pink-walled casita with the charming guest room they entered would have made a perfect place for a romantic getaway.

Claudia began unpacking the clothes she had brought to hold her until the arraignment. "I feel kind of bad staying in such a nice place, knowing Pete's in a jail cell," she said, thinking of her brother's black eye and scraped knuckles.

"We could move to a fleabag motel if you want," said Joel.

"I don't feel *that* guilty."

He laughed. "I didn't think so. Are you hungry? I thought we might grab a bite at Dirtbags."

"Checking out the scene of the crime?"

"Why not? Unless you prefer something fancier."

Claudia chuckled. "I'm not sure Tucson does fancy. Burgers are fine with me."

. . .

THEY SHOWERED off the travel dust together, lingering in the steam. The hot water began to release the tension in Claudia's taut muscles. Joel finished the job.

While she was drying her hair, he checked out the hotel property, a habit she had seen him perform everywhere they went. A cop's habit. He came in from the patio as she was stepping into her sandals. Somewhere on his person, Claudia knew there would be a concealed weapon. Scanning the shirt that hung loose over his Levi's, she couldn't tell where it was.

"Ready to get the investigation started?"

"Ready." She slung her purse over her shoulder. "I keep thinking about Monica."

"Why don't you call her?"

"Ten-hour time difference from home, nine from here. That makes it the middle of the night in Luxor. I'll text her."

Her phone had been powered down since they'd departed the jail. A text from Monica was waiting for her. Claudia read aloud:

'Hey, Aunty C, where's my dad? Too much fun at the reunion?'

"If she only knew." Claudia keyed in a response:

'He said to tell you he's camping, no signal.'

"There. That's not a lie. He did say it," she said smugly.

Joel held the door open for her. "That's a mighty fine hair you're splitting, Ms. Rose."

She landed a light punch on his arm as she passed by. "Better watch yourself, Columbo."

THE BAR WAS under a mile walk from the hotel. On a mid-February evening, the temperature hovered around a pleasant 65 degrees. They took East Elm, strolling past the pink stucco wall that surrounded the hotel, past homes with tall gates, surprised at the number of trees in the desert community. Following Google Maps, they came to a long sidewalk with tall hospital buildings and parking lots, and turned down Olsen to Speedway, and Dirtbags.

As unpretentious as its name, the bar was in a squat stucco

building set back from the street between a Taco Bell and a 7-Eleven convenience store. "Pete said he parked his truck near the dumpster behind the bar," said Claudia. "Should we start back there?"

"Yes, ma'am," said Joel, and they walked around to the rear, where there were two parking spaces next to a low green dumpster, one occupied by a black Jeep, the other vacant. "The cops will have towed Pete's truck to the city impound. The victim's too, if he drove himself there."

"The victim." Claudia loosed a sigh. "Ah, Mitch Graham—"

Joel held up a hand. "Let's not go there until we're sitting down with a frosty beverage, okay?"

"Suits me." She pointed to the building across the alley, craning to look up at the second-floor windows in the plain stucco facade. "That's the building Pete was talking about, where he slept it off. If those are apartments, somebody might have seen something."

Her husband agreed. "Someone might have been awake at that time of night. Let's go see if we can find the doorway where he landed."

Following Pete's instructions, they exited the lot through a gate behind the bar, where bits of yellow crime scene tape fluttered in the chain link fence. They were in the alley he had described, with the two-story building on the other side. Turning right, they went to the corner and saw a long flight of stairs descending to a basement door.

"This isn't it," said Claudia. "Pete said they'd been drinking for a while. He would have fallen down those stairs and broken a leg."

"You're right about that. He said make a left at the corner." Making the turn, they came to a short staircase that led up to a door set into an alcove. "This is the only place he could have crashed. There's nothing else close to what he described." Joel hunkered down and examined the concrete steps for any evidence of Pete's presence eighteen hours earlier. Finding nothing of interest, he repeated the exercise on the landing.

"The crime scene people should have taken anything, but it's not a bad idea to check," he said. "In a perfect world, there would be a Dirtbags' time-stamped receipt lying here with Pete's credit card number on it. Something to prove he was here."

Claudia snorted. "We should be so lucky."

Across the street, several cars were parked alongside a red brick building, a 'Reserved Parking' sign at one end of the block. From where they were, if she squinted, she could read it: Alpha Chi Omega Residents Only. A women's sorority. She had lectured on handwriting analysis to several of their chapters. Such residences were common close to the university. She made a mental note to mention it to Robin Cross. It couldn't hurt to talk to the residents.

To be thorough, they walked all the way around the block, checking out the large building they had seen from the alley behind Dirtbags.

"It's a frat house," said Claudia, a spark of optimism igniting as they came around to the front of the building where Pete had slept. "That late on a Thursday night, there's a good chance someone was up studying. They could have heard something and looked out a window."

"Robin's investigator will want to talk to everyone with rooms on this side," said Joel. "He or she will need to find out what time Pete blew out of the bar and what time he went back to get his truck on Friday morning."

They retraced their steps to Dirtbags. "What are the odds the manager would talk to us, give us his version?"

Joel shook his head. "They'll be concerned about their reputation getting sullied with a murder. Let's lower the bar—so to speak."

"You're the detective."

"And you're a saucy minx."

Claudia had to laugh. "*Saucy minx?* What on earth have you been reading, Shakespeare?"

He gave her behind a pinch. "Have you no faith in me, wench? You think I am fit only for picture books?"

Shaking her head in mock despair, she followed him into the bar.

Dirtbags was larger than it looked from the outside. The waitresses—slender, attractive college age women—wore uniforms of short shorts and sleeveless tees with the bar's name decorating abundant breasts.

"I bet they keep the lights low so you don't know why the floor is so sticky," Claudia complained as they settled at their table. "The food had better be good."

They ordered two bottles of Stella Artois. Their waitress, whose name was Bree, returned with their beers, ready to take their food order. Claudia decided on a Dirtburger with cheese. Joel ordered a Big Tx Burger, which came with BBQ sauce and green chiles.

"Anything else I can get you?" Bree asked with a perky tilt of her head.

"Yeah," said Joel. "We heard all hell broke loose here the other night. What happened?"

Her smile washed away. "Are you a cop?"

Busted.

He gave her a friendly wink. "A couple of curious tourists. Were you here?"

With a glance around as if she did not want to be overheard, the waitress nodded. "We get customers fighting in the parking lot sometimes; never in the bar."

"Sounded worse than a bar fight from what I heard."

She gave him a meaningful look and a slow nod. "Hell, yeah."

"Cops shut it down?"

"The bouncers had it handled until the one guy says he's gonna kill the other one. That's when they went ahead and called the cops." Bree bent down, showing more cleavage than she needed to. No one could accuse her of selling her intellect. "I've seen a lotta crazy shit—oops, sorry—I mean *stuff,* go down. I've *never* seen anyone that wack. Those two guys were in it for keeps. The one guy said he was gonna kill the other one and he obviously meant it, 'cause he came back and did it."

Claudia wanted to yell at Bree that she couldn't be talking about her brother, but yelling would get them nowhere. Following Joel's lead, she bluffed mild interest. "Did you know the guy who was killed?"

"Mitch? Yeah, he was a regular. I heard the guy who killed him was with the reunion crowd. We had a whole crew of 'em here that night."

Joel tipped his bottle and drank. "Any idea what started it?"

Bree scanned her tables, relaxing visibly when she saw the restaurant was sparsely occupied. "It was right over there." She jerked her chin at a table across the dining room. "I was like, about three feet away from that table. That guy—I think his name was Pete—was yelling really loud. You could hear him over the music."

"What did you hear?" Claudia asked with more of an edge than she had intended.

"It was like, 'Say my wife's name again, mother eff word—only he actually said it—'I'll effing kill you,' or something. I guess Mitch got with that guy's wife." She gave a sassy smirk. "He was that type."

"What type? Flirty?"

"More like McGrabbyhands. Us waitresses, we put up with it 'cause he's an excellent tipper and—" Her big brown eyes widened with the excitement of telling her story. "I saw Mitch hit that Pete guy right in the face. Pete shoved him off and was walking away, but Mitch was like, 'go eff yourself,' and slugged him again. So, Pete grabs hold of Mitch and—well, he shoved him, kind of like in the movies. He landed right on that table, and Pete started pounding on him." She pointed again. "People are *sitting* there and here's this guy in their food and everyone's jumping out of the way. The bouncers pulled him off." She paused. "He looked—well, like nobody was home; you know what I mean?"

"Who, Mitch?"

Bree looked at Claudia as if she was an imbecile. "*No,* the killer guy. Pete. When the cops came, we all told them Mitch started it, and Pete's friends said it was self-defense, so they let him go. I guess he waited for Mitch to come out after we closed."

"You close when, two AM?" Joel asked.

"Yeah."

"This all happened close to closing time?"

"Uh huh, around one, one-thirty."

The bartender called her name and Bree excused herself. "Gotta run. Your food'll be right up."

Joel downed a long, thoughtful drink and set the bottle on the table. He leveled a serious look at Claudia. "Now, you want to tell me what happened between Pete and this Mitch Graham dude?"

7

Claudia reached for her beer. Less than twenty-four hours had elapsed since Pete's phone call, their flight to Tucson, the visit to the jail. She prepared herself to tell Joel what she knew. The memory brought with it the heartache of loss.

"It was the day of Pete's wife's funeral. We were at Mom and Dad's house after the reception—that was before they moved to Seattle. Mom and Monica and I were cleaning up after everyone had gone. As you can imagine, we felt like crap. Pete was boozing it up pretty good, which he rarely does. That day, he had a good excuse.

"Out of nowhere, Mom makes some totally inappropriate, horrible crack about Nancy, Pete's dead wife." Claudia huffed a mirthless chuckle. "Not that she ever needed a reason. My mother never met an insult she didn't like."

Joel, who had been acquainted with her mother for a few years now, nodded with understanding. "What did she say?"

"I've blocked out the actual words. It was something like, 'if only she'd been a better wife, better mother;' that kind of thing. It was ridiculous to say that. Nancy was a wonderful wife and mother. In fact, she was a wonderful person and she and Pete had a great relationship."

"What the hell kind of person says something thing like that?"

"A person like Sylvia Bennett. Monica burst into tears. She was twelve years old and had to hear that kind of garbage from her grandmother. We'd just buried her mother, for Chrissake. It was the last straw. Pete went ballistic."

"I can see why," Joel said, letting his distaste show. He had always gotten along with Claudia's mother, but that didn't mean he liked her.

The anguished rage on her brother's face was branded on Claudia's brain. "I thought he was going to strangle her. Dad jumped between them or I don't know what would have happened."

"So. Mitch Graham," said Joel. "I assume that's where we're going with this story."

"We're getting there. I had to get Pete out of the house, away from Mom. I took him to the beach. We sat there for a long time. He started talking about Nancy; how happy they were when Monica was born. What a *fantastic* mom she was." She swallowed the emotion that clogged her throat and threatened to wreck her careful composure.

"Pete's sobbing, I'm sobbing. Then, out of nowhere, he starts saying that Nancy had suffered because of him and he would never forgive himself."

Joel had his listening face on, laser-focused on the nuances as well as what was said.

"You know that when you're shitfaced, it doesn't have to make sense," Claudia continued. "He wasn't talking about her death."

"He was talking about what made him want to kill Mitch Graham."

"Good detecting, detective. Pete and Nance met here at UA in their senior year. He was the computer science geek; she majored in psych."

"Love at first sight?"

"No, but it got there fast. He brought her home on the holidays and we connected like sisters. Mom, not so much—"

"She wouldn't have liked *anyone* Pete brought home."

"Truth. So, here's what he told me happened. They were in his dorm room late one night and had some stupid tiff—no big deal. Nancy flounced off and Pete let her go." Claudia paused, hating to even say it. "She got jumped by three guys on the way to her car."

"Holy shit. And one of them was Mitch?"

He was picturing it. Claudia could see anger building his narrowed eyes, his furrowed brow. She nodded. "She recognized his voice."

"How bad was it?"

"Nance avoided being raped but she was hurt badly enough to be hospitalized. Some random guy rode by on a bike as they were dragging her into an alley. He yelled out that he'd called the cops and they ran off."

"They were waiting for her."

Claudia puffed out a long sigh. "She had never told Pete that Mitch had been coming on to her the whole semester. He wouldn't take no for an answer. She made a big mistake in not taking him seriously."

"And lemme guess *why* she hadn't told Pete." Joel scrubbed a hand across his face as if that would erase the anger he was feeling. "She was afraid of what he'd do to Mitch if he knew." He had worked enough domestic violence cases to make the connection.

"Exactly. He couldn't take rejection, so he took revenge."

"Was the guy on the bike able to identify anyone?"

"No. It was too dark and he didn't know them. Unfortunately, Nancy hadn't kept any of the notes from Mitch, or the phone messages. They weren't overtly aggressive or sinister, just slightly stalkerish."

"I know what comes next," said Joel. "Without any evidence that Mitch had been stalking her, the investigator couldn't do anything."

"They questioned him but he was never charged. His father was a local judge. Pete said there were rumors he stepped in and the whole thing went away quietly."

"So, Mitch got away with it."

"Not totally. He didn't show up for school the whole next week. When he came back, he'd had the crap kicked out of him—black eyes, bruises. It was assumed that the judge had taken the law into his own hands."

"Not much consolation." Joel emptied his glass and signaled the waitress for another. "Pete had good reason to hate the sonofabitch."

"He'd always blamed himself for letting Nancy walk alone in the dark that night, but he'd never said a word about it until the day of the funeral. Mom's comment lit the fuse and he exploded."

"Any decent guy would feel the same."

"You know what's ironic? I doubt Mitch knew Nancy was dead when he went after Pete the other night. Twenty years later, same old jerk pushing the same old buttons."

"Emotions are a funny thing. Being back in the same setting, with the same people, brings it all back."

Claudia gripped her beer bottle by the neck, imagining it was Mitch Graham's neck. She wanted to hurl it across the room and watch it smash against the mirrored wall. "I wish Pete hadn't come to his stupid reunion."

Joel was tapping his forefinger on the table, the way he did when the detective wheels were turning. "Robin's investigator needs a list of the friends Pete was hanging with that night. You can bet the cops have heard about Pete's threat to kill Mitch."

Claudia's earlier spark of optimism fizzled and died like a firecracker in the rain. "It did sound pretty damning."

"When they find out about Pete's personal 'acquaintance' with the victim, which they will, he'll be in even deeper shit."

"No offense to present company, but I imagine Pete was smart enough not to tell the cops anything damning. And you didn't let him say anything that mattered when we talked to him." Claudia let out another deep sigh. "If there's anyone around here who knew what happened all those years ago, they're bound to mention that Mitch was suspected of assaulting Nancy. It provides motive."

Her husband's nod of agreement was a bond between them. His next words brought a chill. "It takes three things to prove guilt: means, motive, and opportunity. They've got two out of three. Let's hope that information never comes out."

8

SUNDAY

Over a late, leisurely brunch at a French Café with excellent reviews that Claudia came across online, she and Joel mapped out their day. He was due back on rotation the next day and had a flight back home that evening.

At the jail, they had been notified that one inmate visit a week was permitted, and it had to be scheduled in advance. She would have to wait to see Pete again after his arraignment.

Depositing phone money into his inmate account dumped a pall of gloom on her. Over the years of her handwriting examination practice, she had dealt with plenty of inmate clients calling her from jail. Her brother did not belong among them.

With the afternoon to kill, they Ubered to Pete's hotel. Joel flashed his badge at the desk clerk and informed him that they were there to collect Pete Bennett's things and close out his account. The clerk didn't look closely enough to notice that the badge was from California, not Arizona where it carried no weight. Handing over the room key without protest, he directed them to the guestroom.

Claudia packed the few clothes Pete had brought—tee-shirts and jeans; a dark suit and tie for the banquet that he would not be free to attend that evening. The memory of the last time she had seen him wear that suit—his wife's funeral—filled her mouth with bitter gall. And now, he had made the five-hundred-mile drive from L.A. to Tucson, excited to attend his reunion, only to be locked up for a heinous crime he claimed he did not commit.

Joel gathered Pete's toiletries and packed them in the Dopp kit on the vanity. Together, they made sure the room was as empty of Pete as it had been when he arrived, and dropped his suitcase at their hotel.

AFTER THAT, Claudia wanted to visit Mostly Books. "It's a very cool bookstore here in Tucson. I want you to meet my friend Tricia Clapp. She and her sister own it. She's a handwriting analyst, too."

"Lead the way," said Joel, and she called ahead to say they were coming.

Mostly Books was located in a shopping center on Speedway, a main drag in Tucson.

"Robin Cross has a great reputation," said Tricia when they arrived at the busy bookstore and brought her up to speed. "She's had her name in the papers a few times."

"For good reasons, I assume?" said Claudia.

"Of course. She's had several not-guilty verdicts."

Claudia raised her eyes to the ceiling. "Please God she gets one for Pete."

"If anyone can, it's Robin," said Tricia. "Hey, I have to get to work. Do you guys want to get together for pizza later with the chapter members?"

Claudia jumped on the invitation. "Joel's going home tonight. I was just asking myself what I was going to do for dinner."

"Cool. I'll pick you up at your hotel after we close the bookstore."

CLAUDIA AND JOEL took their time browsing the store. Cozy nooks, stacked floor to ceiling with used books. Shelves with the latest titles upfront. Racks of cards and funky gifts, tee-shirts with funny slogans. With an owner in the field, the well-stocked handwriting analysis section held an impressive range of lovingly used textbooks and monographs.

"Is this where old handwriting analysis books go to die?" Joel asked, shooting a side-eye.

"No, silly, it's where they go to get resurrected," Claudia said. "The AHAF Tucson chapter meets in the back room. I've given lectures here."

"Wait, what the heck is an AHAF?"

"American. Handwriting. Analysis. Foundation." Claudia enunciated with care. "Kind of a mouthful; thus, AHAF for short. You know. I'm a member."

BACK AT THEIR HOTEL, Claudia called Robin Cross and told her about their visit with Pete, and the information they had gleaned from Bree, their waitress at Dirtbags. Robin had her own report. She had made contact with her investigator, Tim Brody. She promised to tell him about the frat house behind the bar in case someone there had seen what went down in the parking lot.

"It's coming together," said Claudia, a little seed of hope starting to germinate again. Two days until, assuming there was any justice at all, Pete made bail and this part of the nightmare would be behind him. The trial to come was something she did not want to think about.

Joel had done some research and discovered that bail procedures were different in Arizona from California, where there was a set bail schedule depending on the crime. Here, the magistrate had the power to set whatever bail amount he or she deemed appropriate under the circumstances. Pete's clean record worked in his favor, and the fact that he operated a home-based computer business, had family and standing in the community where he lived. The downside was, he resided out of state, so might be viewed as a flight risk. And, as he stood accused of murdering the son of a prominent local judge, his bond could be insanely high. At the thought of him having to mortgage his house to pay for his defense, Claudia's temples started to throb.

She saw Joel off to the airport with a long, soulful kiss and a promise to make it up to him when she got back to L.A. on Tuesday evening.

After a short nap, the headache was gone and a text from Monica had arrived:

How long will my dad be gone?

Her fingers dithered over her phone. Her niece was seven thousand miles away. When she returned home from the dig, it would be impossible for Pete to hide what he was facing. That would be soon enough for her to learn what had happened. Let her enjoy the remainder of her time in Egypt.

Couple days. You can check in with me, xoxo

She couldn't resist adding one more line and a smiling emoji with a heart:

Making any new friends?

Her phone stayed silent.

Tricia arrived to pick her up and Claudia was hungry and ready to go. They were parking at the pizza parlor when her phone dinged with a brief reply from Monica:

Yes, thanks xo

It was uncharacteristic of Monica to be so brief, but with a half-dozen friends waiting in the restaurant, Claudia let it go. The last time this group had been together was at a handwriting analysis conference in L.A. There was plenty of catching up to do.

She and Tricia had agreed in advance to keep things simple, so when someone asked what brought her to Tucson, she had a ready answer: "A California case that ended up here."

With Mitch Graham's father being a well-known judge in town, some of them might have seen the news of Mitch's brutal murder on TV, but there was no reason to connect the name 'Pete Bennett' to Claudia Rose, even if they paid any attention to a bar fight and the arrest of an out-of-towner.

Her explanation was accepted without question, and the friends dove into what had been going on in their various lives. Claudia, having given herself the go-ahead to enjoy the evening and not allow her brother's situation to gate-crash every other thought, laughed freely and reminisced with her friends.

THE KING-SIZE BED felt vast and lonely. Joel phoned to say he'd had an uneventful flight and was home and in bed, too. Claudia told him about her evening. Neither wanted to end the call. Finally, exchanging reluctant goodnights and I love you's, they clicked off and Claudia got out her tablet.

She read until she was starting to get sleepy. Preparing to settle down and turn off her mind, she switched off the bedside lamp. The constant on-off hum and click of the heater made mincemeat of her plans to relax, and the yawning darkness brought back Monica's brief answer to 'are you making any new friends?'

Yes, thanks.

The brevity of the message itched like a flea bite. Normally, Monica's excitement tended to burble into many words. Why had she been so terse this time?

Claudia thought about it for a while. Intuition was telling her that Monica was avoiding telling the whole truth. *Why?* There was nothing specific she could put her finger on, except that her niece was the least successful prevaricator she had ever known. The mildest white lie would stain Monica's cheeks the color of ketchup. What could she be avoiding saying?

Maybe the undergrads on the excavation team were resentful of her presence? They were five or more years older than her and had earned the right to go on this trip. Could they have made her feel unwelcome? She quickly rejected that theory. Her niece had sounded happy and excited every single time they had spoken. What else, then?

Eleven PM in Tucson was nine AM in Egypt. Claudia reached for her phone and opened WhatsApp. Straight to voicemail. She dredged up a smile that would come across in her message. "Hey, kiddo, call me soon. Love you, bye."

She replaced the phone on the nightstand with a nagging feeling that something was off.

Way off.

9

MONDAY

AFTER ONE OF THOSE FITFUL NIGHTS MADE UP OF TOO MANY DREAMS and too few peaceful hours, Claudia slept in and got up late. She ordered breakfast in the hotel dining room and drank three cups of black coffee, feeling the acid burn through her stomach lining. Opening her tablet and checking the local news was a bigger mistake. The headline caused her to choke on her avocado toast: "Tucson Lawyer Murder Victim."

Studying the studio portrait in the link to the article, her chest constricted with anxiety. Maybe she was prejudiced, but with the thin lips and oblique, sneaky glance at the camera, it seemed to her that Mitch Graham had not traded on his good looks. She scanned the story, which said he had been stabbed to death at a popular Tucson location and omitted mention of the bar fight. The article read like an obituary, describing him as a successful estate attorney, detailing his athletic accomplishments and involvement in several civic organizations. It pretty much made him a candidate for sainthood, Claudia thought sourly. His wife, Eleanor, was acknowledged, and his father, retired Judge Leonard Graham. Mitch was predeceased by his mother. No kids.

Reading about the family made the whole nightmare more real. Not that Pete sitting in a cell a few miles away wasn't all-too-real.

If their Dirtbags waitress was to be believed and Mitch was the grab-ass jerk she had claimed—and given what he had done to her sister-in-law, there was no reason to believe otherwise—Claudia could find little sympathy for Mitch Graham. It was the thought of his wife grieving over him that brought the situation into clearer focus.

Her insides were churning as she gathered her things and ditched her half-eaten breakfast. In an attempt to burn off the accumulated tension, she went for a long walk around the block. An hour later, returning to her room as stressed as when she'd left, and with no word from Pete or his attorney, she booted up her laptop.

When life was handing her lemons, work was Claudia's go-to escape hatch.

An email had come in from a new client; a grandmother asking whether anything in her young grandson's handwriting might clue her in on how to help him deal with ongoing problems at school. Claudia opened the handwriting sample and studied it on the screen.

After appraising the amount of space between letters, words, and lines, she examined the movement created by the flow of ink. Rather than a clear, smooth ink line, when she enlarged the image a muddy, blotchy one was revealed—a red flag for physiological issues, maybe substance abuse.

At this boy's age, thirteen, the hormonal condition she was seeing in the handwriting sample came as no surprise. However, there was more than a chemical imbalance affecting his thinking and behavior. Serious problems were brewing that went beyond the range of her expertise. She started and ended her report on a positive note. The tricky part had to be sandwiched in the middle: take him to a doctor for a neurological and general medical work-up. Soon.

When she hit Send, it was close to noon and there had been no word from Monica. No voicemail, no text. Claudia knew that Robin had the bail hearing to attend, plus she was going to meet her new client, so she didn't expect to hear from her for a while.

It was past nine P.M. in Egypt. Monica had told her they worked long hours on the dig—as long as there was light. That meant early to bed and early to rise. Claudia texted a message:

Call me, please. Love you.

The niggling feeling was back, worming into her consciousness. Why hadn't Monica called? The sweetest, most cooperative, obedient girl in the world, didn't normally behave this way.

Five minutes later the phone rang. Pete, calling from jail. His voice dragged. "Hey, sis, how's it going?"

Claudia could hardly blame him for feeling despondent. "Okay here. How are you holding up?"

"What can I say? This sucks."

"Have you seen Robin?"

He brightened at mention of his attorney. "She just left. You were right, she's exactly the kind of hardass I need. The prosecutor didn't want to allow bond, but Robin talked the magistrate into it."

"Dare I ask how much?"

"Two-fifty K. I have to get twenty-five to the bondsman. He gets the rest together and if all goes well, I'm out tomorrow. God, I can't wait to wash the stink off me and get some decent food. We got a baloney sandwich before court, and that's the best food in here."

"Less than twenty-four hours from now," said Claudia, trying to inject cheer into her voice, when inside she was bawling. "I'll be waiting at the jail, ready to whisk you away to the airport."

"I can't believe the grand jury brought back an indictment for Murder One." Pete interrupted himself. "Never mind that right now. How's Monica? Did you tell her what I said about not having cell service?"

No point in worrying him. "I texted her your message."

"Thanks, sis. Hang on a sec." Pete growled at someone on his side of the phone. "The fuck, dude? Can't you see I'm on the phone?" He came back abrupt and irascible. "I have to go. This goddamn place—"

MID-AFTERNOON, Robin texted a message to meet for dinner at Dirtbags; one place Claudia had wished never to see again.

In a consulting business, she didn't have the luxury of ignoring queries. With hours to fill, and her head fully occupied by thoughts of her brother and his daughter, it took every ounce of concentration to get through the next case waiting in her In box—a probate case.

The attorney's client was insisting that the signature on his father's will must be a forgery—the will that cut him out of the estate and left everything to his stepsisters.

The signature, an undefined squiggle, lacked any identifying features that would allow Claudia to authenticate or eliminate it. Nonetheless, she went through a full examination and compared it to the father's exemplar signatures before reaching a conclusion and phoning the attorney with a verbal report. If the case ended up in court, a written report would be discoverable by the opposition, which in this case could work to the detriment of the client.

"Signatures like this have too little complexity," Claudia explained to the attorney. "They're easy to forge and difficult to identify. There simply isn't enough complexity to make a judgment. Anyone could copy this signature, so I can't say whether your client's father did or not sign."

The attorney was philosophical about it. "I wish the news had been better, but this way, I have time to rethink the strategy of my case."

"When the letters in a signature are well-defined and complex, it's extremely difficult for even a talented forger—and talented forgers are rare—to successfully simulate," Claudia said.

And then, it was time to get ready to return to Dirtbags.

ROBIN CROSS, small and slender, was dressed in navy slacks and a shirt tucked in under a jacket. What kept her looking young and innocent at thirty-five was the luxuriant cascade of black corkscrew curls that bloomed around a delicate face and ended halfway down her back. People made assumptions about her based on those looks.

"Bailiffs used to ask for my ID all the time," she had said the first time Claudia had met her in person. "They don't make old white men do that." Those same people were quick to change their tune when they saw Robin in action in the courtroom. *Pit bull.*

Waiting at the bar, a glass of red wine in front of her, she stood and grasped Claudia's hand with a grip firm enough to bruise knuckles. "What can I get you to drink?"

It was the kind of place where they should be doing shooters, but Claudia pointed to Robin's glass. "I'll have one of those, thanks."

Robin ordered another Cab. Claudia perched on the next barstool. "Pete called me. You dazzled him, as I knew you would."

A bright smile lit the attorney's face. "Aw, thanks. Your brother is a sweetheart; got caught up in a circumstantial nightmare. Let's go find a table. I have his permission to discuss his case with you, and we have some things to cover." Claudia's wine arrived and Robin hopped off her stool with her glass in hand.

They snagged a table in the covered patio and ordered grilled chicken salads. Their waitress departed and Robin got right down to it. "I took a look around out back where the homicide occurred. Checked out the alley and the doorway where Pete said he slept."

Claudia feigned disappointment. "I'm devastated. I was planning on giving you the nickel tour."

Robin smiled. "I went to school at the U; been a customer here since I was a baby lawyer." She drank wine, then put her glass firmly on the table. "Let's start with today's proceedings."

"I read the Court's website, so I'm somewhat familiar with what to expect."

"Good. Let's go over it and make sure. Pete had his Initial Appearance on Saturday. Today, the Grand Jury met and, as we expected, based on the prosecutor's recommendation, they returned an indictment of Murder One. The Magistrate set the bail amount."

"Pete said you fought hard for bail," said Claudia, pleased that she had made the right choice of attorney for her brother.

Robin's nod was a modest dip of her head. "I was prepared for the prosecutor to ask for no bail and call Pete a flight risk since he lives out of state, and that's how it went. I moved to reduce the bail amount based on his good record, that he's a productive member of the community who owns a business, and that he has sole care of a young daughter."

"So, he'll be out tomorrow."

"If all goes well. Don't bother to come to the jail in the morning; you won't get to see him. If the bondsman comes up with the bail money tomorrow and he's released, it could take four or five hours before he's out. Unless you have nothing better to do than sit at the jail all day, you should wait until I call you." Robin was chewing on her lip, giving the impression that there was something she didn't want to say.

"What is it, Robin?"

"I've told your brother, you all need to be prepared for the worst-case scenario at trial. The murder has deprived Mitch Graham's wife of her husband and his father, Judge Graham, of his son. The County Attorney wouldn't go for less than Murder One. And there's the 'lying in wait' aspect. They're saying it's premeditated because according to their theory of the case, the killer—in their view, Pete—waited for Mitch to leave the bar and attacked him."

"What about the murder weapon? I read that the victim was stabbed. Where is Pete supposed to have got the knife?"

"Screwdriver."

"What?"

"They don't have the murder weapon. The medical examiner thinks Mitch was stabbed with a screwdriver; something of that type. They made a point that there's a toolbox in Pete's truck with a whole raft of them."

"That doesn't mean a thing. Everyone owns screwdrivers."

"Yeah, but not everyone had a very public fight with the dead guy less than an hour earlier."

"I bet they're not going to find any blood on the screwdrivers in Pete's truck."

"Well, no. But the police have crime scene people going over every inch of the neighborhood."

The neighborhood where they were sitting right now. All of a sudden, the chicken salad was less appetizing. It sat like a stone in the bottom of Claudia's stomach. "You said 'lying in wait,'" she said. "Pete said that after the cops came and told him to leave, he took off. What about Mitch? Didn't he leave, too?"

Robin shook her head and set her curls swaying. "Happens Mitch was buddies with one of the cops who took the call. I had a heart-to-heart with the manager here. He told me they all hung around for a little while. When the cops went away, it was getting near closing. There was no love lost for Mitch with Pete's friends, so Mitch took off right after the cops. He was found the next morning in the parking lot."

"Who found him?"

"A student taking a shortcut to class. The body was right next to Pete's truck. I've seen the crime scene photos. It was pretty grim. The poor girl wigged out."

"I can imagine," said Claudia, wigging out herself.

10

TUESDAY MORNING

AFTER YET ANOTHER RESTLESS NIGHT AND NOTHING FROM MONICA, Claudia made a call to the one person who could be relied upon to know where her niece was: her best friend, Annabelle Giordano.

The conversation was less than satisfactory.

"Hey, Claudia, what's up?"

"Hey, Annabelle, how's things?"

"Fine. Why?" The girl's voice held a tinge of suspicion.

"When did you last talk to Monica?"

"Mm, maybe Tuesday or Wednesday, why?"

"She hasn't returned my calls and texts. That's not like her."

"Have you checked her Insta?"

"Instagram? I didn't know she had one."

"She's been posting ever since she got to Egypt."

"That's good to know. How about the last couple of days? What has she been posting?"

"Oh, you don't have to worry, she's fine."

That answer set Claudia's antenna twanging. She had learned from courtroom training that when someone answers a question that wasn't asked, it's a red flag.

"Why do you think I would worry?" she asked.

"You shouldn't. Her dad's out of town, right?"

"He's at his college reunion in Tucson, but that doesn't change their deal. She's supposed to check in with him every day. Or me."

"What's up with Pete?" Annabelle could be counted on to deflect. "Why can't he call her?"

What was it with teenagers? They always had to answer a question with another question. An uncomfortable one in this case. Claudia reached for the easy response. "He's out of cell range. She's supposed to call me."

"You know she's a legal adult, right? C'mon, Claudia, chill. She can do her own thing."

Another glib answer; another red flag. "What 'thing?' What's she doing?"

Another long pause. "Oh, you know; digging up old bones in Egypt. Or watching the other people dig, anyway. She's recording the stuff they do."

"Yes, I know that, thank you. What *else* is she doing that she might not want to tell me?"

"If you think she doesn't want me to tell you something, why are you asking me?"

"Because you're her best friend?"

"So, why would a best friend blab something her friend didn't want her to?"

"Annabelle—" It was said as a warning. Without doubt, the girl knew more than she was letting on. Claudia couldn't blame her for trying to parry her inquiry. If she had thought she was protecting her best friend, she would not have parted with any information, either.

Annabelle huffed a big sigh. "If I hear from her, I'll tell her to call you."

"I need more than that. Please call her now. Maybe if it's your number she'll answer. I need to tell Pete I'm in touch with her."

"I thought Pete was out of range."

As long as she'd known her, the girl had been a fountain of exasperating sass. Claudia neutralized the stinging retort she wanted to make. "When he's back in range, okay? Will you call her for me?"

"Okay."

"Promise?"

"I said I would."

"Thank you." Not entirely satisfied that to leave the responsibility in Annabelle's hands, Claudia switched subjects. "How's work?"

The change in Annabelle's tone was noteworthy. "It's so cool. The kids are awesome, especially the little ones."

For the past several months Annabelle had been volunteering at the Regina Boles Center for Traumatized Children, which was run by Sage Boles, a friend of Claudia's. Now that she had graduated high school, Annabelle, having experienced more than her share of damaging trauma in her young life, had decided to study child psychology with a focus on helping abuse victims.

"And I've heard you're really popular with them. You're doing really good work there." Claudia let the comment hang there, unacknowledged except for a pleased "Aww." Annabelle had difficulty accepting a compliment, but she was getting there.

"Speaking of work," Annabelle said, "I gotta run."

"Hey, if I don't hear from Monica by this afternoon, I'm calling you back."

"Bye."

The line went dead.

11

Not quite a free man, Pete Bennett walked out of the Pima County Detention Center holding a plastic bag containing his wallet, phone, keys, and miscellaneous pocket junk—property the police had confiscated. Five days in jail had left their mark. He glanced around furtively, as if he expected the cops to show up and re-arrest him. "Let's get the hell away from here," he said.

God willing, he would never have to go back, Claudia thought. Then she remembered—he had the trial to face. After having endured the better part of a week locked up, and having spent his life staving off the unwelcome smothering hugs and lipsticky kisses their mother inflicted on him, Claudia knew that Pete would want his first breath of freedom without a big display of emotion. Fighting the impulse to grab her brother and squeeze him in a bear hug, she refused to consider the possibility of a conviction.

Buckled into the backseat of an Uber driving away from the jail, Pete let out a gusty exhale. "Robin is scary good. I didn't think the magistrate was going to release me. At first, he said no bond, but she argued hard. The prosecutor wanted five-hundred thousand. Robin got it cut down to half." He shuddered. "I don't care how much it is; it's worth not spending another minute in that hellhole."

"I'm glad you don't have to stay in Tucson until the trial," said Claudia.

"I have to come back and report in every month until trial. I can't get my truck out of impound for thirty days, though the magistrate said he recognized the financial burden it would place on me to make me stay here. As if coming up with the bail plus the attorney fees isn't burden enough." Pete caught himself. He reached over and grabbed Claudia's hand. "I'm not the ungrateful prick I sound. You and Joel are the best. Thank you for spotting me the bail. I'll go to the bank when it opens tomorrow and pay you back, promise."

She gave him a watery smile. "I'm *so* not worried about it. Besides, I know where you live."

Glancing at their driver, whose eyes remained discreetly on the road, Pete dropped his voice. "The first couple of days, I had this fantasy, you know? The cops would catch whoever really killed that douche and I'd be off the hook. Truth is, they're not looking for anyone else, are they?"

Claudia knew better than to lie to him. "I doubt it. Robin's investigator will talk to everyone who knew Mitch and look for someone with a motive. As creepy as he was, there's got to be a whole flock of suspects. All Robin has to do is show that someone else had a motive to get to reasonable doubt."

Pete shook his head. "It's a circumstantial case. I'm not optimistic, Claud. He was killed right by my truck. Right after we'd had a fight. With his old man being a judge—retired or not—and Mitch's friends being cops..." He fell silent and Claudia followed his lead. Pollyanna pep talks were not her style and he would not welcome it if she tried to give him one.

They were nearing the airport when Pete roused himself from whatever self-reflection he was indulging in and brought up the topic Claudia had been eager to avoid. "Hey Sis, how's my kid doing?"

She hesitated, looking for an answer that wouldn't make things worse. "I'm waiting to hear back from her."

Pete's body stiffened. "When did you last talk to her?"

"We texted on Sunday afternoon. Annabelle promised to have her call me if she talks to her."

"What the hell? She's supposed to check in every day while she's away." Pete rummaged in the plastic bag for his phone and tried to power it up, dropping it back in the bag. "Battery's dead."

Claudia opened WhatsApp and handed him hers. "You know it's eleven P.M. over there, right?"

"Right." The silence thickened. When the call went straight to voicemail, Pete's message hummed with the tension of a worried father. "Call me as soon as you get this message, Mon. I don't care what time it is, day or night. *Call me.*" He returned the phone to Claudia. "I need to get hold of Frank Booth."

"Who's that?"

"The professor in charge of the dig. His number is in my phone. Dammit, why isn't she answering?"

Claudia didn't say so, but she was starting to worry that something had gone seriously wrong in Egypt. "I expect she's working a lot and not checking her phone," she said, trying to convince herself as well as Pete. "I'm sure she's fine and there's some ridiculous reason she hasn't been able to contact us."

She and Monica had watched dozens of tourist videos together. The comments invariably raved that it was the best place in the world and the Egyptians were a welcoming, happy people. That didn't stop what *could* have happened from curdling in her belly.

"She's a good kid," Pete persisted as they arrived at the airport. "She always calls or texts."

Walking into the terminal, Claudia continued playing devil's advocate. "Wait until you get your battery charged before you start freaking out. If anything major happened, we would have heard. I've checked the news."

"You checked? So, you do think something's wrong."

"C'mon, Pete, give it a rest. You've had a hideous few days. Give yourself a minute to adjust to normal."

Once they made it through security and located their gate, Pete glommed onto a vacant charging station and plugged his phone in. He checked out the fast-food restaurants in the terminal. "I'm going to get something to eat. Want something?"

"Turkey and Swiss on a French roll; diet soda."

He took himself off to the food court and Claudia called Annabelle.

"Have you talked to Monica? We're at Tucson airport and—"

"Why are you in Tucson?"

"*Annabelle,* focus. What about Monica?"

"She hasn't called me back." The unspoken question lingered: 'why are you bugging me about this?'

The spurt of irritation that shredded Claudia's nerves was not for Annabelle; she was used to dealing with her teenage ways. It was for the fear that had started as a nibble around the edges of her gut and had progressed to full out gorging. It didn't take much effort to put on the voice of authority.

"Okay, kiddo, this ends right here, right now. I need you to tell me where she is. You know, and I know you do. Spill it."

"But Claudia—"

"No buts, Annabelle. I don't care what you promised her. Spit it out."

Like Monica, Annabelle was legally an adult now. That didn't stop her from heaving a big teenage huff of protest. "Honest, Claudia, I *don't* know where she's at."

"Then what *do* you know?"

Another sigh. "Fine. I think she's hanging with this super-hot guy she met. She sent me a picture, which is how I know he's super-hot. She's majorly crushing on him. If it was me, I'd sure as hell be turning off *my* phone."

"No, you wouldn't," Claudia retorted half-irritated, half-relieved by the news. "Teenagers never turn off their phones."

"Well, maybe..."

Airport noise blared all around. People running to catch a flight. Southwest Airlines announcing an arrival. A man on the other side of the charging station, complaining in a loud voice into his phone about his escrow problems. Why did people think it was okay to blab their business to the public? Surprised by the news Annabelle had dropped on her, Claudia tuned it all out.

"Who is this guy?"

"It's no big, Claudia. He's a British archaeologist from another dig."

"She never mentioned him."

"Maybe she was afraid you'd tell Pete and he would start ragging on her. You know how he is."

Yes, Claudia knew. Did her niece think *she* couldn't be trusted with the information? "Where'd she meet this guy? How old is he?"

"There was a welcome party for the dig people. They met there. Come on, Claudia, you know Monica's not gonna do anything that would upset Pete."

"What's his name?"

"Why? What are you going to do if I tell you?"

"Give it to Pete and let him figure it out."

Yet another big, breathy sigh came through the phone. "Why can't you wait for her to call you?"

"I'm done waiting. What's his name?"

"Colin." If they had been in the same room, Annabelle would have flounced. Claudia could hear it in her voice.

"Colin what?"

"*Colin.* That's all she said."

Claudia heaved a sigh of her own. "I wish you girls would hurry and grow up. This parenting crap is rough, and I'm not even a parent."

Annabelle giggled. "Aww, c'mon, Claudia, you're killin' it."

That was unexpected and produced a big grin. "Wow, a compliment, thanks. Hey, text me that photo of Colin, please. And let me know if you hear anything from Monica."

"Okay, okay. Bye."

Pete returned with sandwiches from Beyond Bread. "I was jonesing for a burger, but I'm not complaining. Anything is better than the slop I've been eating, not-eating."

While Pete downed half his food and checked his phone battery, Claudia unwrapped her sandwich, dithering on whether to tell him what she had learned from Annabelle.

"Ten-percent," he said impatiently. "That's enough juice."

He wiped his hands on a paper napkin and checked messages. Swiping glumly through the texts, he alternated between bitter smiles and defeated scowls. "My buddies texting, asking what the hell happened to me."

The reunion had meant a lot to him. Hanging out with old friends of his and Nancy's would have brought her back for a while. "They haven't been watching the local news," said Claudia.

"You mean, too busy partying." Pete's expression brightened. "Here's one Monica sent last Thursday night. Says she was going sightseeing with a friend."

"She didn't mention it when I heard from her on Sunday."

He looked up with a worried frown. "There's a message *and* a text from Frank Booth yesterday. He wants me to call him ASAP." He started tapping on the screen and got Booth's voicemail.

"If it was urgent, he would have had his phone on," Claudia pointed out, trying to look on the bright side.

"Today is Tuesday, Claud. You said she hasn't contacted you since Sunday. Why not?"

And just like that, the decision was made for her.

"Um, about that friend she was sightseeing with." Knowing how he was going to take the news, she fumbled for words. "I think I know who it is. While you were getting the food, I spoke with Annabelle."

Pete gave an impatient tut. "If Annabelle's involved—"

"Don't be ridiculous. Annabelle's not in Egypt, is she? She told me Monica has a crush on a guy she met from another dig."

"Oh, that's great. She's infatuated with some 'handsome stranger' in Egypt?"

"Don't jump to conclusions. Annabelle assured me she's not doing anything you wouldn't approve of."

"*Annabelle* assured you? That's setting the bar low."

"How about *lowering* your voice? Annabelle has come a long way."

Wrapped up in his worries, he wasn't listening. "This is not like my kid."

"Maybe you haven't noticed, Pete; your kid is of legal age now.

She's a young adult. I know you don't want to think of her as a sexual being—"

He stuck his fingers in his ears the way they used to do when they were kids and didn't want to hear something. "Stop. I know she's not a child and she's *not* the type to go crazy over 'some guy' she just met."

Claudia had to laugh at what he made sound like air quotes. "Get real. She's away from the restraints of home and she's met someone she likes a lot. A teenage girl with a crush behaves in mysterious ways."

Pete glared at her. "If you're trying to help, please stop. It's not making me feel any better. I'm calling Booth until he picks up."

She put out a restraining hand. "It's four A.M. over there. We'll be home in two hours. Wait until we get there; give him a chance to wake up." As she spoke, their flight was announced. "See, the Universe is telling you to wait. Let's go get in line so we can get decent seats."

Pete opened his mouth as though about to argue, then changed his mind and picked up his trash. "Here's what we know: Monica hasn't contacted us and Booth needs to talk 'ASAP.' Something is wrong and I'm scared shitless."

"I know." This time, Claudia gave him a hug. She didn't say "Me, too," but that's what she was thinking.

12

Pete was a single parent, but his kitchen could qualify for the Good Housekeeping Seal of Approval.

While her brother reached out to Professor Booth, Claudia got busy making coffee. She measured coffee and water, marveling at the lack of errant crumbs and food stains on the counter tops that always popped out of nowhere in her kitchen, and got two mugs from the cabinet.

Maybe it was his computer programmer nature that made her brother a perfectionist who insisted that everything be kept in its proper place. Not knowing where his daughter was, at the same time as facing murder charges, must have been as excruciating as a noose tightening around his neck.

Pete put his phone on speaker to let them both hear the conversation, and proceeded to pace around the center island, waiting for the call to connect. Frank Booth answered promptly.

"Thanks for getting back to me, Pete."

"I've been out of cell range, just got your message from yesterday. Is Monica all right?"

"Erm, well, unfortunately, I'm contacting you because we don't know where she is."

The silence on the line after that pronouncement left Claudia and Pete staring at each other aghast.

"What do you mean, 'don't know where she is?'" Pete yelled at the phone.

"I'm sure you know she went away for the weekend. The problem is, she didn't come back. We haven't heard from her since she took off last Thursday evening. She was supposed to be back Sunday night for work on Monday."

Watching the blood drain from Pete's face, Claudia broke out in a prickly cold sweat.

Pete gripped the edge of the countertop. "No, I didn't know that. Went away where? With who?"

"We don't know where she went. She'd told her roommate that she needed an extra day off, which was fine. We respect the Muslim tradition here, which means our work week starts on Sunday. Friday and Saturday are our off days." Booth sounded apologetic. "To be perfectly honest, I've been distracted by an important find that's kept me occupied day and night, but I phoned you the minute McKenna alerted me that Monica was missing."

Watching Pete struggle with his emotions, Claudia guessed what he was thinking: *I didn't expect you to babysit her, professor, I expected you to keep her safe.* As well as, *how could I have let her go so far from home?*

The strain was evident in his voice. "Didn't Monica tell McKenna where she was going?"

"I'm afraid not. I'll have McKenna call you right away. It's better if you speak directly to her."

"I'd appreciate it."

Signaling to him not to end the call, Claudia stepped closer to the phone. "Dr. Booth, this is Pete's sister. Do you happen to know of a British archaeologist named Colin?"

"Colin Vine? From Hawkins-Whyte's dig?" He sounded surprised.

"We don't have a last name. Monica's best friend here says she's been seeing him. She said she was going sightseeing, and we think she might have gone with him."

"Vine is the only Colin I know." Frank Booth hesitated. "I wouldn't have thought he was her type."

"Why not?" Pete shot a worried look at Claudia.

"Don't get me wrong. Vine is a very bright young archaeologist and popular with the teams. It's, well, there was some trouble last season."

"What does that mean? What kind of trouble?"

"Oh, it was all resolved and Vine was exonerated."

"Exonerated of what? What was he accused of?"

Booth started backpedaling. "As I said, it was all cleared up. It concerned some artifacts, nothing you would need to bother about. I shouldn't have mentioned it."

"Why do you say he isn't her type?" Claudia asked, setting a hand on Pete's arm before he could go off on the professor. She could see him gearing up for it.

"Only that she's a very sweet girl and he's somewhat older, mid-twenties. Colin is a likeable guy; a little on the slick side. Tell you what, I'll contact Henry Hawkins-Whyte and see whether Vine is there, or if not, whether anyone on his team can add anything. I can phone the embassy when they open this morning, too, and report Monica missing. Or maybe you'd prefer do that yourself?"

"Yes, thanks; I'll make the embassy call. They'll need her passport number and other information. If you could follow up and give them anything that might help on a local level, I'd be grateful."

"I will. And please trust me when I say we'll do everything we can to help find Monica. I'll have McKenna get in touch. Stand by."

The call ended. Claudia went through the motions of pouring the coffee in the tense silence and told herself sternly that everything was fine. A jumble of headlines massed in her mind and disagreed with her conclusion: young women kidnapped overseas and trafficked.

"It sounded like he liked Colin Vine," she said in a vain attempt to shut off the headlines. "That was good, don't you think? I mean, it's not like he's a—" Pete's phone rang and cut off her optimistic ramble.

This time, the voice that came over the speaker was youngish and female with a mild Texas twang. "Mr. Bennett? Hi, this is McKenna Ryan, Monica's roommate?"

Pete tripped over her words. "Do you know where she went?"

"No, I'm sorry. All she said was, she was going away for the weekend with Colin. She didn't say where. I tried to warn her about him."

"Warn her—?"

"It's just, since that accident and everything, she wouldn't listen to a word against—"

Pete and Claudia stared at each other, wide-eyed, across the island. *"What accident?"* they asked in unison.

"Oh, she didn't tell you? It happened a couple of days after we all got here. She and Colin went off for the day together and were in a taxi that got into a bad accident. They weren't hurt, but there were some casualties, and Colin got arrested and—"

"Stop. Please, stop," Pete interrupted sharply. "As long as Monica was okay from an accident a few weeks ago, that's something I can deal with later. Colin was arrested, you said. If they went away together last week, obviously, he was released. I can hear *why* he was arrested later."

That was the first thing that came to Claudia's mind. Why would a passenger in a taxi be arrested? Had Monica been arrested, too?

"Well, yeah," McKenna said. "Colin didn't want anyone to know about it, but that kind of thing gets around in a small community like ours."

Claudia thought she detected a note of satisfaction in McKenna's voice. Maybe she was interested in Colin herself and what Claudia was hearing was *schadenfreude*.

"So, it was last Wednesday when she told me they were going away," the young woman continued. "He picked her up right after work. Our permit expires next week and she was supposed to be back Sunday night to help start securing the site."

"And she didn't give any hint as to where they were going?"

"No, but I know she didn't plan on being gone this long. Everything she took fit in her backpack. She left everything else here."

"What about the people at Vine's dig?" Pete asked.

"Frank is checking with them. Don't worry, Mr. Bennett, if one of us gets any news I'll text you."

"Thank you. Thank you for calling."

Glowering, Pete clicked off the call. "She was in an accident weeks ago and never said a word? She's gone away with this guy and didn't tell us she was dating someone? Who the hell *is* this we're talking about?"

"It's not like her." Claudia agreed, preoccupied with a Google search for the US Embassy in Cairo. "The Embassy website says it opens at 9:15. There's a section here for U.S. Citizens Missing Abroad. It says *'most of the time worried friends and family members eventually hear from the person, though it may take several days to get a response.'"*

"It says that?"

"Yes, it actually does." Claudia quoted from the page. "'People forget or are unable to make contact. Due to time differences, busy schedules, lack of cell phone coverage, irregular access to email, or difficulty making international phone calls.'"

Even as she read it, it didn't feel real that the remarks were connected to her family. How could her niece be 'missing abroad?' She answered herself: the same way her brother stood accused of murder. Their world had tilted on its axis and it wouldn't right itself until they heard from Monica and Pete was free of the murder charge.

The embassy wouldn't open for another hour. Claudia used the time to check in with Joel at home and bring him up to date. He was as concerned as she and Pete were, and offered to do anything he could to help.

Next, she texted Annabelle a reminder to send the photo of Colin Vine. Ten seconds later, it arrived: a selfie of Monica and a man. Claudia understood the attraction at once. There was something innately sexy about Colin Vine.

Monica's hand was over her mouth as if suppressing a laugh; her eyes sparkled with happiness. Colin, whose own heavy-lidded eyes had a sensual appeal, was standing behind her, leaning down, his cheek resting possessively on her blonde head. His hair, a deep burgundy color that had not come from nature, was pulled into a Samurai man bun on top of his head.

Monica's father glared at the photo with a silent loathing that said he would welcome the opportunity to rip off the dude's head. "He's way too old for her. She should know better."

"Yeah, like you and I did at her age?"

"Stop 'helping,' Claudia, or go home."

She gave him a good-natured poke in the ribs. "Chill; it's time to call the embassy."

Pete entered the number and she listened with half an ear, guilt gnawing at her as he connected with someone who took down Monica's details. That long-ago conversation she had started with Monica about the cool factor of Ancient Egypt and the old gods—if something bad had happened to her niece, it was she, Claudia, who had kindled her interest in archaeology.

"They'll check the local authorities for any reports of a U.S. citizen being hospitalized or arrested or anything else," Pete repeated after ending the call. He started pacing the kitchen again. He slammed his hand down on the counter.

"I'm gonna book a flight out there for tomorrow, if I can find one. I can't sit around here, twiddling my thumbs until they call."

"You can't go to Egypt. You have to surrender your passport to the court, remember?"

"You can't expect me to do nothing, not knowing where my kid is. I'll deal with the consequences when I get back."

"It isn't going to do Monica any good for you to jeopardize your freedom. I'll go."

"Are you crazy? I'm not asking you to do that."

"I know you're not asking, I'm volunteering."

"What do you think Joel would have to say about that?"

"He'll understand. You can't go and one of us needs to be there."

As they debated, Claudia was logging onto the Delta Airlines website, scanning flights for the next available seat to Cairo, where the American Embassy was located.

Her long-cherished childhood dream, which she had passed along to Monica, was to see Egypt. But not this way.

13

EGYPT

THE DISCORDANT MUSIC OF HONKING HORNS AND PEOPLE SHOUTING AT one another filled the morning air and the acrid smell of desert dust filled Claudia's nostrils. The sixteen-hour flight to Cairo was now a haze of fatigue. Time and again, she had dozed off, jerking awake in a fret over her niece.

During the ninety-minute layover in Frankfurt, she had taken the opportunity to stretch her legs in the terminal and phoned Pete. There had been no news since her departure and he sounded shakier than when they had said goodbye at LAX twelve hours earlier.

Annabelle was next on her list.

Hearing that Claudia was flying across the world in search of her niece, Annabelle had dropped the blasé attitude and went straight to losing it. Her best friend's unscheduled disappearance had just become all-too real. For Claudia, the fact that Annabelle hadn't heard from Monica was far more frightening than Monica not calling her dad or her aunt.

Next, she spoke with Joel. Over their years together, Claudia's habit of rushing into situations he believed were too risky had been a source of friction between them on several occasions. She wanted his company on this trip more than anything, and he had offered to take leave from work and go with her to Egypt. But, talking it through together, it made no sense for both of them to be away when Pete needed support.

In the air between Frankfurt and Cairo, she logged onto the internet and viewed as many videos as she could find about getting around the city; the value of the Egyptian pound—her American dollars would go far—and the local culture. Cairo had Uber and the Egyptian version, Careem. Three hundred miles away in Luxor, where the dig site was located, she would have to use the Nile Taxi service. She booked a room for one night at the Semiramis in Cairo, astonished at the low cost for the five-star hotel.

It was mid-evening when she arrived. She got a visa on the spot for twenty-five US dollars, and purchased a sim card so her phone would work in Egypt. By ten P.M. Claudia was in her hotel room. It was all she could do to find the energy to unzip her overnight bag. Climbing into her pajamas with none to spare, she fell into bed.

The Muezzin and their call of the faithful to prayer woke her at 5:13 A.M. She lay in bed, listening to the melodic tones float across the city from mosque to mosque, and drifted back to sleep. Later, when she drew the blackout drapes in her sixth-floor room, the sky was a dazzling blue speckled with wispy clouds and she was greeted by a spectacular view of the Nile and the city beyond it. The great pyramids of Giza were less than twenty miles away. If her mission here were not so urgent, they would be the first on her 'to visit' wish list.

When I find Monica—Claudia refused to think of the alternative—*we'll do some sightseeing before we go home.*

THE TWO-MINUTE WALK from the Semiramis to the American Embassy was an adventure.

Lanes and traffic signals might as well not exist in traffic the likes of which Claudia had never imagined. When her bleary eyes witnessed a vehicle driving on the sidewalk, she concluded that if there were any rules of the road, these drivers didn't know them, or it simply didn't matter.

Dodging and weaving through the insanity, she arrived at the Embassy's entrance congratulating herself on coming close to getting killed only once while crossing the street.

Saul Wurman, the U.S. Embassy's Regional Security Officer, had the look of an FBI agent. Neat and trim in a charcoal grey suit and tie, he spoke with compassion.

"We're here to protect American travelers and their interests," he assured Claudia, taking her to a table and chair and handing her forms to fill out. "If there's any evidence of suspicious activity with your niece's passport or banking, we'll be able to track it. Please include anything you can think of that might be helpful, even if it doesn't seem important."

"All we know for sure is, Monica went away with a British archaeologist from another dig and didn't come back. They were supposed to return on Sunday night for work the next day. They didn't show up and nobody at either dig has heard from them."

Saul Wurman nodded gravely. "If you can give me the young man's name, we'll contact the British Embassy and ask them to follow up."

"It's Colin Vine. I'll get as much additional information for you as I can."

"Please understand, it might take a while for us to get the information to you."

"What does that mean? How long of a while?"

"A couple of days or so. I know it's difficult to wait. Please try to be patient; we'll do our best to help you."

"I'm heading straight to Luxor from here. That's where Monica and this young man were working, near the Valley of the Kings."

"That's better than hanging around waiting for news; though, there's plenty to see in and around Cairo."

"And I'd love to see it all, but my mind isn't on sightseeing right now."

"I'm sure it's not," said Saul with a sympathetic smile. "We have your contact information and I'll let you know what we find out. I do want you to understand that beyond checking on her passport and credit card activities, we don't have the resources to actively look for travelers or do investigations. When you have a better idea of what's happened, if necessary, we can put you in touch with the local police."

"Thank you. We're grateful for any help you can offer."

"You have my word; we'll do our best."

It was the look of pity in his eyes that nearly undid her. If she was reading him accurately, he was not optimistic about the outcome of their inquiries.

Claudia checked out of the hotel. When the Uber driver advised her that the journey to Luxor would take fifteen hours by bus or train, she directed him to the airport. The flight took about an hour.

MONICA'S ROOMMATE, McKenna Ryan, had texted to say that neither Colin nor Monica had been heard from and she would be at the Luxor airport to meet Claudia that afternoon.

Flying in to Cairo the previous evening, the skies over the city had been dark. Below were the sights she had read about all her life—the pyramids, the sphinx, the jewel-colored Nile. The dense city blocks. The vast desert sands. Even in the face of her reason for being here, seeing Egypt from the air for the first time in daylight tickled Claudia's spine with delightful shivers.

Monica's whereabouts—always uppermost in her mind—stole whatever real pleasure she would have taken from it all. What kind of person was Colin Vine? An archaeologist, but who knew what other activities he might be involved in? Again, she couldn't elude the stories she had seen online of young women kidnapped and trafficked far from home, abused, unable to escape. Closing her eyes, an image came to her of Monica dressed in rags, cowering on a dirty mattress, waiting for a beating between customers. When she couldn't blot that out, Claudia focused on the landscape, which changed as the plane closed in on Luxor.

On approach to the airport, she caught sight of two massive sandstone figures seated on thrones, rising from the desert floor. She knew the sixty-foot-high statues were Pharaoh Amenhotep the third. They had guarded his 'Temple of Millions of Years' for more than three thousand years.

The woman in the middle seat smiled when she heard Claudia's gasp. "Colossi of Memnon," she said in heavily accented English. "Eighteenth Dynasty. One of them sing, you know."

"Sing?"

"Yes, the north statue. The lower part is cracked in earthquake many hundred of years ago. Near the dawn, it would sing. To hear it brought good luck."

"Maybe I should visit it," Claudia muttered to herself. If there was the tiniest chance the statue would bring luck in her search, she would stand in front of it all night until she heard it sing.

For a few blessed minutes, she gave her mind permission to wander away from Monica and transport her back in time to 1350 BC when the statues were constructed. One of Claudia's bookshelves held a book filled with glossy photographs of the remarkable Egyptian art produced during Amenhotep the third's reign. Egypt had been at the peak of its power during his era.

Later, when he ruled Egypt, Amenhotep's son changed his name to Akhenaten, husband of the famed beauty, Queen Nefertiti. He was the father of Tutankhamun, the boy king whose tomb astonished the world in 1922 when it was opened by Howard Carter.

14

LUXOR

THE FRENETIC PACE AND MAD TRAFFIC IN CAIRO WITH ITS POPULATION of roughly ten million was missing from the streets of Luxor. With only a half-million permanent residents, Luxor was a community of mainly tourists.

True to her word, McKenna Ryan, slender and tan with deep blue eyes reflecting a savvy intelligence, was waiting at the curb in an olive-green Jeep. A battered tan felt hat covered shoulder-length black hair. A long-sleeved shirt with dusty jeans and boots completed the Indiana Jones look.

Claudia settled into the passenger seat and thanked her for the ride.

"You wouldn't have been able to find us," said McKenna, welcoming her to Egypt. "Our dig house isn't well-marked. Even the taxi drivers can't find it."

"This made it a lot easier on me. I came straight from spending the morning at the embassy in Cairo."

"We're all worried sick about Monica. She's been our lucky charm —in the best way, you know? We've made some incredible finds since she joined the dig."

"That's so great. Every time I've heard from her, she was having a fantastic time."

Gazing out the window, Claudia blinked away tears that threatened to brim over. If McKenna noticed her passenger's flash of emotion, she was too polite to comment. She waved a hand at an area beyond the neighborhood of mud brick homes they were passing. "Over there to your right is the Temple of Mut. She's the sky goddess, consort of Amun-Ra. Mother of the gods, queen of the goddesses."

Claudia was glad for the distraction. "Like Hera for the Greeks, or Juno for the Romans?"

"Pretty much. Mut is usually depicted as a vulture. Or with a vulture headdress. There's a lot of restoration going on at her temple."

"Sounds like German word for mother, *mutter*."

"It does," said Mckenna. "We're on the East Bank right now. Our dig site is across the river on the West Bank by the Valley of the Kings. The dig Colin is on is located in the same area."

"There's so much I want to see when we get Monica back," said Claudia.

If McKenna thought the remark overly optimistic, she refrained from saying so. "I love the mix of new and old." She pointed to a pair of statues they were passing, standing alone in the middle of an open field. To Claudia they looked forlorn.

"Those statues?" McKenna went on. "The faces were damaged deliberately in antiquity. The nose represents the breath of life. Destroying the nose symbolically killed the person whose statue it was. Sometimes it was tomb robbers who did the mutilation so the dead person couldn't take revenge on them."

"Mutilated or not, they're stunning," Claudia said. "Didn't they also disfigure them when there was a regime change?"

"Yep. Again, to take away their symbolic powers."

Claudia had been delighted when her young niece had inherited from her that same 'wow' factor she felt over the beliefs of the Ancients. She was beginning to regret it.

Areas of greenery that looked as if they might be city parks peppered the spaces around buildings in various states of disrepair. Claudia had to guess at the meaning of the signage, which was in Arabic. Children played in the street. Women in long black gowns—abayas, McKenna said—most in the company of other women, at a distance were indistinguishable from each other.

"In some places, Egyptian women wear very colorful clothes, same as in the West," she remarked when Claudia commented on their dark garb. They crossed a bridge over a long avenue of crumbling statues—rams or sphinxes—she couldn't be sure which, some still on their stone pedestals, others lying on the ground. She couldn't stop gawking. "It's like a movie set. Only it's real."

McKenna laughed. "Everyone gets that feeling when they first arrive. It's pretty mind-boggling."

"Mind-boggling is right. Everything has happened too fast. There's not been enough time to really grasp it. Finding out Monica's missing; flying out the next day." She omitted the part about Monica's father being charged with a homicide. To cover why she had made the trip rather than Pete, Claudia had said he was unable to fly, and let them assume it was a health issue.

She had to chuckle at the scenery. "These flat roofs and desert remind me of Tucson, where I visited recently. The palm trees are the same as where I live in Southern California. Ancient, though—that's something we have none of."

"There's plenty of ancient here," said McKenna with a grin.

They drove through a newer part of town, where nicer apartment buildings and businesses had a fresh, modern look. At the same time, piles of demolished building materials stood in empty lots here and there—reminders of the armed rebellions a relatively short time ago. The silence stretched, each thinking her own thoughts until Claudia had to ask a question that needed answering. "How well do you know Colin, McKenna?"

Monica had dated in groups for quite a while, but had never had a serious relationship. At eighteen and sheltered, away from home for the first time on her own, she was vulnerable. In his mid-twenties, Colin Vine was an adult male about whom they knew next to nothing.

Until then, McKenna had been friendly and chatty. Now, she kept her eyes on the road, the severe set of her chin having the effect of it being locked shut.

When the silence went on long enough, to be uncomfortable, McKenna broke it, but it was clear she didn't want to. "I mean, everyone knows each other some. We do a little socializing when we have time off, which isn't very often. We work long hours and there are always regular chores to do. Laundry, shopping. There's always work to be done in the lab."

Why was she deflecting? It seemed a good guess that a raw nerve had been exposed. There was no point pushing it. They were driving parallel to the longest river in the world—the Nile. Until she could figure out a different way to ask, Claudia decided that gazing out the window would do for now.

With the topic of Colin unanswered, McKenna took up her guide duties again. "The feluccas—those sailing boats you see—they aren't all that different from what they used in Ancient Egypt. Except for the earliest ones. They used bundles of papyrus reeds to make those."

Leaning back against the seat, Claudia viewed the scene through half-closed eyes. The gauzy-mauvy pink sky was the perfect canvas to allow her imagination free reign.

In her mind, the launch cruising up the river alongside them became the funeral barge of the Pharaoh Khufu who ruled in the Fourth Dynasty of the Old Kingdom. Never mind that they were in the wrong part of Egypt for Khufu. It was her fantasy; it didn't have to be correct. The sun, nearing the horizon, was Ra, who ruled all parts of the world. She would not have been surprised to see a falcon—his symbol—diving at them from the sky.

They traversed another bridge, this time crossing over the Nile. McKenna took a corner at breakneck speed and snapped Claudia back to the present. She tried again. "I was about to say 'what does a guy in his mid-twenties want with an eighteen-year-old?' But I guess that's a no-brainer."

"Maybe, maybe not," said McKenna. "Some guys feel awkward

with women their age. Colin knows he's hot and that women like him. I think he enjoys the hero-worship he gets from Monica."

"Hero worship?"

"Oh, yeah. You know the taxi accident I mentioned when we talked on the phone? Colin rescued a teenage boy from the other car that was involved. It was on fire and about to explode."

Claudia gulped. Had Monica told Annabelle about the accident? It had happened weeks ago and she had kept the news from her family. She hadn't told them about Colin, either. "That does sound pretty heroic. And dangerous."

"Heroic?" McKenna gave a scornful grunt. "It's the kind of thing he would do, you know? He's the kind of person who lives on the edge, takes big risks—"

"Am I sensing you don't care for him?"

"No, it's not that," she said, too quickly. "I—well, he rocks at getting people to do what he wants—" she cut herself off as if afraid she had revealed too much.

Claudia tried to picture what Colin Vine's handwriting might look like from the traits McKenna had just described. High velocity with secondary thread forms, the letters breaking down to indefinite and semi-illegible forms. Those who used that general style tended to be good at exploiting the resources and talents of others for whatever ends suited them. As a rule, they preferred not to make commitments, keeping things open-ended as much as possible.

"He sounds like he might be a manipulator," she said.

"Manipulator," McKenna repeated with what might be appreciation that Claudia got the picture she had tried to draw. "That's a good description. I tried to talk to Monica out of going away with him. You know, like a big sister would. I told her right from the start that you can't count on him."

The hitch in her voice confirmed it for Claudia. McKenna was jealous of Colin's attraction to Monica. "How did she take it when you discouraged her?"

"You know how she is. I never saw her in a bad mood or upset; well, except when she called me right after the accident. She was really upset that night. When I said it was a bad idea for her to get with Colin, she smiled and nodded, so I thought maybe she was paying attention." McKenna's lips puckered as if she tasted something sour. "She went off with him anyway, so I guess what I said didn't make any difference."

None of what Claudia was hearing resembled the Monica she knew, who was usually willing to listen to good advice. Pre-Egypt Monica. Pre-Colin Monica. Who the hell was she now? "When a dude comes into the picture, nothing is predictable," she said, and went back to gazing at the agricultural crops growing in fields alongside the road. If she opened the window, what odors would waft in? The Nile, dates, palm trees, sand? The odor of mummies and incense and death. In her fancy, anyway.

Soon, they were coming up on an alien landscape that might as well have been Mars. Towering sandstone cliffs where nothing grew; where so much remained buried, even now.

McKenna honked the horn loud and long at a taxi that cut them off. "Don't get me wrong about Colin," she blurted as if she had been thinking about this for a while and needed to get it out. "I went out with him a few times last season. He's really likeable. I mean, Monica wouldn't be attracted to him if he wasn't—and she *really* likes him. The thing is—" She stopped to gather her thoughts. "He has this almost-smile where his mouth goes up on one side. You get the feeling he's in on a joke that nobody else knows what it is."

Claudia's misgivings about Colin Vine were growing with everything she was hearing. "I've known people like that," she said. "Unfortunately, infatuation brings out the stupid. And trust me, I have personal experience in that department. Not just at Monica's age, either."

"Me, too," McKenna said ruefully. "It's not that I blame her. As I said, Colin *is* hot, not to mention a good archaeologist. I might have gone, too, if he hadn't—"

"Why did you stop dating him?" Claudia asked when she broke off; hastening to add, "If you don't mind me asking."

"The short version? He was accused of being involved in some shady dealings having to do with the antiquities trade. He was cleared, but I guess I was never quite sure of him after that. And, I didn't want to risk my career."

"I don't blame you."

What kind of guy had Monica gotten involved with?

"They talked on the phone just about every night. Mostly about Egyptian history from what I heard—" Again, McKenna interrupted herself. "I don't want you to think I was eavesdropping or anything. I meant when I happened to be in the room while they were talking."

Claudia reached over to give her arm a reassuring pat. "I get it. You can't not overhear when you're both in the same room."

"She was always talking about Hatshepsut. The first thing they did together was to visit the mortuary temple. So, at first, I thought maybe Colin was coaching her on the history. I mean, I'd noticed him noticing her at the meet-and-greet for all the dig people at the Crocodile—that's a restaurant. I think maybe that's what she dug on more than anything else—that he noticed her. It can be pretty flattering."

"You've got the wisdom of experience."

McKenna ignored the faint praise and changed the subject. "Frank rented a villa for the team. It's easier when we live close to the dig. He calls it 'Petrie House.'"

Flinders Petrie. A familiar name in Egyptology. "I've read one Petrie's books," said Claudia.

McKenna jerked a look of surprise in her direction. "You mean you read *about* him, right? You didn't actually read his books from the 1800s?"

"I actually did. Reading about Egypt from the point of view of someone living during those times made it interesting. How he came here in his twenties to survey the Great Pyramid, and ended up spending fifty years here doing very important work."

"Wow, I'm impressed."

"You can blame me for Monica's interest in Ancient Egypt," said Claudia. "I do."

They exchanged ironic smiles. Dusk was closing in as McKenna steered onto a narrow dirt road and into a parking stall next to a property surrounded by a tall stucco-like wall. Two electric motorbikes were chained up out front.

McKenna switched off the engine. "Let's go see about supper. We work as long as there's enough light, and get back to the house around five-thirty. Most days we're up and out by four-thirty in the morning, so we go to bed early."

"That *is* an early start."

"Not tomorrow, though. It's Friday, our weekend. We can't be at the site without a government official and Friday and Saturday are their holy days."

"That must be why the embassy guy said it would take a while to get back to me," Claudia said, crestfallen. "They must be closed on those days, too."

"That would be right. They'll open again on Sunday."

They entered the property through a wrought iron gate, stepping onto a mosaic pathway bordered by green plants. There was a covered seating area, and straight ahead, a new-looking three-story house, the arched doorways recognizable as Egyptian architecture. McKenna told her that one of the two wings had dorms with single beds on one floor and suites for couples or pairs on the others.

"There's a small kitchen and dining area on each floor, said McKenna, "But most of the time, the team eats dinner together." A delectable aroma wafted toward them as they entered through the front door. "We have a local man who cooks for us," she continued. "Smells like Kofta tonight. Mustafa is our *sofragi.*"

Aside from the light snack on the flight from Cairo, Claudia had eaten nothing since dinner on the plane from Frankfurt the previous day, and the delicious smell was making her lightheaded. "I have no idea what that is, but it smells fantastic," she said, looking forward to whatever food ended up heaped on her plate.

"Oops, sorry. He's our house manager and a super-good cook."

They reached a kitchen area with a long wooden table and benches on both sides. A man dressed in a long baby blue *galabeya* and white turban turned from the stove and said something in Arabic. McKenna replied in the same language and Claudia heard her name mentioned. Mustafa made her a small bow and returned to stirring the dish he was cooking.

"Monica was a good roommate. I sure wish we knew what happened to her," McKenna said. She must have realized how gloomy that sounded, as she started over in a cheerier tone.

"I mean, I wish we knew where she *is.* We don't know that something happened to her. I'm sure she'll be fine." The chipper words and game smile couldn't hide her belief that Monica was gone for good. Staying optimistic was becoming an uphill battle.

The entry of a tall, lean man saved Claudia from having to find a response.

"Oh, Frank, there you are," said McKenna obviously glad to put an end to her visitor responsibilities. "Here's Monica's Aunt Claudia. I'll leave you two together. See you at supper." And with that, she hurried out of the room.

With thinning light brown hair receding to the back of his head, Frank Booth's age could have been anywhere from thirty-five to fifty. Not far off skinny, he had the look of a man who didn't concern himself much with the pleasures of food and drink. He reached out a calloused hand to offer a firm handshake.

"I'm sorry we're meeting under these circumstances, Claudia. It's incredibly unfortunate that this has happened."

His words brought with them the gravity of the reason for her visit, and as it hit her, she swayed with fatigue and the desperate fear that the long journey was not going to end well. Booth jumped forward and put a supportive hand behind her elbow.

"Why don't you sit down."

Sinking onto the nearest bench at the table, Claudia closed her eyes.

"Please excuse me; it's been a long week."

Booth fetched her a bottle of cold water. "Don't apologize. We're all very concerned about Monica."

She drained half the bottle and set it on the table, feeling the need to make excuses, to protest that her niece wasn't the type of girl to leave everyone worried sick, especially knowing how hard they were all working. And yet, here they were.

15

When Claudia had recovered her equilibrium, Booth said, "Leave your bags here for now. We'll go through to the Reading Room and talk."

The Reading Room was a pleasant seating area with a loveseat and a pair of armchairs. Shelves holding artifacts and books on Egyptology lined the walls. He offered Claudia an armchair. "With Mustafa preparing supper, this will be more private for us."

Relaxing into the comfortable cushions, Claudia could have easily fallen asleep sitting up right where she was. "I appreciate you sending McKenna to pick me up," she said, rallying herself.

He dipped his head in acknowledgment. "You've come a long way and we want to do anything we can to help. I can't begin to imagine what your family is going through."

"It's no exaggeration to say it's been hell."

"Once we realized Monica hadn't returned, we contacted the local police and the hospitals," said Booth. "The problem is, we had no indication of where she and Vine were going. We didn't have a starting point to go looking. I wish I'd paid better attention and got some information, but by the time I learned she was gone, it was too late."

"It's not your fault, Frank, and I'm sorry about the inconvenience to you. You mentioned on the phone that your team had made a significant find. I imagine you have an awful lot on your plate."

Booth's hooded eyes lit up, shaving years off his age. "There was a major discovery here in Luxor last year. Maybe you heard about it? An Egyptian team uncovered dozens of wooden coffins buried in the Valley of the Kings. Biggest find in over a century. The mummies were in excellent shape."

"Yes, I did hear about it. Monica showed me the story online. The colors of the inscriptions were—even on video—" Claudia blew a puff of air between her lips. "Incredible."

"You're right about that. Well, my team has been digging close to where the Egyptian team was at that time, fairly close to Hatshepsut's temple—I expect you know she was the most famous female Pharaoh." Booth paused, perhaps for dramatic impact. "We've uncovered a flight of steps that we believe may lead to an undiscovered tomb. It could be a priest or priestess of hers."

You didn't have to be an archaeologist to realize the significance of that possibility. "Omigod, that's fantastic," Claudia said, wanting him to know that she was suitably impressed.

For a second or two, pride shone on his face, and then more than a hint of disgruntlement. "It could be the find of a lifetime, but with our permit expiring next week, we have to cover over the work we've done and return next season to see where the steps lead."

"How awful to get so close and have to walk away."

"It's part of the job," said Booth. His mouth curved in a sheepish smile. "Yeah, the truth is, it could piss off the pope. But there you go. I'm due back at the University in Arizona where I teach."

Claudia swallowed. "You teach at UA?"

"Yep. Went to school there about twenty-five years ago."

Thank goodness, that put him there well before Pete. It might have been awkward if he heard about what had happened at Dirtbags. Though it would be hard to be more awkward than it already was.

"I'll use the down time to study the artifacts we've uncovered this season," he said.

"Have you learned anything more about Colin?"

"I did speak with Henry Hawkins-Whyte, the fellow in charge of the dig where Colin is working. He's as mystified as I am about where he's gone off to. Vine has shown enthusiasm and promise—though as I've said, he skirted on the edge of trouble last season."

"McKenna mentioned shady dealings in antiquities?"

"Nothing that could be proved. Henry thinks a lot of him, but was ready to give him the boot. Vine is what the Brits call 'a bit of a lad'—a good talker—and he works his ass off, so he got away with a stern warning about the company he keeps."

Claudia's scalp prickled. "These friends of his; are they dangerous?"

Booth mused on that. "I wouldn't think so, except maybe in a legal sense."

"It doesn't sound good."

"They're being prosecuted, so as far as I know, they're out of circulation—in jail. The interesting thing is, Henry's group has uncovered a tomb robber's cache. It's been producing some phenomenal finds and Vine has been at the forefront of the work."

"So, it would be strange for him not to be here to continue."

"To call it strange is to put it mildly. They've uncovered a hidden chamber in what started as a tomb and was never finished. It's a major find not all that far from ours. Several of the artifacts they've excavated date to the eighteenth dynasty, during Hatshepsut's reign."

"You said a tomb robbers' cache?"

"Yes. These artifacts were hastily buried, so the most likely scenario is that the robbers knew about the unfinished tomb and hid these stolen items there. They would have used it as a bank account and dug up items to sell as needed. The cache went undiscovered until now, and since there are valuable items still there, it's plausible to imagine the robbers were caught and punished."

Claudia chugged the rest of her water, picturing the robbers covering up their loot in an isolated desert tomb, believing they were safe. "I'm afraid to ask what you think happened to the tomb robbers. Something unpleasant, I don't doubt."

"That would be an understatement. Death by drowning or decapitation would be easy, compared to the special penalty for those who plundered the Valley of the Kings. Those unlucky enough to be caught were impaled on a stake. You see, the Book of Life tells us that the robber's body was forever tied to the place where he died and being impaled meant he wouldn't be able to enter the afterlife. There's a special glyph to describe it."

She should have saved some water to wash away the rush of bile. "You'd have to be desperate to risk that kind of punishment."

"Or greedy. They—" Booth displayed a brief smile. "Forgive me. I have a tendency to go off on tangents when nobody stops me. My point was, it was a particularly odd time for Vine to take off and not come back. We're talking about the kind of find an archeologist lives for."

"This is sounding worse by the minute."

"Yes." His tone was grave. "Wherever the pair of them went, it's clear they planned to come back. All of Monica's belongings are here, except what she took for the weekend. And according to Henry Hawkins-Whyte, Colin's expensive camera is in his room."

"I'd like to speak to the Professor myself, if I could."

"He's agreed to meet with you, though to be honest, I can't say he was enthusiastic about it. He's a stickler for protocol, but these are unusual circumstances, so he will allow you to look through Colin's things in case you can find something helpful."

Claudia caught his gaze and held it. "I need you to understand how impossible it is for me to picture Monica doing this. "She's always been levelheaded, maybe thanks in part due to a fairly sheltered upbringing. Taking off with some guy she hardly knows and not contacting anyone to say she's been delayed coming back—it's completely unlike her. She would know we'd be worried sick. Something, or someone, must be preventing her from getting in touch." Claudia's half-smile was wistful. "If they were in a hospital somewhere, there might not be a means to contact us. Is it bad to hope for a smallish accident?"

Booth's spoke in a gentle tone. "News travels fast in Egypt. It would be unheard of if two foreigners ended up unconscious in a hospital and word of it didn't get back to the embassy. The embassy would have contacted her family. And you can be sure that if they had an accident, I would have heard about it. The one they were involved in several weeks ago—we knew of it before Monica got back here."

"I can't say that makes me feel any better. I'm waiting for the embassy to tell us whether her credit card has been used, or her passport. I know they can ping the cell towers if her cell phone is on."

"The NSA is supposed to have the ability to track a phone; doesn't matter if it's turned off. Not that the NSA is going to help in this case. Unless it's a matter of national security." Booth grimaced. "Let's hope it's not that."

"I don't care what it is if it will help find my niece."

"I don't mean to make light of it. I bet she'll show up and have a logical explanation and be all kinds of embarrassed to have caused such a fuss." He stood. "Why don't I show you where her things are?"

"Yes, please."

"We'll go up to the room she shared with McKenna. You'll be taking Monica's bed. We don't have any single rooms to spare."

"Thank you. I appreciate you letting me stay at all."

Booth fetched her bags from the kitchen and Claudia followed him up a narrow stone staircase that ran along the outside of the house. "I should warn you," he said over his shoulder. "McKenna checked her things for any clues to where they went, and didn't find anything helpful."

Claudia let the weight of those words sink in. "I understand you'll be closing up the dig next week. I'll get her things packed up to send home."

"I'd appreciate that," he said as they entered the top floor through double glass doors. He took her along a short hallway to a pleasant, though utilitarian bedroom. There were two single beds, each with a nightstand, a chest of drawers, and a shared desk, where McKenna was currently working on a laptop. She startled when Booth spoke, and swiveled around, yanking out a pair of earbuds. "I didn't hear you come in."

"Would you show Claudia where Monica's things are, please, McKenna; she's going to get them ready to send home."

"You don't think she'll be back, do you?" said Claudia, detecting finality in his tone.

Booth's face was unreadable. "Let's not think that way."

MONICA HAD BEEN TOLD there would not be much room for storage and she had packed light for her stay, taking only one medium-sized suitcase that Pete had bought her for the trip. As thrilled as she was to be accepted as a volunteer on the team, she would have worn the clothes she traveled in every day if that had been necessary.

The suitcase was under the bed and held only a pair of military surplus boots that Monica had purchased especially for the dig. Claudia, having helped her niece shop and pack, could tell exactly what she had taken away on her 'weekend' with Colin: jeans, tee-shirts and a sweatshirt, a black sequined evening top—which meant she had planned for fun—underwear and socks, her anorak. Toiletries.

A weekend getaway that had so far stretched to a week.

Summoning memories of Monica's excitement as she had rolled up each item, making sure everything would fit in her suitcase, a sharp pang of misery made Claudia stop and catch her breath. She emptied the contents of the drawers into the suitcase. If she could find *something*—the mode of transportation the pair had taken or what direction they had gone—she might have been less afraid. As it was, she was poking around in the dark, not knowing what monsters might be lurking there.

In the nightstand drawer was Monica's sketchbook and pen, and a small plush hedgehog that Claudia had bought for her when she was three years old. That her niece had brought it with her to Egypt choked her up all over again.

The sketchbook was filled with handwritten notes. Unlike many of her classmates whose handwriting was either printed because they had never learned cursive, or large and rounded like soap bubbles, Monica wrote with precision. Most of her letters connected and slanted slightly to the right. The m's and n's formed deep cups that made them appear to be w's and u's. The letters were joined by strokes that were curved like open hands. The right margin was wide, the pen pressure medium.

To Claudia, her niece's handwriting revealed a perfectionist who worked her butt off to do the right thing, and also one who had deep compassion for others. She had pressed the pen into the paper slightly more deeply than the average writer, indicating that she had inherited the family gene of keeping her feelings under wraps.

Touching her fingertips to the familiar handwriting made it feel as if a physical part of her niece was right there with her. Monica had made careful notes about Egyptian historical royalty, writing about Hatshepsut, a particular interest of hers; filling a page with hieroglyphs drawn in columns, similar to the ones in tombs and monuments. Claudia paged through the sketchbook, struck by her artistic talent. The margins around the neat handwriting were decorated with skillful drawings: an Egyptian death mask, pottery and jewelry, scarabs, Bastet, the cat goddess. A cartouche—a royal name enclosed in an oval, which designated it as the name of a royal personage.

It had served as a travel journal in which Monica described her activities at the dig and her free time, adding little hearts and flowers to the entries where Colin Vine's name showed up. On one page, she had created a masterful sketch, the deft strokes capturing the essence of the man in the selfie Annabelle had texted.

Had Monica unconsciously recognized the cynical glint in Colin's eye when she drew it, or was she smitten and failed to see it? She would not be the first girl who had lost her good sense in the throes of first love.

Claudia's gut was yelling warnings at her, and her gut was pretty reliable. Wishing she could hold her niece tight and make her safe, she laid the notebook and the toy hedgehog in the suitcase along with her clothing. Nursing her fractured heart, she closed the suitcase and zipped it shut.

"Find anything?"

McKenna's voice bumped her out of her thoughts. "Unfortunately, no."

"If you're ready to go down for supper, I'll introduce you to the gang."

Claudia mustered a faint smile. "I'm starving. let's go."

16

SATURDAY

Frank Booth made a brief introduction and wished Claudia luck on her quest when he dropped her at the house the Hawkins-Whyte team had rented a few miles away. He had errands that would keep him tied up for the balance of the day. The professor would return her to Petrie House when she had finished her quest here.

Henry Hawkins-Whyte reminded her of a bust she had seen at an exhibit of Alexandrian Egypt artifacts at the Ronald Reagan Library. Dionysus, God of Wine, had the same kind of inverted triangle-shaped head and curly hair as the professor, but was lacking the short white beard. The professor's lukewarm handshake trumpeted his reluctance for the meeting loud and clear.

"If you ask me, it's a blasted invasion of his privacy," he said, pronouncing it "*priv*-acy" with a short I.

Deciding it was his Britishness taking issue with the breach of personal space she was requesting, Claudia showed him her professional self. "You didn't have to allow me to do this, and I appreciate that you are."

"I must say, I'm not at all happy to have you pawing through young Vine's things." As he spoke, he reached up and rubbed the nape of his neck.

Claudia, interpreting the gesture as self-soothing, suppressed a grin. He probably saw her as a literal pain in the neck.

"I hate it, too," she replied in a confidential tone. "I hate every day that passes without any information makes it harder to trace them. We have no idea what might be helpful, so if there's anything at all in Colin's things, I'm sure you would want me to find it."

"Yes. Well. I s'pose you'd better get started. I'll take you to his room. Come through this way."

The same as at Petrie House, the second story, where Colin Vine's room was located, was reached via an outdoor staircase. When Hawkins-Whyte didn't bother to introduce Claudia to the members of his team they encountered, she chose to believe it was more a case of 'absent-minded professor' than a lack of courtesy.

The room the professor unlocked was larger than the one Claudia was sharing at Petrie house. Or maybe it was the high ceiling that created that impression. The few furnishings consisted of two twin beds with night tables on each side, and table between them, plus a wardrobe, a lowboy dresser, and a small desk. A bookshelf on one wall held a handful of books related to archaeology and, unsurprisingly, considering the expensive-looking camera on top of the lowboy, photography.

"Is his roommate okay with me being in here?"

"There is no roommate. He wanted his own room, and his father was a highly respected university don. Not that his father had anything to do with Colin's acceptance into my program, of course. Young Colin has top-rate qualifications and experience. Wouldn't have taken him on otherwise. Booth is more willing to relax the rules than I."

Ignoring the poke at Frank Booth's decision to allow the unqualified Monica to join his team, Claudia smiled amiably. "Does the don know that his son is missing with an eighteen-year-old girl?"

"*Doctor* Vine died on an expedition to Peru," said the professor huffily.

"I'm very sorry to hear it. I see Colin left his camera here. Has anyone checked the photos?"

"I can't imagine what that would accomplish."

"I'll take that as a 'no.' I'm sure you've called his cell phone."

The professor gave her the stink eye. "We're not gormless, Ms. Rose. Naturally, when Booth got hold of me and told me your niece was missing with Colin, I telephoned him immediately. There was no reply, nor has there been a response to my messages. The two young people went off together and have disappeared, which is regrettable for several reasons, not the least of which is, his work on the dig has been quite invaluable and we need him."

Claudia considered asking about Colin Vine's having been accused of trading in antiquities last season, but thought better of it. With the professor's less-than-friendly attitude, poking the bear wouldn't help matters.

"I hope he brings Monica back safely in time to help," she said.

The skeptical look the professor shot her said that he suspected she was being sarcastic but was not quite sure. He let it go.

"You'll pardon me, Ms. Rose; I have a lot to do. I'll leave you to it."

The stiff set of his shoulders and the bunching of muscles around his wide jaw broadcast Henry Hawkins-Whyte's disapproval louder than a shout. Now that he had given her permission to search Colin Vine's room, he made to leave, issuing an injunction on his way out.

"When you've completed whatever it is you intend to do in here, I expect you to return everything exactly as it is. Is that clear?"

"As clear as Lake Tahoe. I'm sure it won't take long."

"All right, then. When you've finished, you can find me downstairs in the laboratory."

THE CAMERA WAS a Canon similar to one she used in her document examination work. The display screen filled with a high-resolution image, the last he had taken: A group of people in the desert wearing work clothes, peering into a shaft in the ground.

She swiped through and found several pictures of Monica wearing a pair of pretty butterfly hair clips Claudia had ordered for her on Etsy. They'd had so much fun together, preparing for the big trip.

Colin had handed the camera to someone else to take a photo of him and Monica. His arm was flung around her shoulders and they were both laughing. Seeing her niece's happy face cut deep. She must have been worried about her family's disapproval. Otherwise, why not tell them about Colin?

Claudia's emotions were waging a fierce battle, threatening to get the better of her. If Annabelle had been the one to go missing, it would have been less concerning. She had learned long ago how to take care of herself. Taking off on a whim and not reporting in when she was supposed to would not be unexpected for her. Monica was different.

There were several closeups of a brush-wielding hand clearing the soil from a half-buried piece of pottery, photos of pottery shards, and other items that had evidently been excavated from the ground. One was of a strikingly beautiful gold ring with a bezel in the form of a cartouche. She looked through them all, finding nothing helpful, then returned the camera to the lowboy.

Like Monica, Colin kept a journal in his nightstand. For Claudia, the opportunity to examine his handwriting was akin to finding gold. If his handwriting pointed to him having the potential for homicidal mania—an improbable scenario but you never knew—what could she do? If he posed a danger to her niece, it was too late to do anything about it. She stood there, debating whether she really want to open it and see the truth about him.

He could be an angel, one side contended. *You need to know,* the other side countered.

His name was embossed on the black leather cover. He had signed the inside cover in thick black ink and encircled it with a protective lasso-like stroke. No one could decipher the illegible scrawl as saying 'Colin Vine.' He had used the final stroke on the 'e' to slash through his name in a self-destructive right-to-left movement—not a good sign for his self-image.

The chicken scratch that dotted the pages was a form of cursive writing that was dissimilar from Monica's orderly script in every way.

It reminded Claudia of her English grandmother's saying: "They're as different as chalk from cheese."

The journal's content—notes about the dig—were, for the sake of analysis, inconsequential. After a quick scan, she didn't bother to read them. The handwriting itself was what interested her.

The ink, carelessly spewed on the page, failed to take into account any need to organize it. At times, Colin wrote perpendicular to the printed lines—a sure sign of someone who never went along with the crowd if something exciting came along. Not that this was always a negative trait, Claudia had to admit; she did the same thing.

The space between words were extra-wide. And like trees in a hurricane, the slant wavered from one direction to another, exhibiting impulsiveness and emotional highs and lows. The simplified letters gave no consideration to style, mixing printing with cursive. On the plus side of the ledger, he had excellent intelligence and was a quick thinker with a rapier-sharp wit.

What she saw in Colin's handwriting confirmed McKenna's comments: the secondary thread connections were hallmarks of a clever manipulator who showed a talent for using other people to his convenience. He suffered from an ego that had been damaged in the first two years of life and never recovered. That could explain Monica's attraction to him. Since early childhood, she'd had a penchant for rescuing wounded creatures.

Claudia knew that beautiful handwriting did not necessarily make a good person, and the reverse was also true. Most people with unappealing writing were decent, and her job was to assess personality rather than to judge character. She did her best to be fair with every handwriting she analyzed, and this one was no different.

Bottom line, nothing in the writing could explain why the writer had talked her young niece into going away with him and not brought her back.

The temptation to take Colin's journal with her was strong, but for someone who prided herself on her ethics, it was a bridge too far. The next best thing was to scan some of the pages with an app on her tablet. That done, she closed the journal back into the drawer and took a look under the bed. Colin's dusty, travel-worn suitcase, stored there, was empty.

She opened the wardrobe and found only a field jacket and a sport coat. Rifling through the pockets, she came across a scrap of paper. The words '#9 Flint' and 'Akeem D', were written on it, along with a string of numbers. It was all meaningless to Claudia, but it was in Colin's handwriting—it was consistent with the writing in the journal.

If there was the teeny-tiniest chance the paper was in any way crucial, she owed it to Monica to check it out. The odds that the paper was connected to her niece's disappearance were slim, but Henry Hawkins-Whyte might have an idea of what the writing referenced.

Claudia started for the staircase, halting halfway along the landing.

The professor had made it abundantly clear that her presence was unwelcome. The only reason she had obtained his grudging permission to stick her nose into Colin Vine's room was that Frank Booth had played on whatever sympathy the professor had for the position she was in—or perhaps his conscience. If she bolted downstairs and disturbed what he was doing, her opportunity to finish searching Colin's room would be over.

COLIN HAD USED the bottom drawer of the lowboy in lieu of a laundry hamper. Closing it on the musty, balled-up t-shirts and boxers, Claudia opened the next one more cautiously: cargo shorts and jeans. Not knowing exactly what she was looking for, she moved things around, groped the pockets. The middle drawer was for shirts and sweaters. She pulled out the top drawer: socks and underwear in the top.

Diddly squat.

So, that was it. Unless that scrap of paper and its two words and number string yielded a clue, her trip to Egypt had so far been a colossal waste. She sighed. *Now what?*

She went to close the drawer. It jammed. Exasperation, prickly and intense, pushed up against her, shaking a fist at her self-control.

Professor Hawkins-Whyte would love to know I've broken it. What the hell else can go wrong?

She reached inside and found a sock had caught in the slider. Gritting her teeth, Claudia started working on it, startling when something crackly brushed the back of her hand. Something that did not belong in a sock drawer.

Something bulky wrapped in a lot of plain tissue paper; the type used to line a gift bag. In view of its small size—the little package fit in her palm—it had heft. A cascade of questions fell into her head, starting with why would Colin hide it in his sock drawer?

She told herself she was jumping to conclusions too quickly, but the devil's advocate wanted to know why someone would put a tissue-wrapped object where no one would see it unless he wanted to hide it.

Claudia had never thought of herself as psychic, but some kind of sixth sense was screaming at her now. Whatever was wrapped in that tissue was about to change things in a profound way.

bit of irony for you." He dragged a handkerchief from his pocket and mopped his sweaty forehead.

"This piece is of immense historical value. He must have pocketed it before it could be catalogued." His eyes narrowed with suspicion. "Why leave it behind?"

"Because he didn't plan on it being found while he was away? It was hidden in his drawer. His camera is here, too. He clearly intended to come back."

"He took a ridiculous risk. Aside from the historical implications, antiquities theft is no joke to the Egyptian government. I promise you, Ms. Rose, you don't want to find yourself in an Egyptian prison."

Or any prison, Claudia thought, picturing Pete in the Tucson jail. "How long a sentence are we talking about?"

"Ten years or more."

"Can there be any other explanation?"

"Bollocks." Flapping his hand in dismissal, Professor Hawkins-Whyte gave a contemptuous shake of his large head. "I'd wager a thousand British pounds it's not the only thing he's nicked from the site. It's bloody likely he meant to flog it to the highest bidder, and that's where he's scarpered off to."

Not letting herself think about the implications of what he had just said, Claudia handed him the scrap of paper she had taken from Colin's jacket. "This was in his jacket. Does it mean anything to you?"

He scowled at it. "Number Nine Flynt; Akeem D. That's all?"

"Well, that and the numbers. Could it be an address? Maybe where they've gone?"

"Doesn't sound like any street I know of in Luxor, though I suppose it *could* be an address."

Claudia took out her tablet and entered '9 Flint' into the Maps app for Luxor. "Nothing comes up. Maybe in Cairo?"

"Selling a stolen artifact anywhere in Egypt these days would be extremely difficult." He waved the paper at her. "Who is Akeem D? Not an Egyptian, or it would be *Ha*keem."

"What about the number? A bank account? A phone number?"

"Phone numbers here are eleven or twelve numerals. There are only eight in this number. And as for an account number, the banks are closed today so we can't ask."

The professor shoved the paper back at her. "I'll have to contact the Ministry of Antiquities and alert them. They're frightfully strict about these things. There can be dreadful consequences. My permit could be revoked."

Rewrapping the figurine with meticulous care, he locked it in a cabinet. The violence in his grim brown eyes when he turned back made Claudia take a step away.

"If that thieving sod gets my dig shut down, I'll kill him with my bare hands." The professor fetched his jacket from a hook on the door and jammed a camo hunting hat on his head. "I've got to get to the site and have a look at the area where Vine was working."

Claudia massaged her temple, which had begun to throb with tension. "They've been gone for more than a week. Wouldn't someone notice if anything was amiss at the site?"

"Not if Vine was careful. Don't you understand? I've got to see for myself."

"Whatever he's done, he shouldn't have taken Monica with him. We've got to find him."

The professor jabbed a stubby finger at her. "You're not to mention this to anyone until I've spoken to the government representative."

"I won't."

"Bollocks."

"I said I won't say anything," Claudia protested.

"Not that. I promised Booth I'd return you to Petrie House. You'd better give him a ring and have him collect you here."

"He said he would be busy all day," Claudia reminded him. "I'll go with you."

"*That* would be against regulations," said the professor with a self-righteous sniff.

"If I promise to stay out of your way?"

"I can't possibly take a visitor without asking for a pass from the government."

"Aren't government offices closed today?"

"Yes, but..."

Sensing him weakening, Claudia pressed some more. "The rules can be bent in extreme circumstances, can't they? And you must agree, this is extreme."

"Not at all ideal." The professor looked as though he was debating himself. Then, with a final irritated huff, he capitulated. "I suppose it would save time. Come along, then, and don't dawdle. I'll have to deliver some extra baksheesh to make certain it's not reported."

Claudia followed him out to the Land Rover parked next to the house and settled into the passenger side, glad to be doing *something*. Sitting around all day, waiting to hear what he found would be sheer torture. And, going to the dig site with Professor Hawkins-Whyte might even be interesting.

Once they got on the road, the professor surprised her by behaving as though they were best buds. The discovery of Colin Vine's duplicity had broken the invisible barrier between them, and he talked nonstop—an outlet for the betrayal and whatever else he was feeling, Claudia guessed, letting him ramble uninterrupted. She was seeing a different side of the professor.

Keeping half an ear on what he was saying, she dug in her capacious shoulder bag for ibuprofen and the bottle of water she had carried with her. Her discovery in Colin's room had a brought a whole slew of new questions about where the missing couple had gone; chief of which was, if Colin was fencing stolen antiquities as she feared, why bother to take Monica with him?

The professor's discourse pulsed in and out of her attention. "We're digging close to Hatshepsut's tomb, so it's no surprise the robbers hid their loot nearby," she heard him say at one point. The next time she came back, he was still talking about the tomb robbers.

"Everything we've found suggests they came during the Eighteenth Dynasty, when Hatshepsut was on the throne. Most of the tombs at that time were disturbed, including hers. Her mummy wasn't in it, you know. There were coffins of two women."

"Who were they?" Claudia asked so he would think she was listening. In case he noticed. She had a feeling he could play both sides and hold an entire conversation on his own.

"One of the coffins had been made for Hatshepsut's nurse—her name was on it. At the time it was found, it wasn't known who the other coffin belonged to. When Howard Carter discovered Hatshepsut's sarcophagus in 1903, it was quite empty."

That caught her attention. "The Howard Carter who discovered King Tutankhamun's tomb? I didn't know that. What do they think happened to Hatshepsut's mummy?"

"Zahi Hawass from the Ministry of Antiquities claims to have discovered her." His tone carried the undercurrent of a sneer. "That's not universally accepted, mind you. Hatshepsut's mummy has been ensconced in the Egyptian Museum in Cairo since 2007 with all honors due her. Well, except that after having the DNA examined, Hawass determined she had diabetes and was fat."

"I can't believe she was found after so long," said Claudia, thinking it disrespectful of the Minister to call the impressive pharaoh 'fat.'

"They discovered a box with Hatshepsut's name on it. It contained a single tooth that precisely fit a hole in the jaw of the mummy that had been buried with the nurse."

Engrossed by the story, Claudia told him that Monica had always been a big admirer.

"People tend to think she was the only female pharaoh," the professor responded. "Actually, she was the third, and extremely powerful. Her father, Thutmose the first, died when she was twelve…"

Monica's mother had died when she was twelve, too. Claudia stopped listening again. It was not that the history was uninteresting, but timing was everything. When she'd got her girl home safe and sound—she refused to consider any other possibility—she would happily listen to Hawkins-Whyte lecture all day.

"…large building projects the …Mortuary Temple. Astounding architecture…"

Why did Colin take her with him? Why haven't they come back?

"…in her late forties or so when she died …impressive legacy, although her heir, Thutmose the third, did his best to eradicate her name from every temple and monument she'd had constructed."

They were nearing the Valley of the Kings when Hawkins-Whyte began to complain about the innumerable buses and taxis. Tourists on the road to the public sites, he grumbled peevishly, interrupting himself to make a phone call to the Ministry of Antiquities. "We have to have him there as a government representative," he told Claudia as he ended the call. "It's unheard of to go to the site without him."

She ignored him, staring at the sweeping panorama spread out around them—her first glimpse of the endless barren hillsides that concealed tombs of infinite grandeur. The workers and their families had lived and died building those fabulous monuments of death and the afterlife. No video or documentary could have prepared her for the feeling of reverence.

Where were all those thousands of people buried? Not in the magnificent tombs they had erected for the pharaohs and their attendants. The worker families who were going to build the monuments had first to construct a village to live in. Before now, Claudia had never considered the staggering amount of planning it must have taken. Food storage and preparation, water collection from the Nile, waste disposal, school for the boys, medical personnel to treat illness or injury—all of the various aspects of daily life that would have to be handled during the years of construction.

She thought of the ancients and their belief in a spiritual body, which after death would go on to reside in a world similar to the one they knew in earthly life. The deceased spirit's treacherous journey through the underworld required facing forty-two judges, correctly addressing them by name and reciting the list of sins for which the spirit had been blameless during life. With their purity determined, the deceased could go on to the next step, the final judgment, where his or her heart would be weighed against the feather of Maat.

If a spirit had told lies and committed evil deeds in life, the heart would be heavier than the feather. In such a case, the heart was devoured by the hideous Goddess Ammit; permanently destroyed, with no possibility of attaining the afterlife. On the other hand, if the heart balanced with the feather, Thoth, the Ibis-headed god of wisdom, magic, and writing, would record it and present the soul to Osiris, whose role it was to admit it into the afterlife forever.

"The tourists don't come out this far," the professor was saying, thrusting Claudia back into the conversation as they gave up the main road. They bounced over rough ground for a mile or so, parking near a low wall made of mud bricks and excavated from the desert floor.

She recognized the site from Colin's photos—the square pit, surrounded by sandbags, located between the craggy thousand-foot-high cliffs and the wall of bricks.

"The sandbags stop the sand from slipping back into the excavation," the professor said. He gestured to a large white tent that had been erected a short distance away. "That's where we keep our gear and take second breakfast." He looked around, frowning, his earlier pique rushing back.

"Where's the damned guard?"

Claudia looked, too. No one else was evident in the desolate landscape. "Does every site have one?"

"No, there's one assigned to patrol a fairly large area of land—several acres. He must be in another part of the Valley." Professor Hawkins-Whyte flapped his hands in annoyance.

"Or he might well be snoozing somewhere. You never know what you'll get. Some of these fellows are exceptionally conscientious; others will sleep the day away in their car."

The professor was gearing up for another rant when a Jeep drove up and parked, putting an end to his griping. The driver got out and started toward the Rover. The sight of this Egyptian man in Western garb cheered Hawkins-Whyte in nothing flat.

"Ah, there's the inspector. You'll have to wait here, Ms. Rose. Bad enough you're onsite without a pass. Stay in the Rover, won't you?"

Without waiting for a reply, the professor marched off to meet the inspector. The two men chatted for about five minutes, heads close together, the inspector doing some arm-waving. When the inspector climbed into his Jeep and drove off, and Hawkins-Whyte started back to the Rover, Claudia assumed that the baksheesh the professor had mentioned earlier was discreetly folded into their parting handshake.

"No point in switching on the electricity down below," Henry Hawkins-Whyte said, reaching across her to the glove box. He withdrew a heavy-duty flashlight.

"The inspector has gone off to the Ministry's local headquarters to put in paperwork on this infernal mess. Look here, I shan't be long. Now, you *must* stay in the Rover. Can't have the liability if you took a fall or something equally irritating."

He leaned back down to speak through the window. "Keep an eye out for the guard, won't you? If he comes 'round while I'm gone, let him know I'm in the pit and to wait."

"Are you sure you don't want me to come and hold the ladder for you?"

He shot her a look of exasperation. "Good lord, no. I've told you—"

Claudia grinned. "I know, stay here. Good luck."

"I'll just see to it that everything is as it should be and be back in two ticks."

The professor crossed the uneven ground and moved out of her line of sight. Claudia checked the time. Close to midnight at home. Pete answered right away, sounding exhausted.

"Hey, Sis. I was about to call you."

Her stomach twisted into a tight knot. "Have you heard something?"

"I wish. I went into her credit card and bank account. No need to wait for the embassy on that score. Wish I'd thought of it sooner."

"You hacked in?"

"Didn't have to, we're joint owners. I have the passwords."

"Don't keep me guessing. What did you find?" Afraid of what he was going to tell her, Claudia started gearing up for bad news.

"You're not gonna believe this. Last week, while I was driving to Tucson, my daughter was booking a round trip flight from Luxor to Casablanca."

Claudia's mouth fell open. "Holy crap. Casablanca? In Morocco? You mean like, 'meet me at the Casbah?'"

"Do you know another one? What the hell was she thinking, Claud? Taking off with some dude she just met and flying to frigging Casablanca?"

Claudia's brain raced to catch up with this new information, a string of scenarios sweeping through her head, each one worse than the previous. "This guy she went away with, Colin Vine? We found out he stole a precious artifact from the dig he works on. And that's the one we know about. There's probably other stuff, too."

"He—what the actual fuck?"

Claudia described finding the figurine hidden in Colin's socks, and the professor's reaction. Then, "What the hell are they doing in Casablanca?"

"According to Google, it's a huge financial center."

"Maybe that's where he's fencing the goods. How far is it from Luxor?"

"Almost ten hours by plane." Pete sounded puzzled. "It doesn't make sense. If the figurine was in his room, what was he fencing?"

"I have no idea; it could have been anything. Ten hours—" Claudia broke off at movement in her peripheral vision. Expecting to see the professor returning, she turned to look.

His back was to her as he emerged from the pit, but the man ascending the ladder from the excavation site was not Henry Hawkins-Whyte.

"I'll call you right back, Pete." Claudia climbed out of the Land Rover, calling out to the stranger as he stepped off the ladder onto the sandbags. "Excuse me—"

He whirled, his face a mask of shock.

18

After an instant's hesitation, the man started toward her, halting ten feet away; rocking on his feet as if trying to decide what to do.

He was taller than her, though not by much, and with a powerful build. Egyptian men were so damned handsome. It would be easy to be bowled over by the short curly black hair, the fierce stare, the firm chin. Reading the narrowed eyes and hands balled into fists, Claudia got the message loud and clear: he was not at the dig site to exchange pleasantries.

She stood behind the passenger door of the Land Rover as they took each other's measure. A sudden gust of wind kicked sand into the air and a sparrowhawk in the sky above them called to its mate. The man moved first. "*Imshi ba-ah.*" he shouted. "*Imshi ba-ah.*"

The only implement that might be used as a weapon was a spade in the backseat, out of Claudia's reach. Raising her arms above the doorframe, palms out, she let him see that she was unarmed. "I don't know Arabic. Do you speak English?" A flash of comprehension in his eyes emboldened her. "Where is the professor?"

Wrong question. The man's muscular body tensed with the alertness of a cat about to pounce on a mouse. But as she got ready to run, he stunned her by dropping his fists and spinning around toward the cliffs. Claudia watched the shrinking figure in amazement as he disappeared rapidly behind a hill.

What the hell just happened?

Had the guard returned and scared him off? She looked around at a landscape as empty as ever.

The bad feeling that had hit her when the stranger had climbed up the ladder rebounded like a hard smack in the face. The professor should have been back by now.

Claudia jogged to the pit, where the sandbags were arranged around an incline leading down to a short wooden ladder. From there it was possible to climb down to a stone platform around a six-by-four-foot opening.

Like a grave, and twice as deep.

She examined the second, longer ladder in dismay. Theoretically, from there, one could descend into the pit. If one didn't theoretically fall and break one's neck climbing onto the rickety-looking thing. Hanging onto the side rails, she crouched and peered into the shadowy pit, where a metal gate stood open at the bottom.

"Professor?" Claudia yelled, waiting for his irascible shout for her to go back to the Land Rover and wait for him. Her voice boomeranged eerily back at her.

"Hello," she yelled again, louder. "Professor, can you hear me?"

If Henry Hawkins-Whyte had not taken his car keys with him, she could have driven the Rover to the nearest tourist site for help. She hesitated. Was it overreacting to think emergency help was needed? It took a millisecond to consider the facts: A stranger had come out of the pit where the professor had gone. The stranger had run away. The professor had not returned. Where was he? She got out her phone to dial nine-one-one, then realized she had no idea of the Egyptian equivalent.

Frank Booth's number took her to voicemail. She left a message and followed it up with a text: *Emergency Hawkins-Whyte dig. Bring help ASAP.*

Who was the man who had confronted her and, so strangely, run away? What was he doing at the Hawkins-Whyte site? She had not seen him arrive, so it was logical to assume he had been there ahead of the professor. Had he picked the lock? Did he have a key? Had someone else let him in? And if so, where was that person now? The questions started coming faster: was that man connected to Colin and the statuette? *Is Monica down there, inside the tomb?*

Claudia contemplated the pit again and groaned. It was glaringly obvious that she was going to have to do the very last thing she wanted to. Viewing the wobbly-looking ladder with intense dislike, she reminded herself that the Hawkins-Whyte team was accustomed to trusting it, and that the stranger had made it down and up again.

She dropped to her knees and, holding tight, swung over the lip of the pit and onto the ladder. The descent went faster than she expected. Ten seconds later, she was face-to-face with the heavy metal gate, where a padlock that meant business hung open on the hasp.

Behind the metal gate, the entry to the tomb was cut into the rock face. Booth had described it as abandoned and unfinished. Claudia could see chunks of stone strewn about the chalky passage floor, one the size of a microwave, others as small as a child's building blocks.

About ten feet in, the passage disappeared into pitch black.

Claudia called the professor's name. Why wasn't he answering? Leaning through the opening she called out Monica's name, and the professor's again, louder, rewarded this time by a faint call for help.

Wishing it had been Monica's voice she heard, she was slightly cheered to know that Hawkins-Whyte was conscious somewhere deep in that stygian darkness,

Never a fan of the dark and narrow, Claudia had to dig deep for enough grit to step inside that gate. The uneven excavated rock ceiling not many inches above her brought back the dream of being locked in a small box. She wiped clammy hands on her jeans and reached her out to the sides, her fingertips meeting with rough bedrock walls.

Do snakes or scorpions or huge desert spiders live in tombs, like Indiana Jones movies?

"Not going to think about that," she said loudly, hoping her voice would scare any slithery things into staying in their hiding places as she headed into the darkness.

What if the stranger comes back and locks the gate?

Snakes and scorpions had nothing on being locked in a dark tomb.

Claudia dashed back to the dim rectangle of light at the gate and stowed the padlock behind one of the larger pieces of debris. If her husband knew she had not waited to hear back from Frank Booth and was marching into a place where she was effectively blind, he would be quietly furious. But Joel's big, reassuring presence was thousands of miles away and he couldn't hear the professor's distant pleas for help like she could.

As if invoking Joel had let him drop a suggestion in her ear, Claudia said "Duh!" and launched the flashlight app on her phone. The beam was strong enough to show that the passage—though long and tilting a few degrees downhill—did not continue hundreds of feet underground, as the tombs of some pharaohs did.

"Help. Help me, help me."

Henry Hawkins-Whyte's whimper reached out again. If Monica was down here somewhere, she was staying silent. Holding the light in front of her, Claudia maneuvered around the debris as fast as she safely could, looking from side to side for places her niece might be hidden. A darker rectangle in the rock about forty yards in was the first indication of an opening. The rectangle turned out to be door-sized.

"Professor, can you hear me?"

"Yes, yes, I hear you. Can you help me?"

His voice was shaky, but louder now, coming from inside the opening. This must be the chamber the team had been excavating.

"Hold on, Henry, I'm almost there."

Claudia stepped into the chamber and raised her light high, setting off ear-piercing chirps and squeaks that blocked out her panicked squeal. In a low crouch, she covered her head with her arms, waving away the flutter of leathery wings, the sharp little bat claws that touched her hair.

Scenes from a long-forgotten documentary came back about bat guano spores and the nasty diseases they caused in humans. The colony flew out of the chamber and the noise gradually died away, leaving the professor's plaintive cries bouncing off the walls and Claudia's legs quivering like Jello on a plate.

Her voice was quivering, too. "I'm right here, Professor. We're going to get you out of here; just hold on."

Silently calling on all the gods of Ancient Egypt to help her find the phone she had dropped, Claudia pulled the neck of her tee-shirt up to cover her nose and mouth. She groped the ground near her feet, a slow smile of relief forming when her fingers came into contact with the protective metal case Joel had given her. The flashlight had turned itself off in the fall, but it responded when she called up the app. Thanking the gods and her husband, she scrubbed her hands on her jeans and turned the beam on the professor.

Henry Hawkins-Whyte was sitting propped against a wall. The reddish outlines of an ancient unfinished sketch were visible behind him: a kneeling man cutting bundles of reeds. The professor raised a hand to shield his eyes from the light.

"What's happening?"

"You were attacked."

Blood from an ugly gash in his temple had dripped down and was soaking his beard and jacket. Worried that he might have been stabbed, Claudia knelt beside him, reaching into her jacket pocket for a travel pack of tissues. The next time Joel made fun of her for carrying everything but the kitchen sink, she would piously retort that her tissues might have saved the professor's life. Stanched the blood, anyway. Too bad her bottle of water was in her purse in the Rover.

"Does anything hurt besides the cut on your head?"

Hawkins-Whyte reached up an unsteady hand, wincing when he made contact with the wound. "I can't remember anything."

"Can you press these tissues right here, please, Henry? Don't let go. It's to help stop the bleeding."

While he was doing what she asked, Claudia passed the light over him from head to toe. The scrapes on his hands were likely the result of hitting the ground. A nearby rock the size of a baseball was a good candidate for the weapon the attacker had used. No stab wounds. She let out a long breath.

She found the professor's flashlight, whose cracked lens rendered it useless. There were tools the team used for their work—trowels and spades, brushes and sieves, a stack of labeled baskets. No sign of an eighteen-year-old missing girl or the archaeologist she had disappeared with.

She pictured the stranger, digging in here for contraband; panicking when he heard the professor at the gate. It was easy to imagine Professor Hawkins-Whyte climbing down the ladder to find the padlock open, and rushing headlong into the tomb. The other man must have picked up the rock and waited for him in the dark. He had attacked the professor and fled, abandoning him, injured and bleeding, running into Claudia outside. That certainly accounted for his look of shock when he saw her.

"I don't understand," the professor said again. "What happened?"

Having been hit over the head herself, Claudia was no stranger to traumatic brain injury. Remembering the feeling of disorientation, she set a hand on the professor's shoulder and drew his focus to her, worried by his vacant look and ebbing strength.

"You have a concussion, Henry. Do you think you can walk if I help you?"

"I think—yes, I think so."

"We'll do it together, all right, Henry?"

"All right," he agreed again, although she doubted that he fully understood what he was agreeing to. She could have moved much faster on her own, but leaving him alone in the dark while she sought help was not an option.

Henry Hawkins-Whyte was not a small man, and getting him to follow directions in his dazed condition was no easy feat. Squatting next to him, Claudia pulled his arm around her shoulders. "On the count of three, Henry, I'm going to help you stand up, but I need you to work with me. When I say three. Ready, Henry? One. Two. Three."

He was halfway to his feet when he complained of feeling giddy and sank back to the ground. Ready to burst into exasperated tears, Claudia got his arm around her neck again.

"You're doing fine, Henry," she lied. "Let's try it again."

"What happened?"

"Someone hit you. We're going to get you to a doctor."

"I don't remember anything."

"I know. Just hold on a little longer. We have to get outside so we can get help."

The prospect of help seemed to perk him up. Half-pushing, half-pulling, and bracing the professor's dead weight against her body, Claudia finally got him on his feet and walking.

Together, they stumbled through the chamber and out into the passage. When she saw the rectangle of daylight beckoning at the gate end—a beacon in the darkness—Claudia released a slightly hysterical snicker.

"Look, Henry, it's the light at the end of the tunnel."

19

MONICA

COLIN WAS GONE. SO WERE HER PHONE, HER PASSPORT, AND HER MONEY.

The panic of waking up to that realization gave way to bewilderment. What possible reason could he have for doing such a thing? He had taken his backpack, but all his other stuff was here.

It took a while to calm down and search her backpack a second time. That's when Monica found the note stuffed in the outside pocket. His scribbly, hard-to-read writing didn't offer a good explanation for why he had taken her most important things.

Sweet Mo, please don't be cross, only I don't want you to call anyone or go anywhere til I get back. Stay there, okay? We'll have fun later.
– Col

Baffled, she read it over again. She would have been happy to comply if he'd asked her not to call anyone or go anywhere. The more she thought about it, the more the initial spark of indignation threatened to flare into a conflagration as out of control as a wildfire. Taking her phone was a mortal sin. She wasn't sure she could ever consider forgiving him.

She read the note a third time. A fourth. He had better have a very good explanation.

'We'll have some fun later?' When was 'later' supposed to be? They were due back in Egypt tomorrow morning at the excavations where they were working. They had to get across the border this afternoon and would be flying all night.

Looking at Colin's chicken scratch, Monica racked her brains to remember what handwriting like this meant. She was pretty sure her Aunt Claudia would have had something snarky to say about it. If Annabelle, was here, she would know. Her best friend was good at that stuff. If she'd had her phone, Monica thought angrily, she could have called her.

Why would Colin want her not to use her phone?

'Stay there,' he had written. What else was she supposed to do all by herself in a strange country without phone or money? Until right now, everything had been cool and fun. When he had asked her to go away with him for a weekend, Monica was totally jazzed, especially when he promised not to pressure her for sex.

She had said yes with only a small pang of guilt because McKenna had liked him once. Guilt had not stopped her from packing the sexy undies she'd bought in Luxor, just in case. It was a good thing she had. He hadn't needed to pressure her. She was ready, and it was as mind-blowing and magnificent and amazing as she had known it would be. Colin had made her feel out of this world; connected to her, not just physically, but emotionally, too.

Now, he had ruined it all.

She showered, making it quick so the hot water wouldn't run out, and dressed in fresh jeans and the grey sweatshirt Annabelle had given her. It had a big pink heart on the front and the message 'Be Kind.' A reminder she needed right now. She didn't feel very kind towards Colin.

AN HOUR LATER, he wasn't back. Monica' insides were a rocky ball of jitters. She was crushing hard on Colin, but—and maybe it was because of McKenna's warning—she also recognized something—well, not totally reliable about him. What if he didn't come back?

Don't be stupid. He'll be back.

She dried her hair and pinned it back with the adorable butterfly barrettes Claudia had given her for the trip, then neatly folded her belongings and packed them into her backpack, ready to go. She resisted the temptation to pack Colin's belongings, which were all over the place. He didn't deserve her help.

Finally, there was nothing left to do but double-check the room.

With all that done, and no phone to access the WIFI, Monica sat on the bed, her emotions swinging between furious that Colin had taken her things, and a niggling fear that he had left her marooned. She recorded it all in her travel diary, and when she ran out of things to write, she stood at the window, sketching the hostel's courtyard, pretending she wasn't watching for Colin.

IT WAS PAST NOON, when they were supposed to check out, when a knock on the door vaporized Monica's pique. That's all it took. It was *so* Colin to forget his keycard. His head was always somewhere else—most of the time in some ancient tomb, and she couldn't fault him for that, could she? Monica unlocked the door and opened it with a big welcoming smile.

She blinked in confusion. The man at the door was not Colin.

They were around the same age, but this man was shorter, and stocky. Straight jet-black hair, a chin beard and moustache. Behind his eyeglasses, opaque eyes glittered with hostility.

Wordlessly, he shouldered past her, kicking the door shut behind him.

"Give me the backpack." His English was accented, but nearly as good as hers.

String in shock, Monica's eyes traveled to her backpack on the chair in the corner. She would gladly hand it over, but what was he going to do when he grasped that she was telling the truth—that she had nothing of value because Colin had taken it all?

"I'm sorry, but I don't have any money."

His scowl deepened. "No fucking with me. You get it. *Now.*"

So she handed it over, keeping as much distance between them as she could. "I'm serious, there's nothing valuable in it. And you need to leave. My boyfriend will be back any minute."

The man huffed a short, humorless laugh, his eyes roaming over her with contempt as he tipped the backpack on end and dumped the contents onto the bed.

Mortified when her undies were the first items to tumble out, Monica had to curb the instinct to grab the sexy bra and panties she had worn for Colin last night. Her blingy evening top went next, followed by her spare jeans and toiletries.

The last item bounced off the bed and landed on the uncarpeted floor with a thud. The intruder pounced on the eight-inch-tall resin replica of Anubis, the jackal-headed god of the underworld.

There was no way he could think it was genuine, could he? Monica wondered as the intruder studied the black and gold figure as if it were a work of art. She was not about to break the news that Colin had bought it for pennies at a Bazaar in Luxor. They had been in the taxi on the way to Luxor airport when he had taken it out of a paper bag and asked her to carry the statuette for him because there wasn't room in his backpack.

She was quietly gauging the distance to the door, trying to decide whether to make a run for it, when the Freak—she had named him that in her head—smashed the statuette against the edge of the night table. Once; twice; each time with greater violence. The third time, the inch-thick base broke apart. Resin chips went flying and something small fell to the floor.

The Freak bent to pick it up, and Monica made a dash for the door.

She was turning the knob when he snatched a hank of her long hair and whiplashed her back. Monica cried out as he wound her hair around his hand, tightening his grip as if he meant to rip it out by the roots.

"Where are you going?" he barked at her.

With his hand still wrapped painfully in her hair, the Freak forced her to her knees. He pushed her head down roughly until her nose touched the package on the floor.

"You see this, bitch? You give it to me."

It was scarcely larger than two pats of butter, but she couldn't do it with hands shaking like a palsied old woman. She tried, and dropped it, which earned another round of curses and a vicious slap across the face. Monica recoiled in shock. No one had ever slapped her face.

What was hidden in the statuette? And how did this guy know to look for it there? And where was Colin?

The Freak let go of her hair and grabbed the little package, his flat black eyes gleaming with satisfaction as he dropped it into an inner pocket of his jacket.

She thought he was leaving when he strode to the door. Before he opened it, he said, "You coming with me."

"What? No, I'm not."

He laughed, not in a funny way. "No? Then your boyfriend is dead."

She felt the blood drain from her face, leaving her weak in the knees. "What do you mean?"

"The archaeologist. We have him and we will kill him, slowly and with great pain. Is that to be on your conscience?"

For just a blink, Monica forgot her alarm and started to argue that if they killed someone, it would be *their* conscience that had the mark on it, not hers. Then the threat sank in and she bit her tongue.

We have Colin.

Keeping a firm grip on her arm, the Freak took her downstairs. She could hear voices at the reception desk, where people were checking out; too far and too loud for her to be heard if she screamed. And what about what he'd said about Colin?

They left the hostel and around the corner to a side street, where a car was idling. The driver said nothing when he ordered her into the backseat and slid in next to her. They looked enough alike to be related.

Freak1 and Freak2.

The two men spoke in their own language, which Monica thought was a form of Arabic, but not Egyptian—she had learned only a handful of words. She got the feeling that they were arguing over Freak1 bringing her along to wherever they were going. She didn't dare ask where they were taking her.

They drove for less than ten minutes before Freak2 stopped the car in an alley. There was a long, industrial-looking building on one side and some vehicles parked along a wall on the other. No sign of life as Freak1 ordered her out of the car.

The twitch of a curtain in a second story window caught Monica's eye and she looked up. A face peered down; then it was gone. They hurried her through a dark blue entry door and into an unimpressive hallway. Freak1 opened one of the closed doors that lined each side, and shoved her into what looked like a janitor's closet.

Hunched on the floor in the corner was a man. If it were not for the thick mop of burgundy-red hair pulled up in a man-bun on top, she would not have recognized the misshapen face as Colin's. His right eye was swollen shut, the left, bloodshot. Monica nearly fainted. Blood streaked his face. The lips she had so enjoyed kissing were as fat as tires.

Freak1 pushed past her and delivered a cruel kick to Colin's ribs. "You. Get up and face to the wall. Hands behind you."

Colin, retching wet splatters of blood onto the concrete floor, lurched to his feet.

Monica recognized the thick plastic loops Freak2 used to handcuff him. Her Uncle Joel used the same kind to arrest people. Once, he had asked if she and Annabelle wanted to try on the cuffs to see if they could escape, and Annabelle, who was always up for crazy stuff like that, said, "Sure." Monica was glad when Claudia got annoyed and stopped him, saying he shouldn't play that with the girls. Monica had thought it would be super-shuddersome to be confined that way, even for a minute.

When Freak2 cuffed her, too, she knew she was right.

This was way worse than the taxi accident when Colin got

arrested. The police could be bribed. Monica had a very bad feeling that it wasn't money that the Freaks wanted.

The two of them were ordered to sit on the concrete floor while the Freaks bound them back-to-back by their arms, then locked the door behind them when they left.

Colin sounded mumbly and unrecognizable. "Did they hurt you, Mo?"

Monica was trying not to cry. "Why are we here, Colin? Tell me why we're here."

"—wasn't s'posed to happen. Bloody wankers jumped me, three on one."

"*Three?* Who are they? Why did you leave me and take my phone and stuff? Why did you do that?"

"Sorry, Mo. I couldn't have you talking to anyone until everything was settled here. I thought that was the best way to do it."

"Well, obviously it wasn't. How could you do such a mean thing?"

"Left you a note."

His lame defense infuriated her. "Is that supposed to help? Where did you go?"

"Here; I came here. Had an appointment with this bloke to—" Colin broke off, coughing up blood. Monica turned away. Knowing what it was, the smell made her sick to her stomach.

"We were haggling over price when everything went pear-shaped. He double-crossed me."

"I don't understand. What were you selling? What was in that statue you asked me to carry?"

"I thought I could get it all worked out without having to tell you."

His moan went straight through Monica—nails on a blackboard. Under the circumstances, she put her sympathy to sleep. "You have to tell me, Colin. I'm sitting here, literally tied to you. I need to know. *What did you do?"*

"I know. You're right."

She couldn't see him, but she could feel it when he hung his head. She had to strain to make out what he was saying.

"I wish—look, here it is. You know we've had some fantastic finds.

There was one morning, everyone was at second breakfast, and I wanted to get on with it, so I went back to work early. There I was, sifting dirt, making notes of where an item had been located. Context being critical, of course."

So basic, Monica wanted to clap back at him. Like she wouldn't know that? And what did context have to do with their present predicament, anyway? He was obviously stalling. As usual, she swallowed the ferocious words that wanted to spew out. In her experience, expressing negative feelings tended to upset people and generally wasn't worth it.

When her mom died, she had wanted to scream and yell all the time. She'd wanted to kill the drunk driver who stole her amazing mother's life. Her dad had said the same things himself, but when Monica said them, his eyes would fill with tears and she would feel bad for making him sadder. So, she taught herself not to say those things out loud. Instead, she learned to stomp her anger into oblivion and smile, while inside, her pulse throbbed and her head ached from staying silent.

Once again, Colin had to pause to spit blood. It sounded awful and he apologized. "We'd excavated some really nice pieces—faience ushabtis, scarabs, jewelry—several really lovely things."

Monica knew that scarabs—sacred beetles—were ubiquitous. And ushabtis, an army of small figurines made as stand ins for their owner in the afterlife in case he or she was required to do manual labor, were commonly placed in tombs by the dozens; sometimes hundreds. They were always a terrific find. Any item they dug up was a terrific find. But none of those items would account for what she was hearing in his voice.

"So far, you're not telling me anything I don't already know."

"Right. Okay, then. It's, well, er—"

She listened to him take several labored breaths, growing more exasperated with each one. "Quit stalling, Colin. Just tell me."

"All right, all right. Something I never in my life—"

"What did you find?"

His voice dropped almost to a whisper, and she was sure she must have misheard. Of all the things he might have said, this was nowhere close to being on the list.

"What did you just say?"

"—a gold finger ring with the cartouche of Hatshepsut."

"You've got to understand, I'm not at all proud of this. I—well, I needed money, a lot of money, very badly, and—"

"Oh no, Colin, no. Tell me you *didn't*—"

"Some people I know in Luxor put me in touch with a chap here who deals in these sorts of things—"

"'These sorts of things?' You mean *stolen antiquities?*"

She had been so sure he would never be involved in such schemes. Over the past weeks, while they had been growing closer, she had nudged aside what McKenna said about him being accused of hanging out with people suspected of doing exactly this.

"—offered me seventy-five thousand pounds. That's more than ninety-thousand dollars."

"That's why we're here? For *money?"* The dismay, the humiliation of knowing she had been used, crushed Monica's tender spirit. She let out a pained sigh. "What else did you steal, Colin?"

"Please, Mo, please don't."

"You'd better tell me. The ring wasn't the only thing, was it?"

"There was a small figurine," he said with obvious reluctance. "Nowhere near as valuable as the ring, but worth good dosh. I didn't want to risk bringing both of them out of the country at the same time." He swore softly. "What was I supposed to do, say 'no thanks,' and put it back in the dirt for someone else to find?"

"Yes, that's exactly what you were supposed to do." Humiliation was rapidly mushrooming into fury, as much with herself as with Colin. She should have guessed something was going on when he asked her to carry the Anubis figure for him. She had wanted to ask why he couldn't carry it himself, and why it needed to come with them at all, but she was Monica the Compliant, so she had taken it from him without question.

"You smuggled the ring in the statue to get it out of Egypt and through customs," she said.

Colin leaned back until his head was touching hers. "You've got to believe me; I've never done anything close to this before; I swear it. And I never meant for you to become involved, never."

She tried to shift away from him, but there was no place where the back of her body wasn't touching his.

"Seriously, Colin? *Seriously?* It's only obvious that you did it because *I'm* the one who would have been totally screwed for smuggling if we got caught, not you. You figured customs wouldn't be suspicious of a young American girl. And now we're totally screwed anyway."

"I never thought—"

"No lie."

Monica kept waiting for him to beg her forgiveness, though there was no way on earth he could justify what he had done. She had kissed those Judas lips and given herself to him, fully and willingly—her first lover. Her shame was complete.

Colin was still explaining himself. "See, I wasn't going to hand the ring over until I knew the buyer had the money. That's why I left it at the hostel. I only showed Akeem—the bloke here—a photo of it. I had no clue he was setting me up."

"So, you sent that evil freak to get me?"

"No! I never thought he would do that. Mo, come on—you see what they've done to me. They threatened to cut off my fingers, and they would have, too. I held out as long as I could. They showed me a pair of secateurs—" Colin's voice got watery and broke on a sob.

The first sight of him beaten up had upset her deeply. After hearing his story, she was ready to beat him up herself—a very un-Monica-like feeling. She never stayed mad at anyone, even if they deserved it. Claudia liked to tease that she could have won an award for the most forgiving heart in the world. This was different. Not even Annabelle, everyone's designated 'bad girl,' had ever gotten her into a jam anywhere near this dangerous.

Colin's betrayal of his moral obligation to report finding the pharaoh's ring shook Monica to her core. She viewed every second she spent working at Frank Booth's project as a sacred privilege, every menial chore assigned to her, a thrill. How could a *real* archaeologist entrusted with the task of uncovering ancient history be so mercenary?

And now, Pharaoh Hatshepsut's cartouche ring—a priceless treasure—was in the hands of the Freaks. Which raised the question of why they were continuing to hold her and Colin. They could have taken the ring and let them go. He couldn't report it stolen without implicating himself.

Monica arrived at a chilling conclusion: *We are in big trouble.*

SHE COULD HEAR doors opening and closing. Sometimes the Freaks' voices would sound through the wall, though their words were indistinct. Three of them, Colin had said, although she had seen only the two who had brought her here—kidnapped her.

Hours passed. She lost track of time. The closet had no windows to gauge the arc of the sun across the sky; no hint of whether it was morning or the middle of the night. The rumbling in her stomach told her that a long time had passed since the meal she and Colin had shared in that darling café on the bay.

They had gone back to their hostel afterwards and he had made love to her, gently, sweetly—she put a stop to that line of thought and returned to thinking about being hungry. Not that she could have kept food down if they offered anything to eat, which they didn't.

Dehydration and fear fogged up Monica's brain. She drifted in and out of a light doze, dreaming she was at home in her own room, her own bed, having a nightmare. Then she would jerk awake and realize she was living the nightmare. How long had they been in this dreary little prison, bound together on butt-numbing concrete?

The Freaks had allowed her to use the grungy toilet, though one of them leered at her from the door, which made it super-embarrassing and really hard to pee. Thank God they cut off the handcuffs and let her pull her pants up and down by herself, which wasn't easy when her hands were numb from being shackled for hours; prickling with pins and needles when the circulation started to return.

She made the freedom last long enough to rinse her hands in the rusty trickle from the faucet, and slurped as much of the briny water as she could.

What a sick twist. She had waited forever to be grown up and independent, to insist on making this big trip. Now, all she wanted was to be a little girl again, protected by her daddy's strong arms. He would tell her he loved her and she was the best part of his life, like he always did. She pictured how frantic her dad and Aunt Claudia must be. What hurt the most was, it was her fault. They would have called Frank Booth by now, and learned that she was not where she was meant to be. Even if Annabelle spilled the beans about her trip with Colin, she wouldn't know to look for them here.

Monica choked back tears. She had learned the hard way that when she wept, snot ended up dried on her face because her hands were not free to wipe it away.

If only she had not been so gullible...

20

CLAUDIA

The Ancients may have revered the Underworld, but Claudia Rose was thrilled to step outside the tomb into the bright light of Amun-Ra. Only a half-hour had elapsed since her voicemail for Frank Booth. Or had she been down there for a week and entered the Twilight Zone? It felt that way.

After getting the professor seated on the rough ground outside the tomb, she tried Booth again and got no signal. The wooden ladder taunted her. She was seriously beginning to consider taking the professor's keys, when her ears picked up the distant howl of sirens getting closer.

She jumped to her feet. "Sit tight, Henry. The cavalry's here."

And with that, she shinnied up the ladder to wave at a caravan of emergency vehicles led by Frank Booth's Jeep.

"They'll keep him overnight for observation," Booth said on his return to Petrie House later that afternoon. He had tried calling back when he got Claudia's messages, but she must have been inside the tomb, where the signal could not penetrate. Not knowing what to expect, he had requested both ambulance and police services.

The EMTs had hoisted Professor Hawkins-Whyte to the top of the pit in a litter, and Booth followed the ambulance to the local hospital in his vehicle. At the request of the ENP—the Egyptian National Police—Claudia remained at the excavation site to give her statement and a description of the professor's attacker. When they were finished with her, she was given a ride to Petrie House.

Mustafa, as usual, was busy at the stove, getting the evening meal ready. Booth took two beers from the fridge and held them up, asking if Claudia wanted one. She did.

"Thank God you went with Henry. If he'd been in that chamber alone for much longer in that condition, he would have surely bled out."

Joining her at the table, he twisted off the cap and handed over the sweating bottle. "His people wouldn't have known where he was. They would have gone to work tomorrow and found him too late."

Claudia took a long pull on the beer, savoring the cold brew as it slid down her throat. "He didn't want me to go with him. I had to fast-talk him into taking me."

Booth chuckled. "You must have impressed the hell out of the stubborn old goat to let you persuade him."

"Hah. I didn't get that impression at all. It was more a case of he didn't have any place else to put me."

Booth touched his bottle to Claudia's in a salute. "He owes you his life. It can't have been easy for you to go into that dark tomb, not knowing what you were going to find. I mean, we're used to it—"

Claudia cut him short, embarrassed by his admiration. "That gash on his head looked serious."

"The doc was amazed he didn't have a skull fracture. By the way, the police were impressed with your detailed description of the suspect. You may be called to make an identification at the police station."

"They already caught him?"

"No. I'm sure it won't be long, though. We think we know who it was."

"How on earth—?"

"I dropped by Henry's dig house after the hospital to let the crew know what happened. As you can imagine, the attack on Henry, then Colin's treachery—it was a double whammy." Booth gave Claudia a significant look. "I gave them your description of the man at the tomb in case someone had seen him hanging around there. *That* was the trifecta."

"It was someone they knew?"

"Your description fit their foreman to a tee; a fellow called Farouk Badr. Everyone agreed it described him. As foreman, he is entrusted with a key to the gate." Booth fished for his phone and scrolled through screens. "This is their dig team." He showed Claudia a photo. "Is the guy you saw in this picture?"

Enlarging the screen, she panned around the group photo, studying the faces of men and women arranged in three rows behind the excavation site. Some wore western clothing, others were in galabeyas and turbans. She pointed to a man who stood next to Colin Vine at the far-right end of the top row. Those piercing eyes and sensual lips were something she would not soon forget.

"That's him."

Booth puffed a dispirited sigh. "That's Farouk all right. Damn. I wanted it not to be him. Henry will be devastated."

Claudia was putting it all together. "So, Colin stole the statuette of Hatshepsut, and most likely other artifacts, and has disappeared with my niece. Next, we have the foreman digging in the chamber and standing right beside him in the picture. It can't all be a coincidence; they have to be in it together. Whatever 'it' is." She wanted to put her head down on the table and go to sleep, to pretend none of this was happening.

"If I'd known, maybe I could have talked Farouk into telling me where Monica is. He must know."

"He must have gone apeshit when he heard Henry at the gate. Normally, he would never be at the site on a Saturday."

Again, Claudia pictured the foreman digging in that rear chamber, thinking he was safe on a Saturday morning. Professor Hawkins-

Whyte, seeing the gate open, would have called out, demanding to know who was inside. Farouk must have shut off whatever light he was working by and waited in the dark for the professor to get all the way back to the chamber by the flashlight he had taken from the Land Rover.

She said this to Booth, whose leathery skin creased in a frown. "Farouk never expected you to be there when he went flying up that ladder. He must have thought he could duck out and show up for work tomorrow with no one the wiser and pretend to be shocked when he heard about the attack on the boss."

There was no denying the aura of danger that had emanated from Farouk Badr. The memory of it brought a fresh chill. "He could have done me serious damage if he'd wanted to."

"It must have been quite a shock to see you there. First, running into Henry, then you, a witness. He cut his losses and ran." Booth lobbed his beer bottle into a bin in the corner. "The thought of what else Vine might have made off with besides the piece you described makes my blood boil. They've made terrific finds at their site. It's down to you that Farouk apparently didn't get away with anything today."

"There's no way of knowing, is there?" Claudia started to rise. "If you don't mind, Frank, I'm going to rest for a while before supper."

Booth stood, too. "Could I ask for a quick favor first?"

Inwardly, she groaned. "Of course. What do you need?"

"As you can guess, Monica told us about her famous aunt, the graphologist. I've got a piece of ancient hieratic writing from a scribe named Quasshie. Would you be able to tell me anything at all about the person who wrote it?"

"I can give it a try. No promises, though."

"Whatever you can tell me would be more than I know now. Apparently, this Quasshie was sick. He wrote a letter to the god Thoth, asking to bless him with good health. In the letter, he says he's worried that he would die and his family would be left without a provider."

Her interest rising, Claudia set aside her exhaustion, eager to see what Frank Booth had to show her. "Thoth is the ibis-headed god? The god of writing."

"The god of writing, among other things. Quasshie was the chief scribe for one of the tomb builders' villages. He would have been *very* much respected. Imagine how many thousands of people worked on these building projects, all needing a place to live and bring up their kids during the years the construction was going on. It was the scribes who kept all the village records; the really important stuff. You know—how much you owed in taxes. Or how much beer to order."

Claudia chuckled. "Oh, beer. Definitely the important stuff."

"The *most* important," Frank Booth affirmed with a conspiratorial smile. "I'll go get the letter."

After the stress of the day—days—week—it felt as though her brains were falling out. If he had asked her to analyze *his* writing, that would be easy enough. Ancient Egyptian was another story. At least hieratic writing was done with a reed pen on papyrus, not so different from analyzing modern Arabic. She owed it to him on Monica's behalf to at least look at it.

He left the room, quickly returning with a photocopy.

Claudia studied it briefly. "I've seen some examples where the lines were all crammed together. This is nicely spaced out and the forms are pleasing and somewhat rounded. I'd say Quasshie was well-organized and had a good sense for design and creativity. He was compassionate; truly cared about people. I can't say for sure because of the writing materials, and it's a photocopy, but see here, where the strokes look lighter—that weakness could be caused by illness." She handed back the copy. "I hope Thoth listened to his prayers and gave him a long, healthy life."

"We'll have to see whether there are hieroglyphics in the tomb that tell the story. The Egyptians recorded *everything*. As a scribe, Quasshie would have been very well educated; high up on the social ladder." Booth stood. "Thank you very much. You've really brought him to life."

"I'm happy to help."

"Okay, Claudia, I won't keep you from your nap any longer. I have some photos to download."

A starburst went off in Claudia's brain. "Photos! That's it!"

With the happenings at the tomb, she had brushed aside the subtle tingling that told her she was missing something. It had been lurking below the surface all day. Now, with the unexpected sharpening of focus brought by Frank Booth's announcement, she knew what it was.

"You look as if a lightbulb just went on," Booth said.

"It did. This morning, when I was going through Colin's camera, there were a bunch of photos taken at the dig, artifacts *in situ*."

He sat back on the bench beside her. "Sure; we take photos of every step in the process."

"It didn't occur to me at the time, but when you mentioned downloading photos, something clicked. One of the photos in Colin's camera was a gorgeous gold ring with a cartouche. That photo was taken on the dresser in his room."

Booth frowned. "What do you mean?"

"I mean, the ring was sitting on Colin's dresser when the photo was taken."

"How the hell could you know that?"

"Because there's a blue table runner on top of his dresser. I noticed it had an unusual pattern when I photographed the statuette, but I didn't pay much attention. The ring in the photo was displayed on that runner. And that's the only photo where it appeared. Can you think of any legitimate reason such a ring should have been in his room at any time?"

"None," Booth answered. "A *gold* ring? Are you sure? With a cartouche, you say?"

"Yes. It's the same cartouche as on the figurine."

"What can you tell me about the figurine?"

"Henry said it was Hatshepsut on her throne; it had her cartouche. So, if the ring has her cartouche, the ring must have been hers, too."

Frank Booth's eyes widened. He looked as though his best friend had died. "My God, Claudia, do you have any idea how consequential a find that is?"

"I took a couple of pictures on that same dresser."

She selected and enlarged one of the photos that showed the statuette on the blue table runner and showed it to him. A thundercloud formed between his creased brows.

"This is Hatshepsut's cartouche all right. We've got to get that ring back. And the theft has to be reported to the Antiquities Department."

"I understand your need to get hold of the ring, Frank; truly, I do. But my bigger concern is what Colin has done with Monica."

Her phone rang as Booth was handing it back. Looking at her brother's picture on the screen, she debated whether to answer the call. Her young niece had fallen for what was essentially a modern-day tomb robber. More bad news might just put her over the edge. A wave of sorrow broke over Claudia. Maybe it was being married to a homicide detective that had robbed her of hopefulness. Or maybe it was her own experiences, which had shown her the worst of humanity. It was getting harder to stay optimistic and picture Monica safe at home with them.

Pete was keyed up. "I just heard back from the Embassy."

"What did they say?"

"You won't believe this. The day after they flew to Morocco they went to Gibraltar."

He couldn't see Claudia's double-take. "*Gibraltar?*"

"You know everything I do, Sis."

"I'm sure you checked her accounts again."

"She paid for a ferry ticket from Tangier—in Morocco—to Spain, *a week ago Friday.* From there, you fly from Malaga, take a bus to La Linea, which is on the border of Spain, and Gibraltar, and you walk across Gibraltar airport to the town."

"What the hell is in Gibraltar?"

"Not a lot besides the Rock. The airport is so small, you have to cross the runway by foot when planes aren't using it."

Claudia raked a hand through her hair. Something was not adding up. "She's been gone for over a week and that's all she's paid for—airfare and a ferry? What about food or—whatever?"

"Using cash? Or maybe Vine is paying for food and lodging. Or—" An ominous note crept in. "Something's happened to them."

Claudia told him about the ring. "It's a very big deal, a really important artifact. Maybe Morocco was just a stop along the way and he's fencing the ring in Gibraltar."

"All I know, is, my kid would *never* willingly leave us not knowing where she is. She's got to know we're going out of our minds. If something relatively simple went wrong, she knows to contact the American Embassy wherever she is. In Gibraltar, it's the Consulate. So, as far as I can see, that means she's being prevented."

It was the same thing Claudia had said to Frank Booth. The uneasy vibe she had been carrying around zoomed up to DEFCON 1.

Why Gibraltar, of all places?

An idea worked its way forward. "Remember that paper I found in Colin's room? We know it's not a phone number in Egypt; what about Morocco or Gibraltar? Can you check the calling codes for those countries?"

She could hear him tapping on his computer keyboard as she dashed upstairs to her room and got the paper out of her bag.

"The calling code for Morocco is 212."

"That's not it. What about Gibraltar?"

More tapping. "350."

"Bingo. That's the start of the number string. I bet it's a Gibraltar phone number." She read off the numbers, a puny flame of cheer igniting. They were starting to make some kind of progress; she could feel it.

"I'm doing a reverse lookup," Pete said. Seconds later the energy in his voice lifted. "It's the phone number for a company called Dandachi Ancient Arts. I'm going to their website."

"There's the initial 'D' on the paper," Claudia said. "And 'ancient arts' sounds right." Glad McKenna was out, Claudia dropped onto Monica's bed and reached for her tablet. Pete gave her the URL and she looked at the Dandachi site with him.

The home page featured a series of photographs of crude ushabti figures from throughout Egyptian history. They were marked 'Late Period, 18th Dynasty.'

"It's an antiquities dealer." She skimmed a statement printed at the top of the page. "It says 'Every artifact was legally acquired and exported prior to the 1970 UNESCO treaty,' whatever that means. If Colin *is* trying to sell the ring to them, he has them believing he's got it legally. Or maybe they don't care if it is." She continued browsing. "They claim they sell genuine mummy wrappings, wadjets—"

"What jets?"

"*Wadjet,* the Eye of Horus. It's a symbol of protection." Claudia pored over the site. "Jeez, Pete, you can order a necklace of genuine faience beads for two hundred bucks. They're not picky, they sell items from ancient Rome, Greece, and Israel, as well as Egypt."

"There's no physical address listed. Customers have to order through a form on the website. No email address on the Contact page. You have to leave your information on the form for them to get back to you."

"You've got a phone number," said Claudia. "Gibraltar is in the same time zone as Egypt."

"Hold on. I'll try calling it."

"Good luck."

Two minutes later, he was back, disappointed. "No answer. No voicemail, either, which is weird for a business."

"Are you going to fill out the form on the website?"

"Doing it as we speak. All I can do now is wait for someone to get back to me."

"Well, there's something more *I* can do," said Claudia. "I'm going to Gibraltar."

21

GIBRALTAR

THE LATE FEBRUARY MORNING HAD A WELCOME FRESHNESS. CLAUDIA got off the bus in La Linea, unfolding her stiff limbs and stretching her arms high and wide, not caring who might be watching. She would have preferred to follow the same route as Monica and Colin, through Tangier, but booking a last-minute flight pared down the choices. Now, after three hours trapped on the bus, she looked forward to the brisk half-mile walk to the Passport Control Station at the Spain/Gibraltar border.

The nine-hour red-eye to Malaga and the long bus ride to La Linea had given her too much time to think and worry, and the aching grief of missing her niece filled up her whole being. Knowing something must have happened to her was bad enough. Not knowing *what* had happened was much worse. Would it be better to have a body to grieve over than to wonder every minute of every day whether she was dead, or alive and subjected to horrible abuse? Either alternative was excruciating.

The Gibraltar port of entry was visible in the distance. If it was humanly possible, she would find Monica, and that's all there was to it. If it meant *acting* as if she believed it would all turn out fine, then act, she would.

Near the passport control office, an absurd chuckle burbled up. The familiar Burger King logo and photo of a gigantic Whopper on a squat building across the street suddenly made the world a whole lot smaller. The recognizable aroma curled into her nostrils and made her hungry, but she was too close to her destination to stop walking.

Until Pete briefed her that Gibraltar ranked fifth in the world as a 'most extreme' airport, Claudia had never heard of a busy road intersecting a runway. A runway that was currently closed while an EasyJet prepared for takeoff. Could the nightmare of Monica's disappearance be about to end on this tiny British-owned peninsula? She joined the throng behind the barrier, her nerves twitching as they waited for the all-clear to cross the border.

Across the airport, the majestic Rock rose out of the sea. To the ancient Romans, it was one of the two Pillars of Hercules that flanked the entrance to the Strait of Gibraltar. Having Hercules on your side couldn't hurt, Claudia decided as she hurried across and hailed a taxi on the Gibraltar side.

Pete had booked her into the Rock Hotel and insisted on paying her expenses to make up for not being able to be there himself. She FaceTimed him on the way to the hotel.

The saggy skin under his eyes said he had slept no better than she had. She told him about having identified Henry Hawkins-Whyte's assailant.

Pete made a sound of disgust. "How could his own foreman do such a thing?"

"I just hope he didn't get anything else from the site."

"I'm more concerned that he could have killed you."

"Yeah, that wasn't my favorite part," Claudia admitted. "But he didn't."

"Thank God for that. Any problems getting out of Luxor?"

"Nope. Frank took me to the airport after we went to the police station. I had to make a formal identification of Farouk Badr as the guy who attacked the professor."

She had another item to share that she knew would be a knife to

Pete's soul. The afternoon had included a stop at the Fedex store in Luxor. There was no easy way to tell him.

"I shipped her things home."

He moved the phone away so she couldn't see his face. When he came back, he was breathing hard and his face was red. "Screw the judge's order; I'm coming out there."

"*No,* Pete, you can't do that. I'm going to find her. You need to be home in case—" She didn't want to finish the sentence. Making that shipment had made it seem so final. "Have you heard back from the Dandachi website people?"

"It's too soon. I talked to the Embassy in Cairo, though. They'll get in touch with the American Consulate in Gibraltar. Hotels have to register guest's passports. Unless they're staying with friends, there should be a record of them somewhere."

"We can make a list of all the hotels to call and split it between us. As small as Gibraltar is, there can't be all that many."

"I also spoke to the Royal Gibraltar Police. There haven't been any reports of arrests or hospitalizations; not even minor accidents that involved either Monica or Colin Vine. They've promised to check around again."

"Did you mention the Dandachi site to them?"

"No, and I should have. If Dandachi's is the kind of business where you could fence stolen antiquities, they might be aware of it."

"After I check in at the hotel and get something to eat, I'll go to the address on Colin's paper," said Claudia. "If we're lucky, someone there will know where to find Colin and Monica and I won't have to unpack."

It wasn't much of a joke and Pete wasn't laughing. If Gibraltar was a dead end, what then? Maybe they should have hired a private investigator from the outset. Would a PI have located Monica by this time and brought her safely home?

"Call the police and ask them to go with you," Pete urged, pulling Claudia back to the conversation. "If these people *are* in the illegal antiquities trade, they're probably dangerous."

"The police can't roll out without any proof that someone's

committed a crime. Don't worry, if anything looks unkosher, I'll leave. It's a tiny place. The police can't be very far from wherever I am."

"I know you, Sis," he said with exasperation. "*Please* promise me you won't take any ridiculous risks."

"Who, me?" Claudia protested, as if she had never taken a ridiculous risk in her life. "All right, I promise. I don't want any trouble. Please stop worrying. Yeah, I know; not gonna happen."

Watching him pacing around his house through her phone screen was making her dizzy, but she didn't ask him to stop. He needed to blow off some emotional steam, and pacing was a harmless way to do it.

They ended the call and she made a mental note to ask the next time they spoke if he had heard anything from Robin Cross' investigator, who was working on his criminal case. She spared a thought for how their parents were going to react when they heard the news, which gave her an instant headache. That Pete was to be tried for murder was as inconceivable as Monica going AWOL.

Her taxi driver must not have heard that traffic in Gibraltar was less hectic than Egypt. He whipped around traffic circles and merges with a lead foot, rushing up to the car ahead of them and slamming on the brakes at a red light. Waiting for the light to change, Claudia sat forward to speak to him. "Do you know Flynt Road?"

"You wait one minute." He began tapping the address into his sat nav device, continuing after the light blinked to green and they were moving again. Wishing she had not asked him, she held onto the armrest hoping to make it to the hotel in one piece.

"Is close to airport," the driver said, looking at her in the rearview mirror. "You wanna go back there?"

What I want is to escape your lousy driving.

"No, thanks, straight to the hotel, please."

Not that it made any real difference. All of Gibraltar covered an area scarcely more than two-and-a-half square miles.

They sped along Queensway Road, past the quaint-sounding 'Ragged Staff Road.' Driving through an ancient-looking stone arch, the driver said in his Spanish-accented English, "The Rock Hotel, he is there. He be there since 1939."

Following his pointing finger to the foothill on their left, she saw the name, ROCK HOTEL, in gigantic green letters on a five-story edifice that resembled a big white cruise ship. According to its website, which she had checked out on the Malaga bus, the art déco hotel sat at the foot of the Rock—thus its name—with a panoramic view of the Bay and the Straits of Gibraltar.

"Is most historic landmark of all best hotels on Gib," the driver recited as he must have done five hundred times before.

At Europa Road he made a sharp turn onto a steep driveway and screeched to a halt at the lobby doors. Claudia collected her suitcase from the trunk and to his delight, handed him a cash tip—though she had learned in Egypt that tips were not expected there or in Europe—and thanked the doorman who held the front door for her.

Descending the lobby staircase to the front desk, she had to admit that The Rock was one elegant hotel. Pete had given her a taste of luxury. The most important thing, though, it gave her a place to stow her luggage while she went looking for her niece.

An attractive young woman greeted her at the lobby desk. 'Heidi,' according to her badge. She asked in a British accent for Claudia's passport; made a photocopy and handed it back with a smile, along with the security key card for her guestroom.

"Would you happen to know whether *all* the hotels require a copy of guests' passports?" Claudia asked, filling out a registration form.

"Yes, I'm afraid it's a European Union requirement for us to keep details of our guests on file for twelve months." Heidi was apologetic, unaware of the fillip of excitement this news gave Claudia. "It applies to every guest over the age of sixteen. We have to keep a record of your name, nationality, and your home address."

"I don't suppose there can be very many hotels here."

"You're right about that," said Heidi. "If we're counting one or two hostels, I'd believe Gib has about twenty hotels."

Hostels. *Huh.* Something they had not considered. The kind of place young travelers on a budget stayed. They didn't know Colin's financial status, and Monica had footed the bill for her own travel. It didn't sound like he was throwing money around freely. Nonetheless, if he was fencing antiquities here as they suspected, he must have expected to collect a substantial sum of money; otherwise, what was the point?

It shouldn't take more than an hour to call around and ask if Monica was a guest. Less, if she and Pete shared the task. Right after she checked out #9 Flynt Road.

Her guestroom was as attractive and well-appointed as she could have wished, with windows that looked out onto Gibraltar Bay. Even the line of oil rigs in the Bay could not spoil the view. After the long hours of travel and jumpy nerves, a hot shower, followed by sandwiches on the hotel restaurant's charming Wisteria Terrace, revived her flagging spirits.

Was it selfish to take the gift of a few minutes to sit and contemplate the coastline of Africa, visible through the mist across the water? It was not, Claudia decided. The next step would come soon enough. For now, she allowed a little wandering into fantasyland: a year in the future, Monica home safe. Joel here with her on the terrace. They would explore the bustling streets and shops together; take a cable car up the Rock and visit the famed Gibraltar Barbary macaques.

The chime of an incoming text disturbed her reverie.

Frank Booth: *Farouk has cleared out—in the wind.*

In the wind. Gone. Claudia scowled at the screen. Gone where? He must have been super-spooked to take off that way. He had not known who she was when he saw her at Professor Hawkins-Whyte's vehicle. Still, she could identify him as the assailant. She had a feeling that just about anywhere was better than moldering in an Egyptian prison for antiquities theft.

She texted her thanks to Frank for keeping her in the loop, and asked whether he knew the name 'Dandachi.'

Booth: *"Sorry, no."*

Texting a waving hand emoji as thanks, Claudia scribbled her room number and signature on her lunch bill and gathered her things. Heidi had booked her a taxi. While she waited for it in front of the hotel, she made a call to Joel. Pete had promised to call him and let him know she had departed Egypt for Gibraltar. He would be waking up about now.

"How's the world traveler?" Joel kept his tone light, but Claudia knew her husband well enough to feel the effort it took not to express his true sentiments. He didn't have to say it for her to know he considered her to be on a fool's errand. God, she prayed he was wrong.

"I miss you," she said.

"I miss you, too, babe. I guess it'd be stupid to ask when I'm going to wake up with you next to me again."

"Not stupid. Every morning and every night I wish I was waking up with you."

She outlined the plan to call around the hotels after checking out the Flynt Road address.

"You know how, when you're working on a case and you get that feeling that you're getting somewhere? That's how I feel now."

"I'd feel better if you'd contact the local gendarmes," said Joel, sounding like Pete. "Let them know—"

"It's the Royal Gibraltar Police," Claudia corrected. "I'm going to do a drive-by to check it out, no big deal." Her mind was rushing ahead and his concerns slid off like eggs on Teflon.

They chatted for a bit and said their 'I love you's.' She was slipping the phone into her pocket when the taxi drew up to take her to Flynt Road.

Europa Road became Trafalgar Road, then Main Street. Many of the streets and shops had British names, Claudia observed. Tall palm trees and fresh, modern-looking multi-story buildings lined the roads.

From her driver, a chatty expat, she learned that while some of the locals spoke Spanish, most were also English speakers. He kept up an easygoing patter as he drove, indicating the old barracks from when 'Gib' was a British Garrison, now civilian homes. Talking about the Napoleonic wars. The tunnels. The caves. The monkeys.

She would have loved the history lesson at any other time. With her nerves jangling, it was easier to tune him out.

It was not the grey February day that caused her to shiver when the driver turned onto Devil's Tower Road. The Devil's Bar on the corner reminded her of Dirtbags in Tucson. And that could not be a good omen.

22

"You sure it's the right address?" the driver asked dubiously when the next turn took them to Flynt Road.

It was more of a narrow alley that looked nowhere close to a neighborhood where an 'Ancient Arts' gallery should be situated. A lichen-carpeted brick wall formed a barrier between Flynt Road and the base of the ever-present Rock. Looming over the peninsula, it looked as though a good shake would loose a shower of shale down on them.

Claudia knew the address by heart, but she checked the paper anyway. "Number nine Flynt Road."

On the other side of the short, curved road, a long, industrial-looking building housed several businesses. None had signs or banners to identify them, leaving visitors to guess what they were. She scanned the vehicles parked along the wall. No Dandachi Ancient Arts logo to be seen. They probably didn't want to advertise it if there were valuable goods inside.

The driver braked outside a dirty blue wood door. "Here you are, luv, number nine."

He was right. Next to an intercom box on the wall was a large numeral 9.

"Are you sure this is the only Flynt Road?"

"That's right, luv. The one and only."

"Number nine is supposed to be an antiques business, Dandachi Ancient Arts."

He half-shrugged. "I wouldn't know anything about that."

Clinging to the faint possibility that Colin had got the address wrong when he wrote it down, Claudia asked him to drive around the block one more time. On the opposite side of the Flynt Road buildings, a series of high-end car repair shops occupied the same cheerless building.

When they got back around to Flynt Road, she asked the driver to stop at an open door—a mechanic's workshop down the street from number nine. The man inside saw her and turned off the drill press he was running. Claudia called out to him, "Excuse me. I'm looking for Dandachi Ancient Arts. Do you know it?"

He frowned, concentrating; shook his head. "Never heard of it."

"It's supposed to be at number nine Flynt Road."

"'Ancient Arts,' you say? Nope, never 'eard of it." He jerked his head to the right. "Number nine'd be down that way."

She thanked him and returned to the taxi none the wiser. Asking the driver to wait for her where he was, Claudia walked toward number nine, passing dirt-crusted frosted glass windows that ensured no one could see inside. Just like the grimmer areas of many cities, burglar bars fronted not only the Devil's Bar, but every window.

An old plastic bottle from an office water dispenser had been wedged between the windows and the burglar bars for no apparent reason, and the paint on the grey walls and royal blue door was chipped and worn. With no business hours posted anywhere, it added up to a dismal, deserted atmosphere. The *recherché* showroom she had visualized with gleaming plate glass windows displaying the 'Ancient Arts' for sale was as far from this reality as the moon.

Had it been a mistake to think that the number on Colin's paper was connected to the Flynt Road address? If Dandachi's Ancient Arts was here, it was flying incognito. She got out the paper and entered the number string into her phone, waiting for a voicemail message that never came on.

She pressed the intercom button on the wall and heard a loud buzz inside. When nothing happened, she pressed it twice more, half-expecting a questioning face to peer around the jamb, demanding to know what she wanted.

She rapped on the door, and when it swung open a few inches, the fine hairs on her neck stood up and gave her an eerie chill. She forced a laugh. Whoever closed it last hadn't properly latched it. Nudging it open with her toe, she leaned in and called, "Hello? Anybody here?"

On the other side of the blue door, it was as quiet and cold and musty as the Luxor tomb, although thankfully, not as dark. Leaning back out, she looked down the alley and waved at the taxi, still idling on the corner. The driver was looking down, no doubt texting with someone while the meter kept rolling. For about five seconds, Claudia waffled on the doorstep, Joel's and Pete's urges to call the police blaring in her head. It wasn't breaking and entering. The door was open, and with the driver waiting for her, she wasn't exactly alone. A peek was all she needed. Shrugging off their cautions, she stepped inside.

Automatic fluorescent lights came on overhead as she moved along the hallway. A security camera high in a corner of the ceiling surveilled her through its opaque globe. If anyone was watching live, it was too late to do anything about it. She gave it a thumbs up.

There were several closed doors and she knocked lightly, listening for any sound that might indicate another living soul in the building.

Opening the first and second doors, she saw stacks of boxes. Storerooms. If this was Dandachi's, there were no 'Ancient Arts' on display here. The place was what it looked on the outside: more warehouse than showroom. No wonder there was no signage. The company must use it only for order fulfillment. Maybe they only worked nights.

Behind the next door was a rank-smelling washroom. Who would want to wash their hands in that revolting rust-stained sink, with a hand towel so soiled it could have stood on its own? The condition of the toilet made her want to vomit. It was easy to believe that whoever owned this place might deal in stolen antiquities. Whatever kind of person that was. One who didn't care about being clean, physically or morally, if the washroom was any evidence.

The big fat invisible elephant sat squarely in front of her. If it was true that Colin had brought the pharaoh's ring here to fence, where were he and Monica now? Had they completed their business and were sightseeing around Gib? Lounging by a hotel pool? On their way back to Egypt? Considering that the pair had missed a week of work and not made contact with anyone, that was a nonstarter. There was no question Monica would have called home if she could. And for her to have willingly participated in the fencing of antiquities? No frigging way.

She would never—Would she?

This behavior—taking off on a supposed weekend jaunt with Colin Vine—was about as far out of character as anything Claudia could fathom. To entertain for as much as a nanosecond the idea that the girl she had known and loved every minute of her eighteen years might have changed so completely in a few weeks away from home—to think that she might have become involved in antiquities theft—made her want to sink down on the filthy floor and weep. And that was a complete waste of time.

Her phone pressing against her hip in her jeans pocket reminded her that her brother, forced to sit impotently at home, was counting on her. Weakness was a luxury neither of them could afford.

She took a quick glance into the next room. An empty janitorial closet; shelves built to hold cleaning supplies stood bare. She was starting to close the door. A sixth sense, like the one that had whispered to her in Colin's room, stopped her. She pushed open the door and switched on the light. As if she knew what to expect, her eyes went straight to the floor.

Claudia's mouth went as dry as bone. She had seen enough dried blood to know what the rust-colored splotches were. Then, through the accumulation of dust and grime, a glittery object caught her eye. Something in her cracked and broke.

Long blonde hairs adhered to the clasp of the metal butterfly barrette. There was no room for doubt. Sometime in the past week since she had gone radio silent, Monica had been inside this closet. The pulse in Claudia's neck started thumping hard.

Is this her blood? What the hell happened here? How am I going to tell Pete? And, *What if she's somewhere in the building?*

Her mind flashed back to a time when a fourteen-year-old Annabelle had gone missing and Claudia had recklessly charged into a house that reeked of death, looking for her. She had stumbled across, not Annabelle, but a black cloud of flies feasting on someone else's corpse. Four years later, the olfactory memory was as strong as ever and scalded her throat with acid.

She backed into the passage with the barrette clutched in her fist and rushed outside, leaning against the building, taking huge gulps of fresh, damp sea air. As soon as she could stand on her own again, Claudia stepped back through the blue door before she lost her nerve. Having not spared a second thought when she went looking for Annabelle in that past house of horrors, she could do no less for her brother's child.

There was one more room at the distant end of the passage. A plastic plaque identified it as OFFICE. She knocked, then entered without waiting.

The lights were on, and seated at a desk facing the door was an obese, bald man in white shirtsleeves and a tie, loosened at the neck. He stared in open-mouthed surprise. The round hole in the middle of his forehead said that he saw nothing at all.

23

At the Gibraltar police station, they swabbed Claudia's mouth and took blood to compare to the substance on the janitor's closet floor. They said it was to provide a reference sample.

The splotches were large enough to have resulted from a significant injury. DI Stone had taken the barrette with Monica's hair trapped in it. He wanted to check for DNA, which Claudia considered a waste of time and resources. She knew whose DNA they would find.

She was feeling oddly spacey, as if focusing on the simplest thing was too difficult. She understood that she was in shock. So, rather than requesting the black coffee that would have been her first choice, she accepted the offer of a cup of sweet, milky tea with thanks and answered their questions while the cup sat at her elbow untouched until its contents went cold.

As if observing from a distance, she took note of the polite and businesslike manner Detective Inspector Derek Stone used in asking her purpose in visiting #9 Flynt Road. After trying and failing to marshal her thoughts and grab on to one that didn't want to float off on its own, she casually mentioned that her husband was a homicide detective in Los Angeles in case it somehow added to her credibility.

DI Stone did sit up straighter. "Would you want me to place a call to your husband and let him know—"

"No." Claudia wasted no time shutting down that idea. "No, thank you. I don't want to worry him."

The truth was, she dreaded Joel's reaction at learning she had once again stepped in a big pile of manure. Their very first meeting had been at a crime scene when she had stumbled over the victim of a brutal beating and he was the lead detective assigned to the investigation.

There were other occasions, too, where, in spite of the depth of his respect and love for her, he had looked at some of her choices and decisions and shook his head in despair. She exhaled a deep sigh. Time enough later to figure out how to finesse the latest situation.

She had overheard the uniformed officers hazard a guess that the victim looked as though he had been dead for less than a day. After the initial shock began to ebb, she found that her level of empathy was the same for the dead man as for Mitch Graham—little to none.

Was she getting callous? If he was part of what she assumed was a scheme to sell stolen antiquities, he had brought his demise on himself. Wait. There was never a good reason to murder someone in cold blood. Was there? Her mind was wandering again.

Whether or not Colin had set up the Flynt Road address as a meeting place for the sale of the pharaoh's ring as she suspected, Monica had been at the warehouse—her barrette proved it. Where was she now?

Did Colin kill that man?

Claudia shared the photo Annabelle had texted her of Monica with Colin. Stone listened politely to her explanation for her presence in Gibraltar. She told him everything she knew, except why she was here and not Monica's father. Learning that her brother was awaiting trial on a homicide charge could add nothing constructive to this conversation.

When she had finished the telling, the inspector excused himself and left Claudia to her roiling thoughts. Twenty minutes later, he returned with a severe-looking woman in a dark navy suit and wire-framed glasses. The grey-streaked hair combed off her face put her in her early fifties. DI Darcy Lange.

It turned out that DI Lange was a specialist in antiquities theft and she expected to hear a repetition of the entire saga, not the least of which was the reason for Claudia's journey to Egypt.

Claudia knew well enough the police tactic of asking a witness or suspect to tell the same story over and over, listening for changes to any of the important details. The small amount of caffeine had helped clear the brain fog, but all the tea in Gibraltar was not enough to carry her through another retelling. When Lange asked for what must have been the fifth time about the photograph of the ring, Claudia was on her last nerve and ready to pick up her things and return to her hotel.

"How many times do I have to tell you to contact Frank Booth? He'll get hold of someone at Professor Hawkins-Whyte's house to email you a copy of the photo from Colin's camera." She looked at Lange with a slow burn. "I've told you everything I know, six ways to Sunday. How about you answer me now? What about this Dandachi place? I'm assuming that since DI Stone brought you in, and you're an antiquities specialist, you must know something about it."

"Number 9 has been on our radar," Lange conceded, much to Claudia's surprise. Having expected the other woman to decline to answer, she revised her opinion of the investigator upward a tick.

"We have had our eye on them for a time. There's not been enough evidence to move faster with our inquiries. That will change now there's a homicide on our hands and good reason to enter the premises."

"What about all those boxes in the two storerooms? What do you suppose is in them?"

"All in good time, Ms. Rose. We shall have to open them and see, shan't we? A dealer might acquire a treasure illegally and hold onto it for years until no one is looking. They seek a buyer when the trace has long gone cold. There's a huge illegal trade in antiquities." Lange paused and leveled a speculative gaze on her. "Over the past twenty years or so, much of it has gone to fund terrorism."

A chilly tentacle traced along Claudia's spine. "Terrorism?"

"Your American ICE department believes the Islamic State has organized a very specific set of procedures, especially in Syria and Iraq. They work with illegal excavation operations."

"They work with them? How?"

"Well, in a manner of speaking; it's actually extortion. They get the excavators to dig up works in looted sites and hand them over for sale."

"You said Iraq and Syria. You don't think Professor Hawkins-Whyte is doing that in Egypt, do you? I can assure you he was stunned when he saw what Colin had done."

"Until today, we knew nothing of the professor. We will do our due diligence, but our main focus will be on Colin Vine."

"What about Dandachi? Their website advertises artifacts from several countries."

"Yes, it does. I would hazard a guess that most of the items in the storerooms were legitimately acquired. Mr. Dandachi—it was his body you stumbled onto—operated a reputable import-export business. It's what he did outside of that trade that we are interested in."

"So, you expect to find legitimate artifacts in those boxes."

"We shall have to see. We know that Mr. Dandachi was in touch with a group of Saudis fairly recently. Saudis who are under watch."

"This is all very interesting, but what about my niece?"

"We're doing the necessary, Ms. Rose. As you can see for yourself, Gib is a small enough place that everyone knows everyone else here. We've put feelers out and, you mark my words, it won't be long. Someone will come forward with information and I will be checking with my sources until then."

DI Stone, who had been leaning against the door, listening to the exchange in silence, spoke up. "Our PCs are doing a canvas of the premises and surroundings as we speak, starting with the flats on the first floor, to see if anyone has seen either Monica or Colin going in and out of the last week."

"Flats? People *live* in that place?"

"Above the premises on the ground floor, yes. As it happens, the flat directly over the Dandachi address has been listed for sale for the past few months. We have cause to believe someone has been staying there recently."

Claudia's voice caught. "Monica?"

"Our SOCO—scenes of crime officers—are going over it thoroughly. If there are fingerprints or DNA or any other evidence in the flat, they'll find it. We know there isn't anyone staying there at the time being."

"She's already been taken from that warehouse. Can't you find out whether her passport has been used to leave here?"

"Ah. You don't actually know she's been 'taken,' do you?" said DI Lange, with a look Claudia angrily interpreted as skeptical.

"What the hell is that supposed to mean?"

"She came here under her own steam with this young man, Colin Vine. That's what you said, isn't it?"

"Yes, as far as I know. What about it?"

"So far, there isn't any indication that your niece was held at number nine against her will."

Perhaps seeing that Claudia's head was about to explode, DI Stone took over, playing the good cop role. "I know you're worried about those spots on the floor, which could as well be tomato sauce or—"

"Or blood."

"All right, Ms. Rose, if those spots *are* blood—and as DI Lange said, our SOCO officer is conducting presumptive tests. We'll soon know for certain. What makes you think it's your niece's?"

"The hairclip. What was it doing in that closet if she was never in there? And if she was there, it could be her blood." *And what was she doing in a janitor's closet? Omigod.*

"And, if it *is* blood, it could be anyone's."

"Oh, for heaven's sake. How many people do you have reason to think have been bleeding in there?"

"There could be any number of reasons for those marks." DI Stone spread his hands as if to say, let's be reasonable. "You've said you're married to a homicide detective. You know better than to jump to conclusions without proper evidence."

Claudia leapt off her chair and got in his face. "The *dead* man, Mr. Stone. Have you forgotten the dead man?"

"Please sit down, Ms. Rose. It's *DI* Stone and no, I haven't forgotten. All we know for certain is that a male murder victim was found deceased at an address where your niece and her friend, who *may* have been there, are no longer. We're just beginning to look at what that means to our investigation."

"So, what are you suggesting? That Monica and Colin shot that man to death like Bonnie and Clyde and ran off together? Please tell me that's not what you're saying."

"I ask you to calm yourself, Ms. Rose. I'm not suggesting anything of the sort."

"I'm going to contact the American Consulate."

"We have been in touch with your US State Department. We work very closely with them." DI Stone opened the door. "I'll arrange for you to be driven to your hotel. You can have a lie down and leave it to us to get it all sorted. Or do some sightseeing. We'll be in touch once we have any word at all about Miss Bennett."

24

Claudia was not done fuming over what she deemed the detectives' cavalier attitude.

She entered her room and stepped on an envelope with the hotel logo, her room number written across the front. Not interested in a welcome letter from the hotel, she tossed it on the coffee table. Since walking off the Air Egypt plane at o'dark-thirty that morning in Spain, then the long bus ride to Gibraltar and the discovery of a dead man but not Monica, then the lengthy police interview, she had been on the go. Bone-weary and desperate to wash it all away, she stepped out of her clothes.

The bathroom mirror showed her a drawn face marked by sadness and defeat; limp auburn hair in need of conditioning. Green eyes lackluster with fatigue. "You look way too close to your age," Claudia told her image.

She toweled off, clean in body but feeling no better in soul. It was close to five o'clock when she flopped onto the luxurious mattress, longing for a nap before dinner. Closing her eyes, she was immediately assailed by the grisly death stare of the antiquities dealer and the bloodstained closet floor. With a groan, Claudia revised her plans and rolled off the bed.

A vodka tonic and dinner in the hotel restaurant would either buck her up or put her to sleep. Whichever worked first was fine.

She had packed for the Egyptian desert, not the elegant Rock Hotel. The best she could do was climb into fresh jeans and shirt, add a touch of makeup. The mirror showed a vast improvement.

Stopping on her way out the door to open the envelope that had been pushed through, Claudia was surprised to find, not the standard 'welcome to the hotel letter' she had expected, but a second envelope nested inside the first. Her name was handprinted across the front in black ink. There was no stamp or return address. Inside the second envelope was a sheet of paper folded in half. Written on it was 'Tower of Homage, 5:30. Come on your own.'

There was no signature, but Claudia didn't need one to recognize the handwriting.

"Come on your own," she repeated out loud. "Who else am I going to bring?"

Thumbing to the photos of Colin's notebook on her phone, she compared it to the Flynt Road address on the paper. Having only seven words and three numbers for the comparison was no obstacle in this case. The simplified, idiosyncratic letter forms and mixed slant were consistent in both. She knew it with certainty: the same hand that had written in his notebook had penned the words contained in the envelope. The note was from Colin.

What and where was 'Tower of Homage' and did she have time to get there by five-thirty? She checked the time. She had forty minutes and she would bet that in Gibraltar, she could reach any location in that time frame. Her fatigue vanished, washed away in a flood of adrenaline. The vodka tonic would have to wait.

THE MAN at the front desk—Heidi had gone off duty—took a look at the envelope. His smile showed a set of large white teeth. "Oh, good, you got it I see."

"I did, thank you. Were you here when it arrived? Can you tell me who brought it?"

"Yes, I believe it came in around half-three. I can't say I saw the person, though. Someone had handed it to the doorman and asked that it be delivered to your room."

"Is that doorman around?"

"He is at that. You'll find him outside the hotel. He's called Antonio."

Claudia thanked him and hastened to the front doors. Outside, a middle-aged man in hotel uniform—black trousers and vest over a white shirt—was seated on the edge of a large planter, smoking a cigarette. Seeing her, he stubbed his smoke into the planter and sauntered over with a friendly smile. "Can I do something for you, *Senora*?"

Were the hotel employees all nice people, or had they been trained to be nice? In hotels at home, everyone was too-too busy and uninterested. Claudia went to meet him, smiling, too. "You are Antonio?"

"*Si Senora.*"

"I understand someone gave this to you for me?" she said, showing him the envelope.

He nodded. "*Si,* yes. A messenger, he come on a motorbike and ask me to take it to reception."

"Can you tell me what he looked like? It's important."

Antonio pursed his lips, pondering. "Twenties? Short beard. He was, uh, brown. Mid-eastern. Not a lot dark—um—*moreno.*"

"*Moreno?*" Claudia's Spanish was too limited to recognize the word.

As he thought about it, she saw the light dawn. "Ah, I think you word is maybe uh, swart."

"Swart? *Swarthy?*"

"*Si, Senora, si.*"

Not Colin, with his burgundy hair and British skin. The handwriting in the second envelope was definitely his, Claudia thought, puzzled. Her room number on the outer envelope had been written in a thick green marker pen by someone at the front desk.

Seeing her disappointment, Antonio offered an apologetic shrug. "He was here and gone too quick. I am sorry I do not think of anything else. Everything is all right, missus?"

Claudia showed him the paper. "Does this mean anything to you?"

"Tower of Homage? *Si, si.* This one is *El Castillo*—the Moorish Castle. All the tourists want to see him. If you going to be there at half-five you have to hurry. The Castle close at quarter past six." Antonio checked his watch. "You got car?"

"No, I'll have to call a taxi."

"I do that for you, *Senora*. He come, *pronto*."

"That would be fantastic, thank you."

Promising to be back in five minutes, Claudia hurried to her room and grabbed her shoulder bag and a jacket. She was back as the taxi stopped at the front doors. The British five pound note she slipped Antonio produced another big smile as she jumped into the vehicle.

Here I go again, Claudia thought with a cynical shrug. *Off to meet someone who might be involved in a murder. No surprise that Joel shakes his head at me.*

The driver told her the that Moorish Castle was under two kilometers from the Rock Hotel; a ten-minute ride. According to Google maps, as the crow flew, it was quite close to Flynt Road, but there was no direct ground route from one place to the other. The numerous one-way streets made it a four-kilometer detour. Besides which, the police had cordoned off the crime scene at number nine. Whoever had left the note would not be coming from the warehouse to meet her.

That was the first juncture at which Claudia asked herself what the hell she was doing. The note was unsigned, which meant Colin wanted it to be anonymous. Why? He had no idea she had been through his things and would be able to identify his handwriting.

On the other hand, Antonio had described a very different man from the photos she had seen. The only reason she could imagine that Colin might contact her would be in regard to Monica. If she didn't go, it could end up being the biggest regret of her life.

The bigger question hit her: how did Colin know she was in Gibraltar and where she was staying? The security camera at Number Nine Flynt Road. Claudia began to feel very afraid of the answer.

If things went sideways, somebody needed to know where she had gone. It was the middle of the night in California and she wasn't about to wake Pete or Joel. They would try to talk her out of going to the Moorish Castle, and that conversation could only end in an argument.

Tapping out a text to her brother, she let him know about the note and her destination, ending with a promise to call when she was heading back to the hotel. If he had not heard from her when he woke up, he was to alert DI Derek Stone.

The taxi was still a distance away when the Moorish Castle came into view. A tall, square fortification high on a hill, its current British ownership was evident in the Union Jack flying at the top. Against the backdrop of the Rock, the timeworn walls took on a rosy hue in the setting sun. At the height of its power, it must have been a heart-stopping spectacle to any would-be invader, Claudia thought as they approached through a residential area.

Prince Edward's Road led to Castle Road, winding around and up Willis's Road, a steep incline scarcely wide enough for a row of parked cars along the edge and one moving vehicle at a time. The driver deposited her at a miniature white tower ticket kiosk, where the words 'Moorish Castle' were emblazoned on a banner across the top, and bid her a cheery goodbye.

When Claudia tried to hand over the ten-pound fee, a bored-looking woman at the ticket window waved away the money. "We'll be closing soon. You can go in, luv, bit you've only got half an hour to have a look 'round."

"Thank you. Could you tell me where to find the Tower of Homage?"

Giving her a strange look, the woman jerked her head at the citadel behind her. "Well, there it is, isn't it?"

Feeling a tad foolish for not having known that the 'Tower of Homage' and the Moorish Castle were synonymous, Claudia went around to the entrance, moving aside for a tour group—a dozen or so British holidaymakers exiting through an iron gate, chattering about going to the local for a pint.

Granite steps led down past a wild walled garden and into an open courtyard. A plaque named it 'Queen Charlotte's Battery, 1727'. The black cannon aimed towards the bay gave visitors a taste of what had greeted invading marauders. High above the town, its pitted walls and crenellated battlement spoke of its long history.

From there, a fifty-foot-long walkway led into the castle. At the midpoint, Claudia stopped to look over the side of the chest-high stone wall. Except for the airport with its short runway stretching into the bay, the breathtaking view could have been any modern city: high-rise apartments, condos, hotels, and offices carpeted the peninsula far below.

The Moorish Castle had withstood ten sieges over hundreds of years. Above the entry door, a sign informed Claudia of the Moors' recapture of the peninsula from the Spaniards in 1333. She entered through a metal-screened gate not unlike the one at the Luxor tomb, and through a dark doorway into silence.

The claustrophobic low ceilings and thirteen-hundred-year-old roughhewn stone walls were another reminder of the tomb in Luxor, except the tomb's passage was spacious by comparison. If she put her hands on her hips, her elbows would practically touch three-feet thick walls, built to protect their inhabitants. There was something distinctly prison-like in the narrow, grated window openings. Cold air rushed in, but Claudia's shiver came as much from the desolation of the place as the temperature. With the departure of the tour group, she was the sole visitor in the Tower.

The note had not named a specific location for their meeting, but the cramped passage allowed her to move in only one direction. She descended a flight of stairs, met at the bottom by a large framed sign. Not having time to read the story of "The Tower within the Tower–*La Torre en la Torre*" in English and Spanish, she kept going. Crumbling brick alcoves kept appearing in unexpected places. Openings in floors and walls, pocket-sized rooms that would make good hiding places for a small person if the piles of rubble were to be cleared away.

The next flight of stairs was constructed of modern metal and wound up and around several stories. Looking up showed a rapidly darkening sky through a square opening all the way at the top. No way was she climbing up there. At the second floor, she stepped onto the landing. A glass-paneled door at the end looked out onto the battlement.

As she peered through the glass at a pair of very modern spotlights that warred with the ages and ancient campaigns fought here, the remoteness of the location struck her. Who did she think she was—VI Warshawski? Lisbeth Salander?

Claudia froze. Had she imagined the sound of someone on the stairs? Maybe following the impulse to come to the Tower alone was a bad idea. She felt a sudden movement behind her. Not quickly enough, she started to turn. Strong hands on her shoulders shoved her against the door; a male voice close to her ear.

"Don't scream. No one will hear you."

Her breath caught. She could not have screamed if she tried. Reflected in the glass, he was a shadowy figure, his features hidden; an impression of a man close to her height. Pressed closer than a lover, he gave her no room to move.

"What do you want?" Battling to hold on to her wits, her voice sounded steadier than it had any right to be.

"Why you got to meddle?" It came as a low growl. "You don't want the girl to stay in one piece?"

"What have you done to her?"

The man slammed her face against the glass. His arm went in front of her neck, pushing her chin up. A sharp point pressed an inch below her left ear. Instinct took over.

The position was awkward, but she stomped her foot on his. His grip loosened and she twisted her body, screaming, *"Help me."*

She'd had no expectation of a response, so it was a shock to hear voices from below yelling in agitated Italian. Hearing her assailant's sharp intake of breath, Claudia picked up on his indecision. Another burst of Italian came up the staircase. If he had not struck her, she would have screamed again. The blow to the base of her skull dropped her to the floor.

Lights out.

25

MONICA

SHE OPENED HER EYES A FRACTION, DISORIENTED AFTER THE SOLACE OF dreamless sleep, the great leveler.

In all the days of lost freedom—she had lost track of the number—unbroken sleep was one of the precious things Monica missed most. Too many times to count, bound to Colin, she would start to nod off and either Bashir or most often Omar—the meanest and the one who had taken her from the hostel—would startle them awake with his favorite torment: loud music playing for hours on end, or he would open the door and yell threats at them.

After a while, Monica became less sure of whether she was asleep or awake; in real life or hallucinating. She knew, though, that her body should not feel this heavy. If she had not been so thirsty, she might have guessed something was up when Omar handed her a bottle of water when he ordered her outside to the car—it was the first time he had given her anything. Something had been added to it that had taken away her will to think for herself and gave her a dull headache. Pretty much turned her into a zombie who didn't care about anything.

Figuring that out was a major triumph. It proved that, trapped inside this brittle shell, something of her old Monica self still existed.

Struggling through the fog, concentrating on one thing at a time, her surroundings began to click into place. Not the unyielding floor of the closet. A real cushioned seat. Comfortable. Warm. Tears of gratitude sprang up, blocking the view through the oval window to her right. She squeezed her eyes shut and opened them again, unable to believe what she saw: an expanse of blue sky and bloated whipped cream clouds.

Airplane. Flight attendant. Help.

She dug deep for her voice and told Omar she needed to go to the bathroom. It would piss him off—always a bad idea—but worth the risk. On an airplane, he could not go with her and watch.

Showing her one of his nasty scowls, he made the cold threat she had come to know and hate. "You don't mess up. Do not forget whose life is in your hands."

Grasping the seat in front of her to help her stand, she stumbled on uncertain legs across him, past the empty aisle seat, proceeding slowly to the front of the cabin. Her eyes darted from one passenger to the next, broadcasting a desperate silent message: *Look at me. I need help. Please help me.*

But no one looked up. Or, if someone did, they looked away again, consumed by their mobile phone or tablet, computer, book. The ones who were not otherwise engaged sat with their eyes closed, letting her silent plea go unheeded.

Sixteen rows back, Monica could feel Omar's eyes boring into her. For one single precious minute, she pretended he wasn't there and she was free of having him control her every move.

"Are you wanting the loo, luv?"

Her head jerked up. Someone was talking to her; a flight attendant working in the galley.

"Hang on half a sec; someone's in there." The woman's sharp eyes looked closer. "Are you all right, luv? You do look on the shaky side."

Talk about an understatement; Monica was trembling like a candle flame in a breeze. The temptation to fall onto her knees and beg for this woman's help started deep in her gut and filled every molecule of her being until she was bursting with it.

She darted a look from under her lashes. Omar was leaning into the aisle. She couldn't see his eyes, but she could feel them sending her a harsh warning.

Colin's face pushed into her head as she had last seen him earlier that morning, his eyes pleading with her as they marched him out of that horrible little closet: *don't let them kill me.* They had taken him away—the other two freaks—Bashir and Nasser, one on either side. When she demanded to know where they were taking him, Omar had punched her and told her to shut her mouth.

She thought of his warning—*Don't forget whose life is in your hands.* Unless he was just messing with her head, that must mean Colin was still alive.

"My name's Olivia," the flight attendant said, wrapping an arm around Monica's shoulders. The lavatory door opened and the person inside stepped out. Olivia moved closer, angling her back to the cabin and speaking in a low voice. "Are you being threatened?"

"Yes, yes, but—I—"

"What's your name, luv?"

"M-M-Monica."

Olivia patted her shoulder. "Don't worry, Monica, it'll be all right, we'll see to it, won't we?"

No, it won't be all right, thought Monica, closing herself in the lav. She leaned on the sink, wobbly and breathing fast. When she looked up, shock zapped through her like an electrical charge. Who was that girl in the mirror with the badly cut, dull brown hair? This stranger was hollow-cheeked and pasty, the light in her eyes as dim as a lightbulb about to flicker out. The blue irises, as dilated as they were, did not match the rest of her coloring. This person was someone she did not recognize.

It was hard to make herself leave the tiny refuge. When she opened the door, someone else was waiting to go in and the friendly flight attendant was all the way at the other end of the cabin.

She was buckling herself into her seat when Omar reached over and grabbed her roughly by the chin. "What did you say to that woman?"

"Nothing. I didn't say anything. I swear." She knew he didn't believe her and she would pay for it later, out of the sight of all these passengers. Leaning against the window, Monica closed her eyes and prayed the plane would crash.

A short time later, Olivia came by with sweet tea in a plastic cup for her. "There you are, sweetheart," she said with a bright smile, though Monica dared not look up at her. "This'll make you feel better." To Omar, in a cooler tone: "Can I fetch you anything, sir?"

"No," he said brusquely. He must have heard how rude his tone sounded, as he tried to put on a smile, though it was more of a grimace, as if he didn't know how to properly arrange his mouth. "Thank you for helping my sister. She has not been feeling well."

"Happy to help, sir. Your sister is very sweet. I meant to ask her name?"

He faltered. "Uh—Maryam."

"Ah, Maryam." With a knowing smile, Olivia walked away, back up the aisle, which meant that she was not there to see Omar empty a packet of devil's breath into the cup and order his prisoner to drink it.

The final hour of the flight passed in a haze. At first, Monica's emotions soared with the excitement of believing that Olivia would liberate her. Then came the depths—the guilt of knowing that if she escaped, whatever horrible thing happened to Colin would be her fault. By the time they landed, the drug had done its work and sapped her will to do anything other than what she was told.

Omar wasted no time pushing her along the cramped aisle, passing behind Olivia, the flight attendant, who was helping an elderly passenger retrieve her luggage from the overhead bin and didn't notice them.

Out on the air bridge, Monica was put into a waiting wheelchair and hurtled through the airport as if she were competing in the Paralympics. Pushed through long lines of passengers getting passports checked, her head lolling because she didn't have the strength to pick it up.

Loaded into a windowless van in the airport parking garage, she had lost the inclination to puzzle over why Olivia had failed her.

Colin was in the cargo bay, cuffed to a bar on the side wall. The thick burgundy hair and man bun that Monica had teased was what attracted her to him was a military-style buzz cut with a fade at the back, making him look like someone she did not know. They must have done that so he wouldn't be recognized, the same way they had changed her appearance.

Colin, who must be drugged, too, didn't move as Bashir, his baleful glare bouncing from one to the other of them, climbed in behind Monica and plopped onto a pile of moving blankets. Ordering them not to talk, Omar slammed the doors shut and went around to the front. Nasser was in the driver's seat.

THUS BEGAN the next leg of what to Monica was an unending journey. Had it been the product of her confused brain that she had believed the flight attendant had picked up that something was amiss and she was going to help? What a dumb fantasy that was. No one was coming to the rescue.

She could hear traffic flying past on both sides of the vehicle and no stops for traffic lights. That meant they were traveling on a major highway. At long last they came to a halt and Omar switched off the engine. The pelting sound against the van's roof must be rain. Nasser came around and opened the back door, hustling her, then Colin, out into a heavy downpour.

Dragged along by Bashir, Monica stumbled across a gravel-covered yard to a darkened two-story house, arriving at the backdoor drenched and shocked alert by the freezing rain.

They all trooped inside and someone switched on a light. They were in a plain kitchen, dripping puddles onto the black and white tiled floor. Ordering Monica to go ahead of him, Bashir pointed her up a steep staircase and into a small bedroom. At least, she assumed it was a bedroom. There was nothing more in the room than a sheet of thin foam on the floor, the length and width of a double bed. With no lamp, the only illumination came from a strip of moonlight peeking through wooden boards that had been nailed across the window.

Shivering in the unheated house, Monica asked for a towel, but

Bashir shut the door behind him without answering and turned a key in the lock. She stripped out of her sopping sweatshirt and wrung it onto the carpet, then rubbed it over her inch-long hair. As damp as her jeans were, it would take more effort than she could summon to get out of them.

After spreading the sweatshirt out on the carpet to dry, she pulled the foam around her. It didn't smell very pleasant, but she considered herself lucky to have it—her only means to stave off the cold.

Whether it was exhaustion or the drug Omar had dumped into her tea or a psychological defense or a combination of them all, the instant Monica's head touched the floor, she dropped into a deep sleep.

THE NEXT TIME she opened her eyes, weak daylight showed between the rough wooden boards screwed into place across the single window. The floor was carpeted, albeit dusty-smelling. And she wasn't bound to Colin, unable to move. A definite improvement over the janitor's closet in Gibraltar.

Not as nice as the airplane seat, though.

She wanted to puke. For what must have been hours and hours, Monica stayed curled up in her piece of foam, weak and muddled, waiting for her thoughts to unravel. She struggled to remember who she had been in that other life, where she had a loving family and friends, a pleasant home, good food. That was now the dream; this one the reality.

Between the lack of food and water, the drugs and the threats, all she knew for sure was fear. And that Colin's life depended on her following instructions that she had yet to receive. They took turns impressing it on her, Omar and Bashir: *If you don't do what you are told, we will hurt him a lot, and we will kill him. It will be your fault.* Nasser, who was younger than the others, was mostly silent.

With each exhale, wispy clouds floated from her lips and disappeared. Was it still February, or had the calendar changed to March by now? It didn't matter. Nothing did. She had given up caring whether she was cold or hungry or thirsty. Given up wanting to see her dad and her aunt Claudia and her best friend Annabelle. Given up dreaming of her favorite foods, the books and music she loved, her bedroom at home. Egypt. She had even given up being mad at herself for having trusted Colin.

Monica had given up hope.

26

GIBRALTAR

The sound of running feet on metal stairs reverberated through the Tower of Homage, and a shout in Italian:

"Cosa sucede?"

For an unnerving point in time, Claudia didn't know where she was. The back of her head throbbed and something warm was trickling down her neck. Had she been unconscious?

It all came back in a burst of insane anger. Her attacker had been about to cut her. She pulled herself up and started down the stairway, gripping the bannister for balance. He would be long gone in the time it would take her to reach the ground floor.

Two startled faces gazed up at her from the bottom, a couple. It came back to her: someone had been yelling in Italian.

"Stai bene?"

Claudia met the man's gaze. "Did you see that guy?"

"Oh, American," said the woman in English. "He run down so fast —Oh, you are bleeding. Are you okay?"

Reaching up to touch her neck, Claudia's fingertips came away a sticky red. "You saved my life."

"God send us," the woman said reverently. "Let us help you to the outside."

Between them, the Italian couple got her to the kiosk, which was now closed. In the short time Claudia had been in the Tower, twilight had painted the clouds pink and lengthened the shadows. The man banged on the ticket window until the woman inside opened it. At sight of Claudia, her mouth dropped. "God in heaven, what's happened?"

"There was a man," said the Italian woman. "He attack her. We see him run out. I think he gonna knock us down."

"He had a knife," Claudia said. "He came out of nowhere—somewhere—I think maybe he was hiding in one of those little rooms. These people scared him off." She turned her attention to the couple. "I—thank you. Thank you."

"*Niente,*" the woman said. "I am 'appy we come late to the Tower."

The nick behind her ear burned with the sting of a jellyfish. She dug in her bag for a tissue and her bottle of water and dabbed at the blood. The ticket lady was dialing nine-nine-nine on her phone. "Did you see him come out?" Claudia asked.

"No, I didn't. I had myself locked in, closing out the till for the day. These two were the last ones inside. The sneaky bugger must have gone in straight after you. Or before you. I don't know. Come inside, darling, have a sit down."

The six-foot distance to the chair she was offering might have been a mile away. Seeing her wobble, the Italian man grasped Claudia's elbow and guided her to the low stone wall next to the ticket office. She sat and rested her head against the building, beginning to come to terms with the close call she'd had. Twice in one day. She'd beat her own record.

Paramedics arrived and cleaned the wound, put a plaster on her neck and suggested she go to the hospital for a stitch or two or maybe three. The wound was apparently somewhat worse than she'd thought. When she declined, they supplied her with an icepack to hold against the goose egg on the back of her head, paracetamol for the headache, and called the police.

. . .

DI STONE MADE no bones about how utterly appalled he was to learn that Claudia had responded to the note. "Do you realize what an idiotic thing you did, going there on your own? Especially after what happened at Flynt Road this afternoon."

Claudia held the icepack against her neck. "I thought I was going to meet Colin Vine."

"As if that were any cleverer? And look what happened. You could have ended up dead at the foot of the staircase."

She rolled her eyes, regretting it when pain thundered through her head.

Although Stone was clearly struggling to keep his exasperation hidden, it peeped through the mask of composure. "If it weren't for those Italians, that bloke would have made short work of you."

"I know," she said, chastened. "I'm very grateful they were there."

She had tried to buy them dinner, but they wouldn't hear of it. After giving their statement and saying they would properly explore the Tower another day, they had wished her well and waved goodbye, riding off together on a scooter.

Sitting across his desk, listening to DI Stone's harangue, Claudia's mind wandered. Fragments of memory filtered back. Suddenly, her face went hot, her palms clammy. She interrupted the stern warning he was giving her. "That man—the one who attacked me—oh my God, I can't breathe."

Stone checked himself, pausing with an expression of infinite patience to hear what she had to say.

"He was going to kill me to stop me looking for her and bringing attention to them. They had to be watching on the security camera yesterday when I found Mr. Dandachi's body. He said, 'don't you want the girl *to stay in one piece?*'"

There had been many times in her life when Claudia had been afraid, some of them very recent. This fear that gripped her now was as if someone had reached inside her chest cavity and was squeezing her heart of every drop of blood. She tried to bring to mind what her friend, Doctor Zebediah Gold, had taught her to combat panic attacks, but her mind had gone blank.

She heard DI Stone instructing her to put her head down and take deep breaths. He called for someone to bring a cup of tea.

Monica. Her beautiful, sweet, innocent niece in the hands of that murderous sonofabitch. It was more than she could stand. Claudia, who prided herself on being stoic in the face of stress, burst into tears. The tea was placed in front of her. Thankfully, no one lied and said "There, there, everything will be fine."

They left her alone for a while, and during that few minutes, everything she had worried about, every nightmare that had plagued her while looking for her niece, crystalized into a lump of white-hot fury. If Monica's captors believed that her family was going to leave her to whatever fate they had in store for her, they had made a serious error. Monica's story was not going to end with her aunt tucking her tail between her legs and shuffling home to California, somehow forgetting about her niece.

She took a sip of tea, which had grown as cold as Monica's trail, and scrubbed her face with a fresh tissue. By the time DI Stone returned, she had pulled it together and was ready to do battle.

"Let's start with what we know," said Claudia, brushing aside the inspector's raised brows at her taking over the interview. She counted on her fingers. "Number one, Monica's best friend said she was going on a romantic weekend getaway with Colin. Number two, there's fair reason to believe Colin was here to fence the Pharaoh's ring. Number three, whatever his motive was in taking Monica with him, she's evidently under the control of this other guy who attacked me. Are we on the same page so far?"

Stone gave a short nod. "So far, yes."

Indicating the note she had received at the hotel, which was on Stone's desk in a clear Mylar envelope, she said, "That is Colin's handwriting. And Colin didn't attack me."

"How can you be certain? You said the attacker was behind you."

"Monica and I are the same height. In the photos, Colin is half a head taller than her. I could see enough from the reflection in the window that the man who attacked me was no taller than me, and he had black hair. Colin's is burgundy-ish red. *And* Colin has a British accent. I got the feeling that this guy was Middle-Eastern." She paused for breath. "What we don't know is whether this man and Colin are working together. And we don't know what's next."

"Do you have any thoughts on why he would bother with you? Why not simply take Monica and be done with it?"

Claudia glared at him. "Who knows? Maybe he's afraid of the US State Department coming down on him. What I'd like to know is what you're doing to find the answer. This afternoon, you and DI Lange said you've been watching Flynt Road. She implied that the dead man —Dandachi? was involved with Saudi terrorists. If that's who's got my niece—" The idea was too terrifying to contemplate.

Stone was sympathetic. "Rest assured, Ms. Rose, we are working with your State Department and doing everything we can on our end. As a matter of fact, a few minutes ago, I received some news."

Claudia, starting to droop in her chair, jerked upright. "What happened?"

"A gentleman who lives in the Flynt Road building happened to be looking out his window last Sunday, late morning. He told our PC that he noticed a young woman going inside the premises in the company of two men who we believe may be Saudi nationals."

"Two Saudis. What about Colin?"

"He's not been sighted."

"So this neighbor 'happened' to be looking out and he remembers it a week later? Why?"

"There are such things as coincidences, you know. His flat is next door at number eight, upstairs. It's not such a stretch of the imagination."

"Did he see Monica again?"

"No." Stone gave her a significant look. "We have learned from one of our confidential sources, though, that last Friday, one of these same men was at the airport in the company of a young woman in a wheelchair. She looked unwell. She had short, dark hair."

Claudia thought her heart would stop. "Last Friday? That's *two days* ago. You think the girl was Monica and they've changed her appearance? Why would she be in a wheelchair? What have they done to her? Where were they going? What flight did they board?"

"We're pursuing all that. It shouldn't take long to go through the passenger manifests of the flights out of Gib on that day."

"The man who took her to the airport—he must be the one who delivered the note Colin wrote. Maybe the one who attacked me, too. Antonio, the hotel doorman, can give you his description to check against your informant's."

"Naturally, we will be doing that, too. As for the note, I've taken the liberty of backgrounding you," said DI Stone. "Apparently, in addition to being married to a homicide detective, you are quite a well-known handwriting expert in your own right—not just in America. Yes, I've looked you up. I know you've lectured in the UK and other places."

Claudia shrugged and regretted it. The paracetamol had not kicked in, and the back of her head throbbed at the slightest movement. "It's what I do for a living," she said, trying to stay perfectly still. "And so, when I say Colin wrote the note, I do know what I'm talking about. And I don't give a damn about that. I want to know where Monica was being taken. It's an itty-bitty airport. It can't be that hard to find out. What if he's taken her to Saudi Arabia? We'll never get her back."

"Let's not make assumptions. I understand your, er, displeasure, Ms. Rose. The thing is, if they've changed how Monica, and possibly Colin, look, they must be flying under assumed names, too, with false passports. Don't worry, it should be easy enough to find out which one accompanied a passenger in a wheelchair, regardless if the name is wrong."

"The sooner the better."

"Yes." Stone looked thoughtful. "There is something else I need to ask you about, if you don't mind, concerning some handwriting. Not tonight. You look all in, and no wonder."

"That's not important. If there's *anything* I can do that will help find my niece—"

"Tomorrow morning will do." Stone fixed her with a warning

frown. “Is it possible that if I have you taken to your hotel, I can trust you to stay there?”

Claudia gave him the flat look she usually reserved for Joel when he was giving her a bad time about her adventures. “Yes, DI Stone. I promise I will be good and stay in my room. After I hit the bar.”

Stone’s smile was barely there, but she caught it.

“That’s settled, then,” he said. “Let’s have a chat in the morning, shall we?”

27

When Claudia walked into the Rock Hotel at ten PM, the bar was open and a vodka tonic was calling her name. The bartender was too polite to comment on the icepack she held to her neck, or the blood on her shirt, but she saw him being curious about it.

"Long day at the office," she said, pulling a wry face. He grinned uncertainly and went to pour her drink.

Dreading having to give Pete the latest news, Claudia sat on the terrace with the late diners, nursing her drink, doing her best to fortify herself against the coming conversation with her brother and the one that would follow with Joel. Each would get an edited version. If he knew about her encounter with the man in the Moorish Tower, Joel would be on the next plane to Gibraltar.

And then her glass was empty and there were no more excuses.

Pete's strangled cry when she told him about finding Monica's barrette sliced through to her core. After that, she could not bring herself to tell him about the blood drops on the floor of the closet. Until the results proved whether or not it was his daughter's blood, she was tormenting herself enough for both of them.

Claudia cried with her brother until there was nothing left to say.

LATE IN THE NIGHT, standing at her third-floor window, she gazed down at the twinkly lights on the cruise ships in the harbor, the high-rise condos, the cars whizzing by on the roadway. Where any of their occupants involved in kidnaping her niece? Spiriting off to God-knew-where, in short, dark hair and a wheelchair. If she had arrived in Gibraltar two days sooner and opened the door to that closet, would Monica have been in there? In what condition? Now, her niece was gone.

What have they done to her?

The vodka had done nothing to dampen the dread. And, she was infuriated by DI Lange's implication that Monica had acted with free will in her disappearance. Lange didn't know the first thing about her niece, had no clue what a good, kind girl she was.

With no chance of sleep, Claudia crawled into bed with her icepack wrapped in a towel and cried some more, rerunning memories of the arrival of that precious infant eighteen years ago.

Becoming an aunt had filled a big gap in her life at a time when she had just learned that she would be unable to bear children. She brought that memory skidding to a full stop. The monster who had abused the ten-year-old Claudia was long dead and it was pointless to project those experiences onto Monica. The current situation was plenty dire on its own. What she could do was funnel her energy into locating her niece, and if she was lucky, get revenge on the present-day monsters—the men who had taken her.

When she called Joel and told him what she had learned, he offered to contact an acquaintance of his at State who had access to intel not otherwise available. "No promises," he added.

"At this point, anything could help. *Anything*. Thank you."

Joel cleared his throat, hesitating. "Babe, I can never feel as deeply about Monica as you do, but you have to know I'm wrecked over this, too. We've got to get her back. We *will* get her back."

Hearing her unemotional husband choke up got Claudia going again. She swallowed back her tears. "I know you love her, honey."

"Let me know where you're going next; I'll meet you there."

She smiled at the phone. "I must have banked a whole lot of karma points to deserve you, Columbo. It's bad enough that one of us has to fly all over the world for not-a-vacation. You don't need to do that."

His tone was as serious as she had ever heard it. "These people aren't Keystone Kops, babe. There's a level of sophistication in the way they got out of Gibraltar with Monica and, presumably, Colin. You hunting a terrorist cell by yourself is nuts."

He didn't know she had walked in on a dead man, and had come close to having her throat slit at the Moorish Tower. Mentally, she crossed her fingers so it wouldn't be a lie. "Believe me, I'm taking it seriously. I won't take any unnecessary risks." *More than I already have.*

Ending the call, Claudia punched her pillow, pretending it was the terrorists. She glared at the clock, the helplessness of her situation driven home as she watched the hours pass, powerless to do anything useful.

One. Two. Three. Around four, it dawned on her that she was *not* totally stuck with no place to go until the police or the State Department or someone else came up with something. There was one thing she could do.

WHEN THE PHONE rang at eight, Claudia was up, dressed, had coffee in her room, and was ready to go.

DI Stone. "Good morning, Ms. Rose. Did you manage any sleep?"

"A couple of hours after five."

"That's not a lot, is it? Are you still on for a look at a bit of handwriting involved with the case? I can send a car round for you if that suits."

"I'll be glad to look at whatever you've got. I have a quick errand to run first, so I'll grab a taxi to your headquarters when I'm done. I know where to find you."

"Er, yes, by now, I'm sure you do."

Figuring she deserved the sarcasm, she let it go. "I can be there in about an hour, if that works for you."

"See you then."

FIFTEEN MINUTES LATER, Claudia rang the doorbell at number eight Flynt Road. The door opened on a large man with inquisitive grey eyes in a broad, pleasant face, and close-cropped white-blonde hair. In a smart navy-blue blazer over beige trousers and a dazzling white golf shirt, he peered down at her through gold-rimmed glasses. She hadn't thought ahead to how nervous she would be, facing him. She should have gotten his name.

"I'm sorry to disturb you," she began.

The man crooked one inquisitive eyebrow in a not-unfriendly way. "Hmm. You're carrying a big handbag. What is it you're selling?"

She held up her shoulder bag for him to see. "Nothing, I promise. It's my purse, my travel bag. I don't live here, I'm visiting."

"You're an American. Are you a journalist?"

"No, but there are a couple of questions I'd like to ask you, if I may. It won't take long."

He jerked a thumb in the direction of number nine. "Is this in reference to the goings on next door?"

"Yes."

"But you're not a journalist?"

"Not. I'm the person who discovered your neighbor's body yesterday. My name is Claudia Rose."

This time, both of the man's eyebrows rose into his hairline. He stood back, gesturing for her to enter. "I think you'd better come inside, Ms. Rose. This is much more interesting than breakfast at the yacht club."

"Thank you."

In contrast with the warehouse at number nine, a staircase right inside the front door led to what in the British-owned peninsula was considered the first story of number eight. At the head of the stairs, an open living area was overpowered by a Spanish Hacienda-style sofa and chair. A pleasant room, well-lived in, if the magazines and books on various surfaces were any indicator. The man offered a hand, pressing hers with a doughy shake.

"Do pardon my manners. I'm Charles Ivy. Shall we park ourselves over here?"

He took the armchair; Claudia, the sofa.

"Thank you, Mr. Ivy."

"Please, it's Charles. A cup of tea or a coffee?"

"No, thank you, I won't take up much of your time. And I apologize for showing up unannounced like this. I'm here because the police—they don't know I'm here—said you saw something *last* Sunday that made you suspicious?"

"Well, not *suspicious*, exactly—"

Gauging Charles Ivy, Claudia deduced that he wanted to be drawn out. She went straight for the truth. "I'm here because my niece has gone missing and I believe she was—er, staying at number eight."

The eyebrow rose again—avid curiosity if Claudia guessed correctly.

"*Missing,* you say? I supposed you must be talking about the young lady I spoke about to the police."

"Can you describe her to me?"

"You must understand, I caught but a quick look. They seemed in a hurry to go inside—the two men with her."

"Do you mind if I ask how it is you remember something as minor from a week ago?"

He shook his head, studying her with renewed scrutiny. "I was watching for Stuart, my partner, you see. He'd gone to the chemist to fetch my pills. When I heard a car draw up, I thought it must be him and went to look out the window. That's when I saw a blonde girl climb out of the backseat and a man follow. Another man was driving. She looked up, the girl—I say girl because she looked quite young—a teenager, if I'm not mistaken. I can't say I saw much of her face, but I felt she was upset, though, or worried. That's an uneducated opinion, of course; nothing concrete to base it on."

If he'd seen Monica as a blonde, that meant her appearance had not been changed until she arrived in Gibraltar. Claudia dug out her phone and scrolled through the photos to the selfie Annabelle had sent her. She held it out to him.

"Is this her?"

Charles Ivy peered at it. After several seconds, he gave an uncertain nod. "She does seem to look like the girl I saw. Can't say for certain, though. It was too fast. If I'd known, I would have paid better attention."

"Any chance you can describe the men?"

He tapped the screen, indicating Colin Vine. "This isn't either of them. Both had dark hair, medium build, medium height, nothing outstanding. I didn't see their faces."

"And you didn't see this man at all?"

"No, that's definitely not one of the people in the car. Not that I make a habit of watching the window, understand. With the Rock on the other side of that wall down below, and this flat situated as it is, there's not much to see. I only saw the girl because I happened to look down when I did."

"Did you notice anything at all unusual over the next few days? Hear or see anything that stood out?"

"What I told the police was, a good deal of shouting went on, and loud music late at night coming from downstairs, which *is* unusual. Stuart banged on the wall several times and told them to pipe down. Until that lot arrived, it's always been as silent as a mouse over there."

"The shouting—could you hear what was being said?"

"I'm afraid not. Young men carrying on in a foreign language. Not one I knew, either, and I speak several myself; all European. My guess is, and—it could be that I'm being influenced by the looks of those two—I'd say it was an Arabic dialect."

"I don't suppose you heard the gunshot that killed Mr. Dandachi?"

Ivy shuddered delicately. "No, thank heavens. I would have had a heart attack. Poor chap; I didn't know him at all, except to nod hello on the rare occasion we ran into one another. He was never especially friendly, you see."

"And you didn't see Monica—the blonde girl—leave at all?"

"'Fraid not. I saw her the once when she arrived and not again." Charles Ivy tapped a thoughtful finger on his chin. "She's missing, you say? D'you think she's run off with those blokes?"

"No. I believe they've kidnapped her."

His mouth gaped open. "*Kidnapped?* Oh, my dear lady, that's ghastly."

"Yes, it is. If you can think of anything—anything at all—would you please call DI Stone at RGP headquarters and let him know? My niece's name is Monica Bennett." She gave him her phone number and WhatsApp, too.

"I had no idea such things were going on over there," he said.

His professed shock notwithstanding, Claudia got the idea that Charles Ivy was rather titillated by the idea of criminal activities next door.

28

The Royal Gibraltar Police Headquarters was a large two-story building constructed of rough-hewn stone with an arched entrance fit for a castle.

Claudia was once again seated at a table in the same interview room she had occupied the previous afternoon and evening. Again, DI Stone took the chair opposite her, placing a dark brown envelope sealed with evidence tape on the table between them. Ignoring the envelope, he reached down to haul a large evidence box, similarly sealed, from the floor and placed it on the table.

"We'll get started on the handwriting in a tick," he said. "First, though, I have something to show you."

"What is it?"

"I've learned that we took a call last Tuesday from the Hostel el Mar. It's located about a kilometer from Flynt Road. A fifteen-minute walk. Your niece and Colin Vine were registered there a week ago for the Friday and Saturday night. They didn't turn up to check out at midday on Sunday and the duty manager assumed they were late back from sightseeing. When they failed to return and pay the room charge, the manager first thought they'd done a runner. Later, as their belongings had been left behind, she began to suspect something was wrong and phoned us to file an incident report."

Stone tapped the box lid. "The items in this box have been in our property room ever since. After your niece was reported missing yesterday, her name was flagged in the computer and I saw the report this morning. So, I'm opening this for the first time, with you."

Stone scribbled his name on the evidence slip attached to the box and sliced through the tape with a scissor blade. "I'd like you to tell me whether you can identify any of the items."

Claudia stood up, trying to mentally prepare for whatever was inside. Stone opened the flaps, revealing a turquoise canvas surface. It was one of the items they had purchased together. Claudia had joked that it was big enough to work as a sleeping bag, which Monica thought was pretty funny. She squeezed her eyes shut, forcing tears back.

"That's Monica's backpack."

Stone went through all the pouches and pockets, finding nothing. In the box underneath it were the items that would have filled it. Claudia rifled through them. The blingy top was evidence that Monica had been expecting to party in Gibraltar. The lacy lingerie was new. She took a deep breath, getting her emotions under control.

"These are her clothes. This is her makeup and toiletries bag. Here's her travel diary. She never goes anywhere without something to write and draw on."

She opened the small sketchbook with the expectant feeling she always got from holding someone's handwriting. It was akin to shaking hands and getting an impression of the person's essence. Leafing through the pages, she again marveled at the talented illustrations drawn in the margins, as she had done in the larger sketchbook Monica had left behind in Egypt.

Monica had written about taking four days off the dig in Egypt, half of which would be travel time, to go to Gibraltar.

"I hate not being up-front with Dad, but he would go ballistic if he

knew I was taking off with Colin. It's not like anything major is going to happen between us—but maybe it is."

She had written about seeing a glimpse of Morocco, and taking the ferry to Gibraltar. The last page where she had made an entry told some of what they were looking for. Claudia read it aloud:

"I can't believe this. Colin bailed while I was asleep and he took my phone, passport, money, everything important!!! He left me a stupid note—in my backpack where I wouldn't have even seen it if I hadn't looked twice. It said to wait for him (what else am I supposed to do?!). I don't think I can ever forgive him. This is sucky. I hope he comes back soon."

Reading in Monica's own words what had happened aroused Claudia's fierce protective instinct for her niece all over again. "What a rotten thing to do. She must have been petrified—a young girl, alone in a strange country with no identification, no money, no means to contact her family."

Stone, who was continuing to examine the contents of the box, held up a torn paper. "Here's Vine's note to her." He handed it over to Claudia. By now, the scrawly writing was familiar.

Sweet Mo, please don't be cross, only I don't want you to call anyone or go anywhere til I get back. Stay there, okay? We'll have fun later. — Col

"How could he think she wouldn't be upset?" Claudia fumed. "What an asshole."

"It was an awfully rough thing to do," Stone agreed. "Does this handwriting match the note you found in your hotel room?"

"Yes. I told you it was his." She showed him the sketchbook. "And this settles it. Monica would never have gone anywhere without it. She was taken."

DI Stone nodded, the lines around his eyes deepening. "There is one other thing. In the report, the hostel manager mentions a broken statuette. Egyptian."

"One of the items he planned to fence."

"No joy on that score. The hotel maid said it was a cheap thing you can buy at any junk shop. Regrettably, she binned the broken bits, so no fingerprints. But she felt duty-bound to report it to her manager in case there was violence involved."

"She didn't want to be blamed if they showed up later to claim it."

"Fair point."

Something puzzled her. "Why would he have a cheap statue?"

"DI Lange has a theory."

"Well, what did she say?"

"Smugglers carry precious artifacts through customs by hiding them in cheap tourist trash. Given the information you've provided about the gold ring, Lange thinks it very well could be what happened in this instance."

"So, you're thinking that Colin broke the statue to get the ring out, which he had brought to sell the terrorists?"

"That's our current working theory."

"It doesn't work. According to what Monica wrote here, Colin took her things and left while she was asleep. If he had broken the statue to get the ring out, it would have woken her up. So, it was broken sometime later. And I can't picture her going along with him to sell a stolen ring."

"Assuming she knew it was stolen. There's a lot about this incident that we haven't sussed out yet."

Claudia started thinking out loud. "Colin's note said he was coming back for her. Why destroy the statue at the hostel? Why not take it with him to Flynt Road?"

"We don't know that's where he was going."

"He did go there. We have proof Monica was there—her barrette. Why not take the statue with him?"

Stone's lips twisted. "No honor among thieves? Perhaps he wanted to make sure he had a deal, rather than tipping his hand and letting the buyer see it."

"The upstairs neighbor saw Monica getting out of a car with two men and neither of them was Colin. Maybe they went to the hostel to get the ring from the statue and took her, too. For insurance? For—I can't think about it."

"Let's not," said Stone kindly. "No need to think up frightful stories that probably aren't true. We'll have some information soon, I assure you."

"I don't understand where Colin was in all of this, if not in the car with them."

"In that custodian's cupboard in number eight, I daresay. The results of the blood test are presumptive for Vine's blood. Male, at any rate."

"You couldn't have told me that sooner?"

Stone looked uncomfortable. "We've covered quite a lot of ground so far. I should think you must be happy to know it's not your niece's blood. Gender is quite reliable in typing. We also have indications of dark hair dye in the lavatory sink there. And a bagful of blonde hair in the rubbish tip."

In the overall scheme of things, it was silly to feel a pang over such a minor matter as her niece's hair. It was the last thing to worry about. But like most teenage girls, Monica took pride in her beautiful, shiny mane. To lose it that way had to be humiliating.

"Vine's hair as well," Stone added when Claudia said so. "His particular shade of red is rather unusual. From the amount we found, it's cut quite short; might even have shaved his head."

"What about his belongings?"

"His clothing and toiletries were at the hostel with Monica's. His backpack was found at number nine. Nothing of interest." Stone hesitated. "Ms. Rose, I want you to understand, it's not standard practice to share this sort of information with a witness. It's because—"

"I get it. You have handwriting you want me to look at—tit for tat."

He pinched his lower lip between his thumb and forefinger, pulling on it. "You work with your American police; you're married to a detective. It's a professional courtesy."

Claudia summoned a sardonic smile. "And I appreciate it, thank you."

Stone returned Monica's things to the box and re-sealed it. "There are several handwritten items to show you. I should like to know who wrote them, if possible."

"Let's see what you've got."

The inspector signed his name on the evidence card attached to the envelope on the desk and unsealed it. Withdrawing several transparent Mylar envelopes, he handed them to Claudia. Inside each envelope was a sheet of what she knew to be A4 paper size—standard in the UK and slightly larger than its American letter size counterpart.

"These were in the rubbish. It appears they were composing a letter of provenance and had done several practice ones. DI Lange has already had a look at them. We'd like to know whether Colin Vine wrote them."

"Provenance for what?"

"Several artifacts, among which is an ancient gold ring."

"The Pharaoh's ring. Do the letters mention the cartouche of Hatshepsut?"

"Yes, they do."

"You found them in the trash?"

"The flat over the warehouse was owned by Akeem Dandachi, the dead man. As I told you earlier, there was evidence of recent occupation. They must have neglected to put the rubbish out prior to going."

"Or didn't think about it. Most criminals are not all that clever."

Claudia took a seat at the table and ran a practiced eye over each sheet to get a basic idea of what she was looking at. The in-depth analysis would come afterward.

Her experience with letters of provenance and letters of authenticity had been for autographed rare books or photographs, not ancient relics, but the principles held true whether for artwork or an ancient artifact. The intent of such a letter was to show a record of ownership for an item. A new owner would know whether it had been acquired legally or in questionable circumstances.

"From what DI Lange said yesterday, you believe the sale of the ring and whatever else there might have been, is to fund terrorism," she said.

"It's a credible scenario."

"Letters of provenance are supposed to show a detailed history of where the artifact was found and wherever it's been since. The actual facts about the ring would track it to Professor Hawkins-Whyte's dig in Egypt, which means that information is definitely fabricated. I'll leave the other items up to you."

Claudia pointed to the first letter. "This is definitely not Colin's. It was written by one of the Saudis."

"How can you know that? It's written in English."

"There's a style Middle-Easterners tend to use when writing in English. It's not hard to tell if someone is more comfortable writing in Hebrew or Arabic. Or any other language for that matter." She went on to the next letter, a list of artifacts with supposed details of their history. The many cross-outs made a path as he changed his mind about the fictional particulars.

"This is a different writer. We know he's lying about the ring. This says it was obtained from a collection at an English estate. I bet some of the items on the list are in the boxes in the warehouse."

"I expect you're right," Stone agreed.

Claudia launched a magnifying app on her phone and looked closer at the handwriting, analyzing out loud as she examined it. "The upper loops are too tall and thin—it's a sign of ultra-strong idealism. No surprise if the guy *is* a terrorist. What adds to fanaticism is the extreme slant and heavy writing pressure."

Turning the Mylar sheet over, she showed Stone how the pen had cut grooves on the reverse side of the paper. "His handwriting in Arabic would be quite different. It's like me trying to writing in Arabic if I knew only the basics. And this sample shows how he was feeling at the time he wrote it."

Stone watched over her shoulder as she pointed to similar features on the next page. "This is more rigid than the other. There's a lot of anger here. Plus, rigidity makes it more dangerous than the other one. He's idealistic, too, but he gets fixated on an idea and nothing will get him to let it go. And unlike the first one, this guy has the energy to carry out any plans he makes."

"That could describe any terrorist, couldn't it?"

"Maybe so." Claudia tapped her finger on the mylar sleeve. "There is one other thing that might help you identify him."

"Oh? What's that?"

She showed him the upstroke on the letter 'y' in several words. "See how the ink gets very light in this area? That tells me he had an injury to his right leg. It could have been a long time ago that it happened, I don't know when; just that it's causing him a problem. I wouldn't be surprised if he walked with a limp."

"You can't be serious." Stone's skeptical tone was nothing new to Claudia.

"What? You don't think physiological problems can be seen in handwriting? Fine. Don't use it. But if you ever get him in custody, check out that leg."

"I'll keep it in mind." Stone placed a pad of paper in front of her. "I don't suppose you can get anything out of this?"

At first glance, the page appeared blank. Claudia lifted it near eye level and saw what he was talking about: heavy-pressured writing had been done on the prior sheet, creating indentations on this one. Something similar had been discovered in the case of the Jon-Benet Ramsey ransom note when the six-year-old beauty queen was murdered in 1997.

"You wouldn't happen to have an ESDA machine here at HQ, would you?" she asked

"A what?"

"ESDA. Electrostatic Detection Apparatus. It develops indented writing so you can read it." Stone's blank look indicated that further explanation was needed. "It's a piece of equipment similar to a portable photocopier. You set the paper with the indented writing on the glass and sprinkle charge-sensitive toner on it. When you switch it on, the toner is vacuumed into the indentations and allows you to read what the indented writing says."

Stone looked doubtful. "I shouldn't think we have one here. I imagine it would have to be sent out to our forensics department."

"If not, there are other ways to develop the writing. I can try photographing it with oblique light; at a glancing angle. The writing might show up that way. Or, and with this third method, there's no turning back. I can run a pencil lightly over it. The writing should develop."

"The way we did as children?"

"Just like that."

"You're the expert here. What do you recommend?"

"Let's start with the oblique photograph. If that doesn't work, pencil it is. I'll need a table lamp. With a bendable gooseneck if you have one. And a computer."

While Stone was off rounding up supplies, Claudia replaced the practice letters of provenance in their evidence envelope and cleared the table in preparation. He was back in under ten minutes, bearing the equipment she had requested.

"We're partly in luck," he said, crawling under the table to plug the cords into a jack. "No ESDA, but one bendable gooseneck lamp. One laptop computer."

Claudia set the lamp to shine at an oblique angle on the paper and positioned her phone to take a picture in the shadow. She snapped several shots at different angles, then emailed them to the computer Stone had brought.

"Not good enough," she said, disappointed after viewing the images. "We'll have to try the pencil method. At this point, there's nothing to lose."

Stone crossed his arms, signaling reluctance, but conceded. "All right, let's do it. I mean, you do it."

Claudia lightly rubbed the pencil he gave her across the indentations. Two words on the first line came up in contrast as light grey, clear enough to read: Piccadilly Circus? And the third: Trafalgar Square? The second line was trickier to make out.

She squinted at it. "I think this word could be 'Tower?' There's not enough detail to reach a firm conclusion, except you can see it also has a question mark, like the other two."

Stone scrunched up his eyes, frowning at the scribbles. "By God, I think you've got it. The Tower of London. These are potential targets."

"And these people have Monica," said Claudia with dread rising like a riptide. "This is bad. This is really, really bad."

Stone blew out a breath. "I've got to get hold of the Commissioner. Thank you *very* much for your help, Claudia. I'll have someone see you out."

"What about—" The question died on her lips. Stone was gone and she was alone in the room.

29

A TIDY YOUNG PC ESCORTED CLAUDIA TO THE FRONT LOBBY AND ASKED whether she needed a lift to her hotel.

"Would you mind dropping me at the cable car station?"

"Brilliant," said her driver, who was obviously pleased to get out of the police headquarters for the short ride. "You won't need a reservation. They go every ten to fifteen minutes."

A ride to the top of the Rock to see the Barbary macaques while she waited to hear from DI Stone was an infinitely better plan than moping in her room or at the bar, where she would drive herself up a wall over Monica's situation. Time enough for that later.

Claudia bought her ticket and ended up sharing a cable car with a family of three from the US.

"Where you from, honey?" asked the mother, a petite blonde with a Long Island twang.

Not in the mood to chat, Claudia smiled briefly. "California. L.A."

The woman whacked her husband on the arm. "What a hoot! Did ya hear that? Ya fly across the world to a pee-wee island and five minutes later, you meet someone from the good ole US of A."

"It's not a island, Ma, it's a peninsula." Their son, about ten years old, was as tall as his mother. She ruffled his hair affectionately. "Same difference, baby."

The operator locked the door and they began to rise at a leisurely pace, proceeding past a series of colorful apartment buildings. Across the street was a salmon-hued church. Houses painted olive green, light blue, pink, deep red made it appear the sort of neighborhood where cheerful people should live. People not like Claudia Rose.

Claudia jerked at something that had just filtered through her ears. Her head snapped around to the Long Island woman. "What did you say?"

"I said, didja hear about that little American gal who got snatched from here?"

"When—"

"It was Breaking News on the TV this mawning while we were getting dressed. A teenager, like sixteen or seventeen, they said. Some terrorists grabbed her right off the street."

Her husband corrected her. "She was at a hostel, Roz."

The woman went on undeterred. "I bet they wanna marry her off to one of those—what are they called—amiras or something like that? That's what they do with those girls, isn't it, Angelo? Or sell them." Without waiting for Angelo to reply, she prattled on. "She was real cute, too, a blondie like me. They love the blondes, those A-rabs." She took off her sunglasses and peered closely at Claudia. "Are you okay, honey? You look like you saw a ghost."

Gripping hold of the thin railing that crossed the window was all that was keeping Claudia on her feet. "They showed a picture of her?" she asked faintly.

"Yeah, a group photo. They blurred the other people's faces." The woman tut-tutted solicitously. "You really oughta get a bottle of water, honey. Someone told me there's a gift shop up top, and a café, too."

"Thank you, I will." She kept her expression blank but her mind was racing. *It was on the news.* She had left the police station twenty minutes earlier. DI Stone hadn't said anything about releasing the information to the media. What did this mean for Monica? Her kidnappers would certainly see or hear about it. Would it push them to get rid of her? Forget a bottle of water. Claudia was going in search of alcohol.

They were nearing the docking station at the top of the limestone monolith. The boy started pulling on his mother, jumping up and down for her attention. "Look ma, it's a monkey; can I pet it?"

A silky brown Barbary Ape the size of a small child sat on the railings, unafraid of the cable car as it slid to a smooth halt. A second one joined it. In any other circumstance their antics would be amusing. Not today. The question was spinning in Claudia's head like a Ferris wheel on steroids: *how did the media get wind of Monica's abduction?* Was there a leak in the police department? Had the hostel manager contacted the media?

The Ferris wheel ground to an abrupt halt.

Charles Ivy. She remembered her impression that hearing Monica's plight had supplied something of a thrill in an otherwise dull life in his flat on Flynt Road. She could easily picture him contacting the media to tell how he had seen the girl as the abduction was taking place. He would relish his ten minutes of notoriety. And if it was him, she, Claudia, was to blame. She had given him Monica's name and told him she'd been kidnapped. Considering how little she had gleaned from the man, she should have left him to the police.

"Omigawd, look at that—running around as free as you please." The Long Island woman wagged an admonishing finger at her son. "No, you can't pet it. I told you, Mikey; you don't touch the monkeys. They'll bite ya face awf."

The family exited the cable car and moved toward the observation deck. The wind was stronger than it had been the previous evening at the Moorish castle and seagulls wheeled around the brushy trees, looking for scraps. Claudia walked swiftly to the Top of the Rock Café and bought a Gibraltar Beer.

She took her bottle to the observation window and sat at one of the tables, staring out. The Rock looked like a gigantic whale breaching fourteen-hundred feet out of the sea, but with Monica uppermost in her mind, Claudia scarcely noticed. If the terrorists went to the effort of changing Monica's appearance, they must not plan to kill her. At least, not yet. She took a healthy slug of beer, wishing the alcohol content was higher.

She twisted around and scan the Café. Tourists buying food and souvenirs; nothing out of the ordinary. Then why did she have the eerie feeling of being watched? Her experiences at the Moorish Castle and number nine Flynt were making her paranoid.

Tossing her bottle into the bin, Claudia went out into the crisp morning, following the pathway to a sheltered area that looked out over the peninsula. Sightseers passed behind her, chatting together and laughing at the monkeys' capering while she tried to picture her niece with short, dark hair. The woman on the cable car had described Monica as blonde, which meant the media didn't know about the change in her appearance. Claudia opened a browser on her phone to see what they were reporting.

The story had blown up the internet. Every major news outlet shouted a similar headline:

'US TEEN KIDNAPPED ABROAD.' And the subhead: *'Who took Monica? Isis? Al-Qaeda?'*

Under the lede was a photo of Monica Claudia had not seen before. She was with the team at Frank Booth's excavation site, her booted foot on a shovel, long blonde hair in a ponytail, a big, happy smile on her face.

The conversation with Annabelle circled back. She had talked about Monica posting about her trip to Egypt on Instagram. For reporters, social media was child's play. They would have located her account in under thirty seconds. Pete would wake up to the news in the morning, unless the media was already swarming him.

His voice mailbox was full. Text messages, too. She sent him an email and trusted that he would get it. Otherwise, she would be stuck waiting for him to call.

An ape popped out from the bushes, startling her. An adorable baby clung to its back, looking at her with inquisitive eyes as the pair bounded up the hill. Monkeys everywhere she looked: on the walls, sitting on rocks, grooming each other. Catching a ride on the roofs of the cars and tour buses making their way up the steep road. Running up and down, scavenging for tourist leftovers, undeterred by the fact that they were well fed and cared for by nature societies. Monica would love them. Unless she and Colin had come up here as soon as they arrived in Gibraltar, it seemed doubtful she would have. The two men Charles Ivy had spotted with her at number nine Flynt Road didn't sound like sightseers.

"Quite a view, isn't it?"

Even before she swung around, the American accent registered. Claudia had not heard this woman approach, yet there she was, two yards away, having materialized from nowhere. Like her attacker at the Moorish Castle, except this was a Halle Berry clone in a business suit. The confident hazel eyes didn't quite match her bland smile. Not a tourist. A reporter?

She thought of the feeling she'd had in the café, of being watched. It wasn't paranoid after having a knife at her throat to be wary of strangers. Mumbling something about it being amazing, she started to walk away; halted by her name on this woman's lips.

"Ms. Rose—Claudia—please wait."

Claudia turned around, all her senses on high alert. "How do you know my name?"

"Let's just say you have a friend and leave it at that."

"I don't have friends here," she said coldly. "What do you want? Are you a reporter?"

The woman leveled that impassive gaze at her and seemed to read her mind. "No, I'm not. And I'm not with the people who took your niece. I'm here to give you a heads-up."

"About what?"

"You need to go to London right away."

"Why?" The tourist spots she had identified for DI Stone blinked in Claudia's head like neon signs in Vegas: Piccadilly Circus, Trafalgar Square, the Tower. Terrorist targets.

Halle Berry shook her head. "All I can tell you is, there's new chatter about MI5 elevating the threat level for a terror attack. The news will be released very shortly, so you'll want to get a head start. Take the first flight out you can find."

"Wait—what am I supposed to do when I get there? It's a big city."

"You'll work it out," said Halle. "Good luck."

And like a spy in a cheap thriller, she spun on her heel and strode rapidly up the hill toward the cable car station. Irked that she had dropped a hint without enough information to be really useful, Claudia started to go after her. Her phone buzzed. DI Stone.

"We've had a word with the airlines. Monica was traveling under the name of Maryam Amari with a man claiming to be her brother. He's calling himself Omar Amari. British passports and visas. False ones, obviously."

"Where? Where did they take her?"

"They flew into Heathrow."

Heathrow—among the world's busiest airports. *In London.* Stone was humming and hawing. "Er, unfortunately, we didn't get the information soon enough to stop them."

Once his announcement made it to her frontal lobe it was hard work not to scream at him.

"You've got to be kidding. You let them get away? We'll never find them now."

"There are CCTV cameras all over the UK. It's a matter of time before—"

"A matter of time? By the time you find them, Monica could be dead or—God knows what they're using her for."

"No need to panic, Ms. Rose, we're on the case."

"I'm definitely panicking. Have you seen the news? The story is *everywhere.* How did it get out?"

"I've seen it. It wasn't us."

The non-answer pumped up her anger at herself. She would have hated for the police to release it, but this was worse. A queasy feeling laid the blame squarely at her feet. It had to be Charles Ivy. She wished she had never met him.

She started running toward the cable car station. "I've got to go and pack. I have to call the airport and book the next flight I can get. Oh, God, is there one out this afternoon?"

"There's no need—"

"Yes, there is, I—"

"Please, Claudia, stop. We've arranged a booking for you. Your ticket will be waiting at the British Airways counter. I'll send a car for you. You can be in London in time for dinner."

30

LONDON - MONICA

SINCE THE DAY AFTER THEIR ARRIVAL AT THE HOUSE—SOMEWHERE IN the south of England, Monica guessed—her life had improved fractionally.

That first morning when Bashir came for her early, had still been swaddled in the stale-smelling foam mattress. She pulled on her sweatshirt, which felt no less damp and cold as when she had removed it the night before, and followed him downstairs, worried about where he might be taking her; worried about what they might have done to Colin.

Omar and Nasser were seated at the kitchen table. A half-dozen bulging shopping bags with the Tesco grocery logo were lined up on the worktop.

"You will do cooking and clean it up afterwards," Omar informed her. "Washing the clothes, too."

The residue of drugs in her system had left her dull and logy, but Monica scraped herself together enough to nod acknowledgment. Inside, she was celebrating that they were not taking her somewhere else or taunting her with some horrible fate, as they so enjoyed doing. Not right now, anyway.

The prospect of having something to occupy her after the

boredom of the hours and days of nothing to do troubled her not at all. It was way better than being bound to Colin on the floor of the utility closet in Gibraltar. And better than being alone in the frigid room upstairs. The cold had seeped into her bones and settled there. Knowing she would be standing at the worktop, soaking up the heat of the stove while she cooked was positively exciting; something to look forward to.

Omar directed her attention to the two shiny new deadbolt locks on the kitchen door, and the boards covering the kitchen window, the same as in the room upstairs.

"You don't try to go outside. Do what you are told and no problem for you."

From that time on, Nasser was always in the kitchen with eyes on her while she worked, instructing her in broken English how to prepare the dishes they wanted her to cook. Sometimes he would talk on his phone in Arabic or read what she assumed was the Koran—it had the look of a religious text, kind of like a bible. Mostly left her alone, for which she was thankful.

After observing the Freaks for days, Monica had deduced there was a hierarchy. Omar was in charge, Bashir was his second in command, Nasser was the gofer. She figured them for Islamic extremists, which had been covered during the last semester of her World History class. She was fully aware of the lengths such people went to achieve their evil aims, and now she and Colin had become part of the plan.

Where is Colin?

After breakfast, Omar and Bashir went somewhere and did not return until lunchtime. Monica could hear the tires crunch on the gravel drive. Under Nasser's direction, she had food ready for them when they returned. A bowl of lentils and yogurt, potatoes, a couple of dates, shredded chicken, hummus, Kuboos. The aromas were heavenly.

She was surprised that she was allowed to share in the meals she prepared—though not sit with them at the table. That arrangement pleased her. Who wanted to sit with terrorists, anyway?

After all the days with nothing to eat other than stale pita bread, she expected a proper meal to feel fantastic. It didn't. Her stomach ached for hours after eating. Yet, despite the discomfort, she began to notice something good taking place. The nourishment swept away the cloudy haze of drugs and dehydration. Her mind began to clear.

And as she started to rebound, the anger that had been smoldering in her heart burst into a flame that burned strong enough to cauterize the hole Colin's betrayal had left there. With startling clarity, Monica saw how the ever-present threat against him had crippled her thinking. Her loyalty to him was a danger to her life.

The last thing she wanted was to be responsible for anything bad happening to Colin, but if there was any chance at all of escaping the Freaks, she was going to need all of her wits and physical strength. So, whether she felt like eating or not, when food was on offer, Monica resolved to force it down.

At the end of the first day, the thought came to her: *This* is who I am. *This* is how I feel. I'm not a pathetic rag doll who lets things happen to her.

She dried the dishes and put them away, looking for knives in the drawers and cabinets, refusing to be discouraged when there was nothing more lethal than plastic utensils. The Freaks had planned ahead. Nasser had cut up the raw food before she cooked it, removing anything with sharp edges.

Monica two-point-oh, the new version of herself, swore silently that if she were to come across anything that could be used as a weapon, she would do anything to make her captors suffer, and not show the tiniest speck of remorse.

Making the time away from her cell, as she thought of it, last as long as she dared, she stirred the rice and meat dishes as slowly as she could get away with. When any of the Freaks addressed her, she was meek and docile, secretly staying vigilant for any weakness she might be able to exploit.

. . .

On their second evening in England, Colin was brought to the kitchen and Monica was required to serve him at the table with the other men. This was the first time she had seen him since their bumpy ride in the back of the van the night before. She noticed how loose his clothes hung on his lanky frame, giving him the look of the hollow-cheeked starving prisoner he was. The bruises on his face were a sickly yellow, shading his ashy skin with an unhealthy cast. But knowing he was still alive and relatively unharmed made her feel better about her intention to leave him behind if she could get away.

The Freaks spoke to each other in Arabic while they ate. Colin, who was fluent in the language, ate in silence and gave no indication that he understood the conversation.

Monica watched him wolf down every last scrap of his serving and gaze at the empty bowl like a hungry mongrel who would lick it if he could. Even as furious as she was at him, she would have warned him about the stomachache, but she knew better than to speak when the Freaks were there. It wasn't worth getting her face slapped or having some other indignity inflicted upon her.

Still, as glad as she was to have the food, Monica wanted to know why she and Colin were being treated marginally better. Why had the Freaks stopped yelling at them and playing loud music to keep them awake, as they had in Gibraltar? Was that, and starving them, supposed to soften them up? Made them compliant? For what purpose?

While the men ate and talked, Monica scoured pots and pans, wishing Colin could tell her what he was learning from their conversation, and whether anything of significance was being said for—

"Maryam," Omar called out, making Monica jump when she realized he was addressing her. "Come here."

As infuriating as it was to be called by a name that was not hers, it would have been foolish to challenge him. Rinsing her soapy hands and wiping them on a dish towel, she moved over to the table where the men sat. Omar rose and thrust his face close to hers for the daily warning:

"When it's come time for you to do what you are here to do, I want you to remember this: if you fail in your mission, this one—" he jerked a thumb at Colin. "He will die in a very bad way and it will be your fault."

Yada. Yada. Yada.

Monica wanted to spit in his face. Lowering her eyes, she asked in a timid voice, "What do I have to do?"

"Be quiet, woman," Omar hissed at her. "When you need to know, you will be told." He reached out to touch her, slapping her when she flinched. He smirked, an evil leer. "After you have prove yourself, maybe I take you for my bride."

Bashir laughed as if Omar had made a hilarious joke. Colin looked fixedly at his bowl and said nothing. The flicker of hatred that crossed his face may have bypassed their captors, but not Monica. She pictured stabbing Omar in the eye with a big, sharp fork.

31

LONDON - CLAUDIA

The wheels touched down on the runway and Claudia switched her phone over from airplane mode. Her voicemail box overflowed with calls from well-wishing friends who had seen the reports of Monica's abduction. The reporters had done deep background and uncovered the news that the victim's aunt was a world-renowned handwriting expert.

Most of the messages were requests for interviews. And one she most wanted to avoid—her parents, begging her to call and tell them what the hell was going on.

Deleting them all, Claudia phoned Joel. Given the speed he jumped on her call, he must have had the phone in his hand.

"Where are you? Why aren't you answering your phone?"

"I've been on a plane for the past four hours, just landed at Heathrow."

Claudia heard him expel a long breath, which she knew came from a deep well of worry.

"Have you seen the news?" he asked.

"I saw it in Gibraltar. Colin Vine barely got a mention." She kept her voice low. "Something weird happened this afternoon. I was at the top of the Rock and this woman walked up and told me that MI5 had raised the threat level and I needed to go to London. Which is why I'm here."

"That had to be a message from my contact at State. He promised to follow up on the QT. It's not something he could do openly."

"I appreciated the heads-up. I wish I had a clue what to do for the best."

The plane continued its long, slow taxi to the gate. Making sure that her seatmates were otherwise occupied, Claudia turned to the window and quietly described the three potential targets she had uncovered with DI Stone.

"I've checked Google Maps. Piccadilly Circus and Trafalgar Square are less than a half-mile apart and the Tower is three miles from Trafalgar Square. I'm going to get a room at the Motel One Hotel at Tower Hill. That way, I'll be right around the corner from the Tower of London and close to the other venues, too. I won't get there until after nine tonight, but tomorrow, I'll walk around to the Tower, and take the tube to the other places."

"Claudia, *please* don't do anything by yourself."

She reached up to touch the band-aid on her neck, the feeling of the knife pressing into her flesh still very much alive. She kept her tone light. "You don't think I'm going to run into these people while I'm traipsing around London, do you? I've been to all these places before. I want to refresh my memory of the layouts. I have friends who live here, so I'm not totally alone, like I was in Egypt and Gibraltar."

"Monica's face is plastered all over everywhere," said Joel. "They'll be more careful than ever. We know they're in the UK; we don't know what plans they may have for her."

"They've cut her hair short and dyed it dark so she won't be as recognizable. If they were planning to traffic her, they could have taken her home to Saudi Arabia and disappeared."

Could she really be talking about someone she knew and loved?

Joel glossed over it and went for his bottom line: "You're everything to me, Claudia. I can't afford to lose you. Be careful, please?"

Hearing him say those words melted her into a gooey pile of

marshmallow. She smiled. "I love you so much. I promise I'll be careful, and I'll text to let you know when I get to my room, okay?"

"I'll be waiting to hear from you. Listen, I'm taking a few days off. I'm going to Pete's place right now. Moral support."

"Please tell him to call Mom and Dad. They're frantic. They have news shows in Seattle, too." The plane came to a halt and the fasten seatbelt sign blinked off. "We're at the BA gate, gotta go."

"Love you, babe; 'bye."

HEATHROW WAS a city-sized labyrinth of endless corridors and passages, people-movers, escalators, and lifts. With only hand luggage, Claudia marched straight through the British Airways terminal, ordering an Uber on the way. At last, she walked into the cold, drizzly night, ready to sink into the backseat of the Prius that pulled up next to her.

Her driver was a Romanian giant—he had to be six-five or taller—named Romulus. As the car left the colossal airport and headed into the City of London, he surprised Claudia with the news that his day job was working at the Met—the Greater London Metropolitan Police. He was driving for Uber at night to save money and take the detective's test.

Weird synchronicities happened, she thought after lobbing a series of questions at him that produced reasonable answers. When he took out his wallet and showed her a picture of his eight-year-old son and wife, she decided he was on the up-and-up, and told him about Monica.

"That girl is your niece?" His English had a strong Slavic edge. "I see this today in the briefing. I hope you get her back."

"There's talk that the people who took her are planning to attack one—or some—of the monuments here. I'm scared to death."

"Yeah, I hear that, too. We get an alert today. Some places have extra security. These people, they don't play games, you know? They are very violent and they want to do as much damage as they can."

Claudia shuddered, wishing he hadn't mentioned violence. "I was at the Charing Cross tube station a few years ago when there was a bombing. Too close."

Romulus eyed her in the rearview mirror. "Hah. You one of *those* people?"

"What people?"

"The kind who trouble follow you around everywhere."

"No, I'm the kind who wants to find my niece. They've had her for more than a week already."

"Even she get rescued, it gonna be tough for her, such a young girl. You know about the Stockholm Syndrome?"

"I do. The prisoner starts to relate to their captors, maybe develop affection for them. That happened in a famous case in the US in the 70's. An heiress named Patty Hearst was kidnapped by a terrorist group."

"I don't know her. What happen?"

"They held her for a long time—over a year. They got her to say she supported them. She helped them rob banks. Eventually, they were all captured and she went to prison."

Romulus whistled. "Prison less risky than bank robbing, maybe."

"Spoken like a policeman," said Claudia. "I should know, I'm married to one." They drove through the rain, which had grown from drizzle to downpour. Tower Hill, her destination, was about twenty miles from the airport, Romulus informed her. Between the weather and the traffic, which was no better than L.A., it would be an hour's drive. He shifted the conversation back to Monica. "She's a nice-looking girl," he said. "I saw the picture on TV."

"They've cut and dyed her hair." Claudia could not hold back the big sigh that gusted out of her. "Hair style and color make a huge difference to someone's looks. Where the hell do I start looking?"

Romulus' eyes met hers in the mirror again. "You call the Met," he said sternly, sounding like her husband. "Tell them you are here. I give you the name of someone you talk to. They take care of it. We got more than half-million CCTV in London alone. We find her."

"That's a helluva lot of cameras," said Claudia, undecided whether to be impressed or appalled. If the authorities were to check the CCTV at Heathrow, they should be able to identify Monica in her wheelchair. DI Stone had said the fake passports showed British citizenship, so they would not have to go through immigration.

"Six million camera all around UK. If these people go anywhere outdoor in London, we find them. Facial recognition."

"We don't know what the men look like and with Monica looking different—"

"Don't matter; they didn't change her bone structure, right? The men, there are many photos. Some will come from Gib, from the passports, fake ones, too. Everywhere, there are photos. The computer can compare. We find them."

Claudia was skeptical, but his confidence improved her mood. When he dropped her at her hotel, Romulus took out a business card and scribbled a name on the back. "You call the Met, ask for this guy. I wish good luck to you. You don't have to do nothing; they do it."

She didn't bother to tell him that for her, 'do nothing' was a non-starter. Handing him a cash tip that raised his brows and made him smile, she thanked him and dropped the card in her bag. It was a small comfort to know she had someone official to call at the Met.

THE MOTEL ONE was nothing like an American motel. This was ultra-modern glass and chrome, German-designed and owned; a full-service high-rise hotel. The nearly two-hundred-pound rate seemed a lot for the pocket-sized guestroom, but it was worth it for someone who needed a shower, a cup of hot tea, and to climb into a bed as soft and comfortable as a puffy cloud.

Once she had done all that and texted Joel, it was past ten and Claudia had one last phone call to make. If she could stay awake long enough to make it, she was certain Elliott Fields would not object to the late hour.

As she had told Romulus the Uber driver, trouble had followed her on her last visit to England. She had been running away from problems at home when she accepted an invitation to present a paper at the British Institute of Graphology Conference in London. The presentation went well, but afterwards, she'd had the bad luck to be at the site of a tube station bombing. On top of that, her involvement with the Irish leader of an eco-terrorist group Joel was investigating for murder became an unintended consequence.

In the midst of everything, she had met a journalist, and while her instinct was to avoid getting chummy with a reporter, Elliott Fields had proved himself a useful ally when she needed his help. Hopefully, he would be willing to do the same again.

"Elliott? It's Claudia Rose."

"Claudia, I'm pleased you've rung. You got my message, then?"

"No, my mailbox is crammed full of—"

"I couldn't believe it when I saw your name in the story," Elliott continued over her as if she hadn't spoken. "What's happened to your niece is just awful."

"That's why I'm calling. I thought that maybe with your credentials, you'd have access to information that I don't."

There was a moment of silence. "You do know I'm not working for the paper anymore?"

Disappointment hit her with a hammer blow. "Oh. No, I didn't know that."

"Listen, I've been doing a podcast on terrorism in this country. It's getting quite popular—the podcast, not the terrorism. Your niece's situation is right up my street. Don't worry, I've kept all my old contacts. How can I help?"

The relief was as strong and swift as the disappointment had been. "Have you heard that MI5 is looking at three tourist sites as possible targets for attack?"

"No." One word that telegraphed his eagerness to hear more. "What sites?"

"I can't share that at the moment. It would give the game away if these people are watching the internet, and it got out. We have to assume they are."

"You know you can trust me, Claudia. If you keep me informed, I'll do the same for you."

"If you could keep your ear to the ground and let me know if you hear anything at all, I'll give you the names as soon as I can."

"You know I will. What are you going to do?"

"I'm going to look for Monica."

32

LONDON - MONICA

MONICA CONTINUED TO DO HER HOUSEWORK AS SLOWLY AND meticulously as she was allowed. Over the course of the day, she had cooked three meals, cleared up the debris each time, washed the dishes and put everything where it was meant to go, did two loads of the Freaks' laundry. She had swept the kitchen floor and was scrubbing the table when Bashir came in and ordered her to stop and go upstairs. It was not quite eight o'clock when he locked her in for the night.

She went, pleased that this kind of tired came from expending energy on mundane chores, rather than a chemical substance thrust into her body. It felt good, she thought, peering through the narrow openings between the wooden slats over the windows. The full moon, low in the black, cloudy sky, peeped through.

"Star light, star bright, first star I see tonight, wish I may, wish I might, have the wish I wish tonight."

Monica whispered the poem her Aunt Claudia had taught her as a child. Every night since then, she had gone outside into the backyard and said the poem, then made a wish. Over the time she had been under the control of the Freaks, she hadn't seen any stars to wish on.

Maybe wishing on a full moon made up for it. She closed her eyes and made the biggest wish ever.

"I wish I was home safe with my family."

The sound of knocking downstairs jerked her out of her dreamy state. A heavy door opened and closed. Unfamiliar male voices floated up. The Freaks had company. The now-familiar stirring of fear vibrated in Monica's chest whenever something new was introduced to her shrunken world. Who were the newcomers? Why were they here? Would they all sit around the kitchen table, or would the guests be invited into the lounge?

Wishing she had her notebook to record her thoughts and make some sketches, Monica sank onto her piece of foam. She felt gross, wearing the same grubby jeans and Annabelle's 'Be Kind' sweatshirt that she'd had on when they took her. Everything she was not wearing had been left behind at the hostel in Gibraltar. The closest she'd come to a shower was the rainwater on their first night here. She had no idea what had happened to the items Colin had taken from her backpack—phone, passport, money.

Asshole.

Monica never used profanity, not even in her head. Sparing a wistful thought for her friends at the dig in Egypt, she could not think of a single reason why she shouldn't use profanity right now. She was meant to have been there to help them pack up the excavation site. They would be getting ready to leave and go home. Did they think badly of her for not returning? What had they done with the things she had left behind in the room she'd shared with McKenna? Shipped home to her dad, she suspected. Poor dad.

None of that mattered anymore. She refused to feel sorry for herself. It was her own damn fault for listening to Colin's sweet talk. *Shit.* She tried the epithet out and it felt good. *Shit.* She couldn't quite make herself say the 'f' word, but the way things were going…

"Mo? Monica, are you there?" The soft voice came from somewhere close and down low.

"Colin?"

"Mo, can you hear me?"

Dropping to her knees, Monica crawled around the small room. Colin's voice was coming through a heating register on the interior wall. With no heat emanating from it and the room poorly lit at the best of times, there had been no reason to notice it.

After being silent for days on end, her anger had shrunk around the edges and she was desperate for someone to talk to, even if it was the dude whose fault it was that she was a prisoner of a terrorist cell. She stretched out flat on the carpet and put her mouth close to the metal grate. "Colin?"

She heard his sigh of relief.

"I was afraid you wouldn't be able to hear me. Or that you wouldn't talk to me."

Monica put her mouth close to the vent. "I hope *they* can't hear us."

"Our voices won't carry if we keep them low. Anyway, they're busy talking downstairs."

"Who do you think the visitors are?"

"Some of their lot, I'd say." Colin cut himself short. "Are you all right, Mo?"

Though he couldn't see it, she made a sour face at the grate. "All right? No. I don't think so."

"Yeah. I'm sorry. I know I've said it—"

"Actually, I don't think you have."

"Well then, I'm saying it now. I'm sorry. A complete bloody plonker I am, dragging you into this."

She heard him blow out another unhappy sigh.

"I've had a lot of time to think about it. Obviously. In any case, if I don't have another chance to say so, I'm truly, truly sorry."

"All right, thanks. Good to know." Monica hoped the sarcasm wasn't lost on him. "Why did you have to take my phone and my passport?" She had asked it while they were in that horrible closet in Gibraltar, but Colin had never given her an answer she could live with. "I was totally defenseless. And that Freak, Bashir, showed up..." Her voice cracked.

"Oh, God, Mo, I'm so, so sorry. Again, and again and again. Honestly, I thought you'd still be asleep when I got back and you'd never have to know what I'd done. In any case, I didn't want you phoning your friend or your aunt and letting them know where we were until it was all settled. Look, you can't make me feel any worse than I do."

"Too bad your regrets can't help us escape."

With no inclination to soothe Colin's feelings, and determined to armor her emotions, Monica could find nothing to say to him. She was getting acquainted with the new Monica, who was a lot more powerful than the old one, and she liked her.

Laughter and loud voices sounded from downstairs, filling the awkward silence that fell until Colin said, "Won't you talk to me? Please?"

"We're talking, aren't we?"

"I know you're annoyed, and I can't blame you. Er—" Colin appeared to be searching for something to say. "You're an excellent cook, you know?"

Like that kind of compliment was supposed to make everything better? She would rather he said something about the night they had spent together in that narrow bed at the hostel. The one wonderful night before everything went to hell.

"I'm glad you got to eat," she said, relenting a touch.

"God, I was starving," he said, then hesitated. "Ah, Mo. I wish things could have stayed the same as they were."

"Yeah, me, too."

"I always loved our chats, you know? I mean, you're such a good listener."

Why was he skirting around that night as if it hadn't happened? Had it meant nothing to him? McKenna's words came crawling back: *'He lays women like bricks.'* Apparently, Monica Bennett was now one of those bricks.

"You're a good teacher," she said dispiritedly. "I learned a lot from you."

"You're brilliant, Mo. I hate myself for letting you in for this hell. I should have—"

"Should have what?" She couldn't hold it back any longer. "Should have stayed with me in bed all weekend instead of trying to sell a precious artifact? Yeah, that would have been a whole lot better for both of us."

The days of captivity had given Monica plenty of time to think about their relationship. She was inexperienced, not stupid. She had recognized his charm for what it was, and it had been clear from the start that no mind-blowing love affair was going to come of what they had—they lived thousands of miles apart. The attraction she felt for Colin was about fun and excitement and yes, growing up.

Their talks about Ancient Egypt had been the highlight of her day. He *was* a good teacher and always showed an interest in what she had to say. She had learned loads of cool stuff about archeology from their discussions. His casual bravery in saving that boy in the car accident had made him even more attractive. Bottom line, she sensed a basic sweetness that made her believe he might actually care for more than just getting her out of those sexy undies she had bought for their trip to Gib.

The memories that had been precious were unbearable. Monica pressed her hand over her mouth so he wouldn't hear her choking on the emotions that welled up. If she was going to die soon, as she suspected, she wouldn't die a virgin. Despite everything, she couldn't help being glad about that.

The silence from the other side of the grate went on for too long. It was better to keep this conversation anchored in the present. She swallowed her tears. "What were they saying at the table?"

"Oh, mainly complaining about having to stay for too long in Gib after they took us. They'd thought they would grab the ring from me and come to the UK straight away."

"Why didn't they?"

She could hear him through the grate. One, two, three breaths. Psyching himself up?

"Omar had the bright idea that since there was the ring, there must be other valuable kit to be had at our site. So, while we were tied up in that shithole in Gib, Bashir buggered off to Egypt."

"Why? He couldn't get onto the site."

"Yeah, well. Remember Farouk, our foreman—the bloke who paid off the cops when they arrested me? They 'persuaded' him to have a look."

"He's not an archaeologist."

"He's worked on digs for years; probably knows more than any of us. They paid him to have a go at the dig himself; see if there was anything he could nick that they could sell. He's got a key to the site gate."

"You sent them to Farouk?"

"I wouldn't say I 'sent' them. They 'asked' me, and none too politely, who was the easiest one to bribe. Remember those secateurs I told you about? I'd like to keep my fingers on my hands as long as possible."

Monica wrestled with that. The whole thing was wrong. Not that she blamed him for wanting to avoid being tortured. He'd been beaten more than once.

"Did they get anything?" she asked.

"Not a bloody sou," said Colin, sounding satisfied. "Too bad for Farouk, though. Some random lady saw him at the site and scared the holy bejezus out of him. Or more like the holy Allah. He wasn't having any of it after that; told Bashir to piss off."

"How did Bashir take that?"

"Cheesed off, but what could he do? The Saudi blokes had sold the ring to a private buyer while we were still in Gib. They had to be content with that. From what they said, I've got a feeling it's going to one of their princes."

"You mean like the one who ordered that poor journalist killed, Mr. Khashoggi?"

"Yeah, like that."

"Our lives are worth the price of a pharaoh's ring? I'd love to know how much they got for it. I hope it was a lot."

"With Hatshepsut's cartouche—"

"Seriously, Colin? Is there *any* amount that's worth our lives?"

Even though she couldn't see him, she could tell he was uncomfortable talking about it. If they had been in the same room, she guessed, he would have been looking away from her, refusing to meet her eyes.

"You're right. I was being stupid. Look. About the ring. I know you think badly of me about that—and I can't blame you at all." He faltered. "I—I never told you *why* I did it."

"You said you needed money," Monica reminded him in a cold voice. "You stole the ring for—"

"No! I'm saying I had a good reason; it *wasn't* for me."

"What 'good reason' could there ever be for what you did?"

When he hesitated again, Monica could feel him getting his nerve up.

"All right, here goes. It was to help my mum."

"Your *mom?*" Had she misheard? "Help her with what? Is she sick or something?"

"Not like that. Not physically. Like I told you, she's got a bit of a gambling problem."

"And—?"

"She goes down the casino most nights. Blackjack, craps, roulette, anything she fancies. A few weeks ago, she phoned me, crying, begging me to help her out of a jam." Colin's voice was ragged with emotion. "It's my mum, don't you see? What was I supposed to say to her?"

The new Monica's outrage pushed her to be more blunt than the old Monica would have been. "How about 'it's not your responsibility to dig her out of a jam?' 'A bit' of a gambling problem? That sounds like 'British understatement' to me."

"Fair enough. She's got herself into a load of debt with some very bad people. It's illegal loan sharking; doesn't stop them from doing it. They don't play nice if you don't come up with the dosh."

"Why doesn't she report them to the police?"

"She's too frightened. It's not the first time it's happened and it's gotten a lot worse."

This time, Monica snapped her mouth shut on what she was thinking: that as harsh as it sounded, his mother needed help and not the kind Colin was trying to provide. She knew that's what her dad would have said.

"If you'd sold the ring and gave her the money, why wouldn't she gamble and lose it all again instead of paying them off?"

"She couldn't. I've spoken to these people myself; promised I would see to it that they got their money."

"How much does she owe?"

"More than a hundred and fifty-thousand quid. It might not sound like all that much, but the thing is, if she can't raise it, she'll lose the house and everything she has. They've said they'll hurt her, too. And me. I thought I could give them the ring money and sell the statuette later."

Again, Monica stopped short of saying what was on the tip of her tongue: 'It's your mother's fault we're here.' True or not, she couldn't be *that* self-righteous.

"By now, those people must know you're missing," she said. "They'll *have* to give her time."

Colin's tone was somewhere approaching hopeful. "The cops will be looking for us."

Monica had spent hours thinking about this. "Frank Booth and Professor Hawkins-Whyte had to report to our embassies and our families when we didn't show up after the weekend. The embassies can track our passports to Gibraltar."

"Yeah, and that's as far as they can track. Those vile sods down-stairs got us here on false passports."

That made Monica ask the Big Question that had plagued her from the time the drugs had drained out of her system and she started thinking for herself again.

"*Why* did they bring us here? Did they say anything about that? What they're planning to do with us?"

The silence from Colin's side of the grate went on until she said his name softly.

"Yeah, Mo, I'm here."

"It doesn't do me any good not to know what's going on. If you know something, you've got to tell me."

The restraint in his voice was a clue that she wasn't going to like the answer.

"They mean to attack some of our historical sites. They mean to use us in killing as many people as they can."

"*That's* why we're here?" Monica had to stop her voice from squeaking up higher. She wanted to get up and run around the room, screaming. "Oh my God. There's no way I'm driving into a crowd—that's how they do it, isn't it? They can't make us—"

"No, not that. They're talking about using some sort of explosive device."

Monica felt as if she had been punched in the gut. "You don't mean like those crockpot bombs they put in backpacks?"

She had been eleven years old at the time of the Boston Marathon bombing. That was before her mom died. She had tried to stop Monica from watching the chaos on TV, but she'd seen it anyway and it made a big impact on her tender young soul.

It was something she would never forget: the people joyfully running their race, getting near the finish line. The explosion. The camera filming them had wobbled and a cloud of white smoke rose behind the brightly colored flags lining the sidewalk.

Monica had wept over the people who died, and the young woman whose foot was blown off—a dancer.

"They didn't talk about what kind of explosive," Colin said. He gave a self-mocking snort. "God. I thought the ring was the answer to a prayer."

"What gods were you praying to?"

"I told you, Mo, selling it was the way out. She's my mum. I had to do what I could to save her."

"Well, you can't save her, and you can't save us."

"I didn't *want* to do it. I'm an archaeologist, not a thief."

Monica could feel what Annabelle called her 'judginess' bristle. To her mind, his desire to help his mother was not a good enough motive for stealing the pharaoh's ring, even if the woman had not been a gambling addict.

"Excuse me," she said tartly, "You *are* a thief. And a coward, too, planting it on me in case we got stopped at customs."

"I didn't—" Colin began to protest.

Monica was having none of it. "Yes, you did. And you let a gang of evil freak terrorists take it from you. And here we are."

He heaved one more, longer sigh; this time, of surrender.

"Yeah, here we are."

33

LONDON – CLAUDIA

On the back of his card, Romulus the Uber driver had written 'D.O. Neil Wyatt, MI5.'

'James Bond,' Claudia thought. No, that wasn't quite right. Bond was MI6, whose mission it was to combat threats overseas. MI5 was the foreign intelligence security service for the government of the United Kingdom; the agency that dealt with threats at home.

When she called the number and asked to be transferred to him, Claudia learned that Neil Wyatt was the Desk Officer in charge of the team overseeing the operation involving the Saudi terrorists. And by extension, Monica Bennett and Colin Vine.

"I've heard something about you from Gibraltar," said Wyatt. "DI Stone seems to think quite well of you and your particular set of skills."

"I'm glad I could be of help."

"Mm, yes. Thanks to what you were able to uncover, we've got our strategic teams positioned in the various locations."

"How's the facial recognition hunt going? Any progress identifying the men who took Monica?"

"As it happens, progress *is* being made, and I'm not at liberty to discuss that aspect of the investigation."

What an annoying man. Claudia was pretty sure he had never had someone he loved ripped away from the family and—she stopped her thoughts there. "You do realize my niece's life is at stake, and probably her friend's, too?"

"Understood, Ms. Rose, and we are doing everything—"

Bureaucracy drove her crazy. And understanding their need for secrecy did nothing to help soothe her. "I've heard that from DI Stone. Isn't there anything at all you can tell me about your strategy?"

Wyatt had the grace to be mildly apologetic. "I'm afraid that's impossible. Nothing to do with you. It's policy."

"And policy is king, right?" When he failed to respond, Claudia forged ahead. "Here's what worries me, D.O. Wyatt. My niece is being held against her will. I don't want to see something happen to her because you grab her up in your net. Friendly fire. Collateral damage."

"Ms. Rose, this is not America. MI5 officers are not armed and don't have police powers of arrest. Our Operational Command and Tactical Commands are in place. We work in partnership with the Met's Counter Terrorism Command in New Scotland Yard, and the police Firearms Team. That's who will effect any arrests."

"Assuming you identify the terrorists in time."

"I have every confidence we will."

"Because of facial recognition?" Again, silence on the line. "What if I were to ride along with your team?"

"Out of the question. We can't put members of the public in that kind of danger."

"I'm not a regular member of the public. Monica is my only niece. She's an innocent eighteen-year-old—a baby. I'd be more than happy to sign a waiver releasing your government from any liability."

"It's simply not within my power." Neil Wyatt was beginning to sound like a man whose patience was wearing thin.

She was not going to get anywhere with him. Glad he could not see how her shoulders drooped in defeat, Claudia gave up. "Fine; I'll find another way."

"I see what DI Stone meant about your persistence," Wyatt

snapped. "Ms. Rose, if you impede our operation in any way, I can assure you, it won't be looked upon kindly."

Angry heat flared into her face. "Don't worry, Mr. Wyatt," she said with phony sweetness. "I'll stay out of your way."

THE EARLY MORNING buffet was served in the front lounge area of the hotel. Claudia sipped excellent coffee and nibbled on a hard-boiled egg with toast, watching through the front windows as people bustled past on their way to work. When there was no reason to put it off any longer, she pulled on her slouchy knit hat and snatched up her jacket.

Neil Wyatt's refusal to share information wasn't going to stop her from doing some intel gathering of her own. It would have been nice to know whether he had any indication of when the attacks were planned or what form they might take, but without that information, her aim was to scout each of the three target regions, starting with the Tower, and get to know the surroundings better.

The mist that dampened the air was not heavy enough to bring an umbrella for the short walk from Tower Hill to the Tower of London. Striding along the Minories, where her hotel was located, Claudia could not resist checking the face of every young woman of her height with short, dark hair coming towards her. Not that she reckoned on encountering Monica, but it cost nothing to look.

She had toured the Tower of London on previous trips to England and knew something of the nine-hundred-year-old fortress' history as a royal residence and prison. The Beefeater's tour patter about the Tower's long and bloody history had enthralled her. She had viewed the spectacular crown jewels, and the chopping block where in 1532, Queen Anne Boleyn was said to have lost her head—though there was controversy around that legend. On this visit, her plans did not include going inside the great stone walls that surrounded the Tower.

These days, bollards kept the street safe from a vehicle attack, which meant the terrorists would have to enter on foot. Everyone who went in had to buy a ticket at the ticket office across the way, then join the queue and file through the gates. Considering the number of locations for a possible attack on the Tower, it seemed as if waiting around outside the entrance was the most practical. From a vantage point near the ticket office, it would be easier to keep an eye on visitors as they entered.

Strolling the cobblestoned street outside the Tower entrance, no one in the long line of people buying tickets or queuing up to get into the grounds looked like either Monica or a Saudi terrorist. With no guarantee that she would recognize her niece or Colin Vine with their new looks, and not knowing what these particular Saudi men looked like, she would have to watch anyone who appeared Middle Eastern. As distasteful as racial profiling might be, it was a way to spot them.

Claudia followed the path around to the rear of the Tower, steering away from the entrance to the Millennium Pier and taking the other direction, toward Tower Bridge. To her right, the Thames was the color of pewter today. Intrepid joggers braved the heavy cloud cover and threat of rain. Tourists took photographs. At the Traitors' Gate, where many prisoners had arrived at the Tower's riverside entrance for over three centuries until the mid-1800s, she could almost hear the Beefeater Guard from the tour she had joined on her last trip:

"The Tower was a prison as late as the 1950s, ladies and gentlemen, when the infamous Kray twins were held here. Ronnie Kray was the dominant twin, and a paranoid schizophrenic psychopath." The Beefeater had paused for the crowd to react. *"They were the East End's most notorious gangsters, only held in the Tower for a few days for failure to report for national service..."*

What if the attack came on Tower Bridge, rather than the Tower of London proper? It wouldn't be the first time. A terrorist had stabbed two strangers to death on the Bridge and wounded several others as recently as 2019. Two years before that, a vehicle had rammed a group of people, killing eight and wounding forty-eight. Fast-walking it, Claudia figured she could be there in about a minute.

MI5 would certainly have teams in place around the area. Not that she would be able to spot them. They would be well hidden.

She was starting to get edgy. If this were a chess game, it was one move away from checkmate, not knowing what that final move was to be or who would win.

With nothing to keep her at the Tower, Claudia took the Tube to another of the sites on the target list. Trafalgar Square was a short two miles from Tower Hill, but the ride was eighteen minutes long. If it hadn't taken twice as long to walk it, Claudia would have. Descending the long escalators deep into the underground, she began to wish she had opted for a bus or taxi.

Having had the misfortune to be at the site of the tube bombing, taking the Underground set her nerves on edge. She was pretty sure most of London was standing shoulder to shoulder with her this Tuesday morning, many rows deep on the platform. Had the stations always been so jam-packed?

The Tube trains were no longer all painted red, but she still thought of them as big red caterpillars. One emerged from the tunnel and whooshed to a stop, setting off a palpable twitching of the human tide, and announcements over the tannoy:

The train is arriving at the Tower Hill Station. Stand clear of the closing doors. Mind the gap.

Commuters flooded onto the congested platform; the waiting crowd surged to take their place. Claudia's philosophy was 'last in, first out.' Better to be squashed up against the door than in the middle of the sardines.

TRAFALGAR SQUARE, built to commemorate the 1805 Battle of Trafalgar, was situated in the very heart of London, with roads leading from it to Parliament and Buckingham Palace. The National Gallery and the National Portrait Gallery were there. In addition to being a major tourist attraction, demonstrations and celebrations were frequently held there. A terrorist attack at this location could do untold damage.

At the center of the Square was Nelson's Column which, not counting the regal statue of Admiral Lord Horatio Nelson at the top, rose 170 feet. Four bronze lions guarding the base symbolized Nelson's heroism in the Battle of Santa Cruz de Tenerife. Claudia had published an article about Nelson's handwriting before and after the battle, where he lost his right arm and went on fighting.

The sheer numbers of people continually moving and changing made it implausible to pick out a girl who might be Monica, especially not knowing what she looked like now. That was no deterrent for Claudia. She took a quick walk around the Square looking for her, just in case; only throwing in the towel and giving up when she arrived back where she started.

The third potential target was less than a half-mile away on foot.

Smaller than Trafalgar Square, Piccadilly Circus was the UK's version of Times Square. Claudia saw the former Ripley's Believe It or Not Museum across the street well before she saw the iconic statue of a winged Eros poised on his toes, bow ready to shoot his arrows at unsuspecting mortals and incite erotic feelings.

Scads of people surrounded the monument, thumbing their collective noses at the gloomy weather. Eating lunch from paper bags, talking on phones. Once again, Claudia scanned the faces of the younger crowd, elbowing her expectations down another notch when Monica was not among them.

Pretending to believe she would spot her niece was a foolish distraction. It wasn't as if she would be allowed to wander around London on her—

Claudia froze, her gazed fixing on two men standing outside the Lillywhites emporium across the road on Regent Street. Neither showed any interest in the footballer displays in the store windows. The way the shorter one was checking out the Eros statue was—the only word that came to mind was 'furtive.'

Outside the Criterion Theatre next door to Lillywhites, a tall, robed Yoda had attracted a small crowd. Taking care to stay outside of the two men's direct line of vision, Claudia strolled to the pavement to catch a better look. Staying at the back of the crowd, she edged nearer until she was close enough to describe them.

The one who had caught her notice was medium height with black hair, neatly trimmed beard, sunglasses; a swarthy complexion.

Swarthy.

Huh. That gave her a jolt. The doorman at the Rock Hotel had used the word to describe the man who delivered the note that had taken her to the Moorish Castle. The man who had pressed up against her back and would have slit her throat if the Italian couple had not appeared in time to save her.

She had not seen his face then, but an instinctive fury boiled up; a volcano primed to erupt. As if his intent to kill her had left a taint of evil behind, Claudia was certain it had drawn her eyes to him.

His companion was taller, younger, and thin, his clothes hanging loose on him. He sagged, half-turned away from Swarthy, his body language making it clear that he was not there willingly. Swarthy was talking to him from behind his hand, apparently trying to get him to look at the statue without appearing conspicuous; making himself conspicuous in the attempt.

The tall man suddenly straightened and started to walk away; halted after a few steps by something the other man said, and returning to his place alongside him. Claudia tried to gauge what she saw on the pale, haggard face. Misery? Despair? Desperation? All three.

The photos and Monica's sketch of Colin Vine had shown him wearing a burgundy topknot. Hair—the color, the length, the style—made a tremendous difference to one's looks. This man's was a muddy brown and cut close to his scalp, shaved on the sides. As best she could from where she stood, Claudia studied the shape of his eyes, his nose, his lips. For a good sixty seconds, she tried to persuade herself that she was wrong, when ninety-five percent of her knew she was looking at Colin Vine.

But if this *was* Colin and one of the terrorists, where was Monica, and why was she not with them?

She wanted to grab hold of Swarthy and beat it out of him. She wanted to hear him beg for mercy before she stomped him to—Claudia pulled her panic up short and swallowed the scream that threatened to burst out of her throat. They would not have gone to the trouble of changing Monica's appearance and transporting her to London in a wheelchair on a fake passport and visa unless they had plans for her there. *She must be alive.* Her aunt refused to believe otherwise.

The men were unlikely to recognize her, but she pulled her knit hat down over her auburn hair and acted as if she was photographing the statue of Eros. As if sensing the camera, Swarthy started to pivot in her direction.

Quickly turning her back, Claudia flipped her phone camera to Selfie view and strolled around the monument watching them behind her. Her circuit was just about complete when her two quarries started walking away up Regent Street. If she'd had any doubt, it was erased in that moment. just as she had predicted to DI Stone from his handwriting, Swarthy walked with a slight limp.

The traffic was heavy, but not as crazy as Cairo. Dodging between vehicles, Claudia made it to the other side of the street. If Swarthy looked back, she was far enough behind that the crowds weaving in and out of the high-end shops would provide cover.

When the pair halted some fifty feet away, she stopped at the window of a trendy women's shop and watched them from the corner of her eye. Swarthy was talking on his phone, gesticulating, while Colin fidgeted from one foot to the other with the miserable demeanor of a dog on a too-tight leash.

Punching in D.O. Neil Wyatt's number, Claudia left him a clipped message when he didn't answer, then texted the photos she had taken of the pair.

Then, they were on the move again. An unmarked white van veered to the curb. The men stepped into the road. Swarthy pushed Colin in through the back door and followed him.

Shit! Shit! Shit!

The van was moving back into traffic.

Fumbling to get a photo of the number plate as the van drove away, Claudia knew she had blown it. Her hands had been shaking with nerves. She stepped back onto the curb and tapped the images onto her phone screen. As she expected, the numbers were too blurry to make out. She texted them to Wyatt anyway. His forensics people might be able to do something about it. She also sent one of the nearest street sign. If they could get the make and model of the van, a CCTV camera in the area would have captured the number plate.

ELLIOTT FIELDS WAS WILDLY enthusiastic when Claudia called from an Uber on her return trip from Piccadilly Circus and asked him to meet her for lunch at the Three Lords Pub across from the Motel One. She was waiting for him there, chafing over losing her quarry, when Neil Wyatt returned her call.

"I thought I made myself clear about not interfering with us, Ms. Rose."

"You did that, Mr. Wyatt, and I don't see how my walking around London is interfering with you in any way. I thought you'd be glad to get a photo of Colin Vine and one of the kidnappers."

"Oh, you thought that, did you? And you coincidentally 'happened' to be in a target location."

"I didn't know they were going to be there. I was careful to stay at a good distance. They didn't see me."

"How do you *know* they didn't get eyes on you? Your face is in the media along with your niece's. Do you think terrorists don't watch the news?"

"I was never in their line of sight. I'm not an idiot, D.O. Wyatt. Nothing I did compromised your operation. Oh, and you can check with DI Stone. I told him that the terrorist who wrote the materials I examined probably walked with a limp."

"A limp?"

"Yes, his right leg. The man I followed today had a limp; his right leg."

"Astounding," Wyatt said. "I'll let our people know that."

Claudia got the feeling that the grudging admission didn't mean the D.O. wasn't hanging on to his skepticism.

"You can track the van with your CCTV system, can't you?"

"You can be sure we are on it." He took a pause. "I suppose I should thank you for the photos. Nevertheless, Ms. Rose, you are an infuriating woman."

"I suppose DI Stone told you that, too."

"Look, if it *was* the terrorists you were following—and I'm not saying it was, mind you—you put yourself in a very dangerous position. Again. Is it necessary for me to have you arrested to keep you from interfering?"

"That's not the first time I've heard that threat, Mr. Wyatt. You have no grounds to arrest me. Tell you what; next time I see something, I'll keep it to myself."

He thought she was infuriating? She thought no less of him. She ended the call without waiting for his reply, and was putting her phone away as Elliott Fields arrived at her table.

Tallish and wide across the chest, he wore a soft black leather jacket and jeans. His dark hair was clipped nearly as short as Colin Vine's, but curly. Stubble—less than a beard—peppered his round cheeks. His eyes hid behind dark glasses, which stayed on inside the pub. His smile was brief and close-mouthed. It all gave him an air of anonymity. His podcast dealt with terrorism, after all. Maybe he fancied himself a spy. Over the past few years, they had been in contact several times by phone and webcam. This was their first in-person meeting.

Elliott fetched beers from the bar and they ordered burgers. Claudia had considered lasagna but changed the order in the nick of time. British restaurants used cheddar cheese in lasagna and while cheddar was as British as John Bull, it didn't feel right in an Italian dish.

While they waited for their food, she filled Elliott in on her morning. Any sentimental loyalty to MI5 had dissolved when Wyatt figuratively showed her the door. And, knowing nothing of their operations, she felt free to divulge what she had learned on her own.

"I can't believe I lost them," she said winding down her story. "The tall one was Colin, I know it." She showed Elliott the photo of Monica and Colin with his burgundy hair and man bun, and the ones she had taken at Piccadilly Circus.

His eyes narrowed in concentration. "Yeah. Definitely. The hair makes a huge difference. Still, even without it, the rest is the same.

Look at the shape of the mouth. And the ears." He raised his eyes and looked across the table with admiration. "It's fucking amazing that you went after them like that."

"It would have been *really* amazing if the license plate number had been clear. I was shaking too hard to get a good shot." Claudia held out her hands, which were steady, and shook them to demonstrate.

"Lucky they didn't turn around and snatch you into that van."

"I hadn't thought of that," she admitted. "But if they'd taken me to where Monica—"

"That's not going to help get her away from them, is it?"

Her phone pinged. A text from Joel.

The Russians are funding the Saudis.

Claudia's heart sank. He must have heard from his contact at the State Department. Russian terrorists were famous for their paramilitary-style training and violence, as well as for their habit of poisoning Putin's enemies. If she hadn't thought her fear for Monica could get any worse, Joel's text had just doubled it.

She sent an acknowledgment and dropped the phone back in her bag, refusing to think about it for now. She brought her mind back onto Elliott and their conversation. "If MI5 can get something from that lousy photo—"

"If anyone can, it's them. You say this D.O. Wyatt warned you off?"

Claudia gave him an exasperated eye roll. "He can't tell me not to walk around Piccadilly Circus or anywhere else. He should be glad I spotted them."

"Except you could've scared them off that site if they think they're being watched."

"Don't be ridiculous; there's no way they saw me." Elliott was parroting Wyatt without knowing it, and it ticked her off. "That list of sites didn't say whether they were going to attack one or two or all three of them. Or any of them, come to that matter. We're assuming. And if they do, we have no idea which one or when. The attack could come at any time of the day or night."

Elliott took a big bite of his burger and spoke as he chewed. If he hadn't been wearing the dark glasses, Claudia guessed his eyes would be screwed up in concentration. "When the most people are around, I don't doubt," he said.

"When might that be?"

"Saturday."

"That's four days from now. The Muslims in Egypt don't work on Saturdays. The Saudis are Muslim." She got out her phone. "There's nothing Siri doesn't know."

Siri replied: "Here's what I found on the web."

Claudia read the answer aloud from her screen. "Friday and Saturday are the official days of rest. So, maybe tomorrow or Thursday. More plausible than our weekend."

"That's all well and good," said Elliott, stuffing a fistful of chips in his mouth. "With only the two of us, I don't see how we're going to manage the problem of having three sites to watch."

She pushed away her plate, her appetite gone. "Aren't you a bundle of optimism."

34

MONICA

"Maryam."

Monica turned from the sink where she was washing the dishes and imagining she could see through the boarded-up window. She missed the sunshine of Egypt and the fun of the dig. And at last, she was allowing herself to be as angry as she wanted at being deprived of her life.

"That's not my name," she said, unable to stop. "My name is Monica."

To her surprise, Omar let her retort go unanswered. He was studying her with a speculative gaze as if she were a specimen he had collected for an exhibit. "Take off the sweatshirt," he said.

Her mouth dropped open. "What did you say?"

"You heard it. Or, you want me to take it off for you?"

"No!"

Faster than she could process, he crossed the space and shoved her against the table. Her feet went out from under her and she screamed, grabbing for his hands, which were wrestling the hem of her sweatshirt. Her bare back pressed against the table's hard edge. She screamed again, but Omar outweighed her by a good thirty pounds and was as determined as she was. The shirt was up and over her bra in two seconds flat.

Monica's teeth clamped on his hand and she bit him hard enough to draw blood. She was done with being a helpless victim. Omar let go with a yell of pain. His nostrils flared; his mouth turned down in an ugly snarl. He reached back to punch her, but he was off-balance, and as she rolled off the side of the table, she pulled him with her. He hit the floor first with a loud "Ooof" as the breath rushed out of him and she landed on top.

There was no time to think; only to act. Monica jumped to her feet. Every torment, every insult, every fear she had suffered at Omar's hands went into the kick she delivered to his groin. His gasp came out a squeak and he curled onto his side, his hands cupped over his genitals. His mouth was working, but all that emerged was a series of agonized moans. Monica didn't need a translator to catch the meaning when he recovered enough to spew a string of Arabic at her.

The scrappiness she never knew she possessed evaporated; the adrenaline leached away, leaving her spent. Smoothing her sweatshirt down over her body, she edged as far away from Omar as possible, but there was nowhere to go in the small kitchen. She had no choice other than to wait for the inevitable punishment.

A sound made her turn her head. Nasser was standing in the kitchen door.

Maybe because he was younger than his cohorts, he had shown some sympathy for her. He never pushed her around like the others did, and when he told her how to cook the dishes they wanted, he spoke to her like she was a human being. He came in and helped Omar to his feet, speaking in a soothing tone. Omar, bent over, panting and groaning, pushed him away.

"The shirt must come off first, to put it on her," he growled when he had could speak.

"Let her do it," Nasser reasoned with him. "It will be easier."

Hunched into her sweatshirt, Monica hated having them talk about her as if she wasn't there—as if she were a doll, not a person. She had to dig her teeth into her lower lip her to stop from saying so.

It was better to act like a doll and not draw their attention to her. And what were they talking about, anyway?

Switching to Arabic, the two of them continued the conversation. Omar did a lot of hand waving, scowling at her from under those beetle-brows as if he would like to kill her right then and there. They were still going at it when the last voice Monica expected to hear spoke from the kitchen door.

"She can't do it," Colin said loudly. Bashir, standing behind him, gave him a shove.

Omar sneered at him. "What are you saying? Why can't she?"

"She's not strong enough to carry it without drawing attention to herself. I'll do it. Put it on me."

Colin didn't know that she had been strong enough to throw Omar off her, Monica thought, a little annoyed that he would think she was weak. That kick to his—she couldn't bring herself to think the word—but it had been worth it, even though she would certainly suffer for the act. Then Colin's eyes met hers and she got the message in them: he was trying to protect her from whatever they had in store for her.

The terrorists eyed each other, telegraphing messages between them. Omar jerked his head toward the door to the lounge. His curled lip showed his contempt; his opinion that the prisoners were lower than vermin.

"A guard is waiting outside. You try to go, they kill you."

The three of them filed out of the kitchen, into the lounge.

Monica didn't care whether Omar was telling the truth about the guard or not. She and Colin were alone and he opened his arms to her. He held her, the first touch of human warmth in—she had lost track of how many days they had been captive.

"You're going to escape, luv," he whispered urgently. "I don't know how yet—it'll take a miracle but, look, when the time comes, you must do as I say. All right, little Mo? Promise?"

He could have asked her anything and she would have said, "I promise." She held onto him with an intense longing to never let go. He leaned away and gave her a jaunty wink.

"What they were saying in Arabic—is it true? Did you really kick that manky prick in the bollocks?"

Her first smile in a long time came with a burst of pride. It had all happened so fast; she had hardly known what she was doing. Ten minutes ago, she was elbow-deep in soapy dishwater, and then she was fending off Omar. The smile fell away. He was not going to forgive and forget what she had done to him. His ego would be as sore as his genitals.

Colin pulled her close again, resting his chin lightly on top of her head. "Well done, Monica, luv. Well done."

She reminded herself about protecting her heart, but her hands were clasped around his slim waist and she couldn't let go. They were connected in a way she had never been connected to anyone. With her head laid against his chest, she could feel his heart beating. The heart of the only person in this whole country who cared about her.

"Where did you go with Bashir this morning?" Monica asked softly. "You were gone for so long—"

"We were all over London. Piccadilly Circus, Trafalgar Square, the Tower."

"The Tower of London?"

"Yeah, the same."

"Why?"

"He wanted to have a look round where he wants the explosives. They're deciding where to do the deed."

"Why didn't you run, Colin? With that limp, Bashir couldn't have caught up with you. You would have got away."

"If I could have told the cops where this house is—where you were —I would have done. Trouble is, you can't see fuckall in the back of that van. I haven't a clue where we are." He shook his head slowly. "Besides, after all the aggro I've caused you, I couldn't bugger off on my own and leave you to it, could I?"

"You volunteered when you knew they were going to make me do it."

He avoided her eyes. "Call it atonement."

"Omigod, Colin, what are we going to do?"

He stroked her tears away with his thumb and brushed his lips against hers. "Don't give up, luv. I'll think of something."

Through the closed lounge door, they could hear what sounded like an argument in Arabic. The Freaks were always arguing. Or maybe it was nothing more than a discussion, and that's how they negotiated. Monica started to ask Colin what they were saying, when the voices in the other room quieted. Colin heard it, too.

"Shh, they're coming back." He stepped away from her; not fast enough.

Omar entered first and took in the scene. "Ah, the lovebirds," he mocked. To Colin, he said, "Sit in the chair. Take off the shirt."

Wordlessly, Colin righted the chair that had been knocked over in the struggle between Omar and Monica. He removed his jacket and sweatshirt, stripping down to his bare chest, and sat on the chair. He laid his clothing across his lap, outwardly impassive, and waited.

Bashir entered the kitchen carrying a garment that looked a lot like the fishing vests Monica's dad and Uncle Joel wore when they rented a boat to go lake fishing. This one was khaki-colored and had larger pockets than those that were intended to hold lures and hooks. Bashir tossed it at Colin, who silently pulled it over his head.

While he was doing that, Nasser brought in a cardboard box, which he set on the table. Reaching into it, he took out several large metal ball bearings and handed them to Omar, who stuffed them into the vest pockets.

Watching Colin stare straight ahead as mute and immobile as an Egyptian statue, their conversation from the previous night flashed back: the terrorists intended to use explosives in their attack. All at once, Monica understood.

"No," she shouted. "You can't!"

Omar backhanded her across the face and she fell backwards.

Colin leapt off the chair. Punching with both fists, he drove Omar against the Aga.

35

CLAUDIA - THURSDAY

JET LAG HAD SET IN. ALL THE DIFFERENT TIME ZONES—EGYPT, Gibraltar, England—made it hard to sleep at the appropriate times, and hard to wake up.

Claudia awoke groggy, fifteen minutes early for the eight o'clock alarm. She dragged herself from under the warm covers and stumbled to the window, met by the standard grey drizzle wetting the streets. London in March. What if she and Elliott were right and this was the day of the attacks?

What if they weren't?

After yesterday's lunch, they had spent the afternoon making the rounds between the Tower of London and Trafalgar Square, surveilling both locations without result. Since Colin had been at Piccadilly Circus earlier with one of the terrorists, it seemed improbable they would go there twice on the same day, so they had crossed it off their list.

SHE HEADED down to the breakfast buffet, her stomach churning. Anything more than a slice of dry toast and two cups of black coffee would certainly make her puke.

"He's probably one of them, you know," Elliott said, sliding into the chair opposite her and pouring himself a cup of tea.

Claudia eyed the scone on his plate, slathered with clotted cream and jam, and turned green.

"Colin?"

"Yeah. I mean, look, he's prancing around free as you please with them. Either he was with them from the beginning or he's gone over to their side, that's what I think."

"I don't think so. He didn't look at all well when I saw him yesterday at Piccadilly. He might not have had a choice."

"Well, then, where's your niece? Why wasn't she with them?"

The question made her want to punch him in the face. When had she ever been so violent?

"I don't *know,* Elliott. If that's all you have to say, why don't you go home? I don't need that in my head. I have enough crap to scare me without you adding to it."

He shrugged, not at all contrite, and ate half his scone in one bite. "Sorry then; I'll shut it."

"How about you go to Trafalgar Square and I'll hang out here. We can cover two of the bases, anyway."

"If you think—" Elliott broke off as her phone rang. He popped the rest of his scone into his mouth as she put up a 'wait' hand.

She checked the screen. "It's D.O. Wyatt."

The last time they spoke, the Desk Officer had been exasperated by her. She answered the call, her stomach churning anew. If there was news of Monica—

"Good morning, Ms. Rose," Wyatt said in his crisp manner. "I'm having a passport photo texted to you. It's of a young woman traveling under the name of Maryam Amari, who we believe to be your niece, Monica Bennett. After you've had a look at it, we'll continue the conversation."

A text pinged in Claudia's phone. The unsmiling young female face on the screen was at the same time recognizable and unfamiliar. A face she was accustomed to seeing with a sunny smile and shiny blonde tresses. This girl with the short, choppy, dull brown hair and vacant eyes could have been a runaway crack addict.

Claudia showed Elliott the photo. He gave her two thumbs up while another piece of her heart crumbled.

"The hair changes her looks a lot, but it's definitely Monica," she told Wyatt.

"Right. That's what we expected." He made a 'harumph' sound. "I thought I ought to let you know that last Friday, a British Airways flight attendant alerted the pilot that she believed a young woman was in some sort of difficulty, possibly being trafficked. The young woman identified herself as 'Monica.' She indicated that she needed help and then apparently changed her mind. She didn't provide any additional information, but she was traveling with a man who claimed to be her brother. After they landed, the pair disappeared before the flight attendant could see her again. The pilot put the message through to the authorities, but there were some communication balls-ups and it took too long to get to the right person. They had deplaned."

Claudia listened in silence; every sentence ratcheting up her blood pressure. "They could have rescued her?"

"Well, er, I suppose so. It's one of those unfortunate things. The message slipped through the net. I felt you ought to know."

"Unfortunate," she repeated, anger making her voice as frigid as the North Pole. "Slipped through the net."

"Er, yes…" Even over the phone, Wyatt's obvious discomfort tipped her off.

"What else? There is more, isn't there?"

"We got several hits in our facial recognition system using your photos. The man with Colin Vine—you were right, it *was* Vine—is in our database. We have a clearer idea of who we're dealing with thanks to your, uh, detective work. Well done. My apologies for being a mite brusque when we spoke earlier."

Taken aback by the compliment and the apology, Claudia stammered thanks and asked if they were able to get anything on the van.

"There was enough of the number plate visible along with the make and model that our people were able to give us what we needed through the CCTV cameras. We have eyes on the van now."

"Now? You know where they are?"

"We do. And they're on the move. We're following them."

"This is the day, isn't it? We were right about the monuments. Is it one we talked about?"

Wyatt paused, possibly debating the wisdom of sharing information a civilian would ordinarily not be privy to. Maybe it occurred to him that without her work they might not have the intel on the three monuments. He coughed a little; cleared his throat. "It would appear the Tower of London is the intended target."

"I'm at Tower Hill right now."

"Look here, Ms. Rose, I'll let you know if we need your help. Until then, you *must* step away. We've got this."

"What am I supposed to do, sit around until I see something on the news?"

"Yes, exactly that. Look here, I know it can't be easy when it's your niece, but it's best that you let us deal with it." Wyatt's tone said he was losing patience.

"We're getting snipers into position and there are other personnel around the area in plainclothes. We don't want anything to alert these people, and we don't want to put civilians in danger any more than necessary."

"You said your people weren't armed?"

"They're not. This is a different division. Obviously, we have to outman them."

Claudia listened with growing apprehension. How could an eighteen-year-old girl stand a chance in the face of what was coming? She squeezed her eyes shut and pretended he was talking about a movie, not real-life snipers looking for her niece.

"According to the witness in Gibraltar, there were three terrorists, plus Monica and Colin," she said.

"Three we are aware of; there are probably others in this cell. Now, you must listen to me, Ms. Rose. We'll be ready and we'll be watching them. Any wrong move by you could spoil the entire operation. I need your assurance that you won't interfere."

Claudia knew she wouldn't get anywhere by arguing, and she couldn't blame him for doing his job. If she was in his position, she wouldn't have welcomed outside interference, either.

"I won't interfere." There was one final question. "D.O. Wyatt, please tell me. Do you have *any* new information about Monica?"

His longsuffering sigh told her he was holding something back. All at once, her woolly pullover was too hot and tight. She stretched the neck wide, trying to get more oxygen. "D.O. Wyatt?" she pressed. "Are you there? What about Monica?"

"Your niece is in the van with them."

36

MONICA

Omar's arms were up, covering his face defensively like a boxer in a match. There was no chance to hit back against the stored-up rage Colin was channeling into his fists.

Bashir and Nasser thrust Monica aside and between them wrestled Colin back onto the chair, pinning his arm behind him.

In a fast move, Bashir stopped Omar's fist, which was aimed at Colin's face. From the gestures he made, and the shaking of heads, he appeared to be urging Omar not to injure Colin where it showed. The older facial bruises were nearly gone. If they were going to send him to detonate the suicide vest, drawing attention with a messed-up face was the last thing they wanted.

So, Omar aimed a brutal kick at his ribs instead, where bruises wouldn't show.

Monica's cheek was throbbing from the backhander, but three against one was such an unfair fight; outrage won over fear. "If you need a martyr, do it yourselves, you cowards," she shouted. "You got the ring. Why should he have to die for your stupid cause?"

For a second or two there was stunned silence. Monica had been a shadow, a mute observer, not expected to express opinions. Bashir was first to recover.

"Shut your mouth, woman. You infidels are dirt underneath our feet."

Fully expecting to end up beaten, or dead, Monica had nothing to lose. "I won't shut up. I did everything you told me because you said you wouldn't kill him."

Omar's sneer was a taunt; a punishment for embarrassing him. "I lied. And now, you will go with him."

"Leave her out of it," Colin roared from his chair. "You don't need her. You've got me to do your filthy work."

Bashir's ferocious slap whipped Colin's head to the side and stained his cheek with a scarlet imprint of his hand. Monica's hand flew to her own face. She didn't need to know anything about explosives to understand that the terrorists' plan to kill as many people as they could included her and Colin. Her family would pay with their heartache for the mistake she had made. Her mouth was dry, her breathing fast and shallow. She was starting to panic.

Colin had promised she would escape somehow, that he would make it happen. The Freaks were packing the vest pockets with explosives, each wired to the next. Sweat, hot, then cold, trickled down her back. Escape? Not a prayer.

Omar pointed a warning finger at Colin. "No more tricks. The vest will not be armed until we go to the target."

Colin gave a bored yawn. "Oh fuck. I was going to blow up the house with all of us in it."

"Funny man," Bashir mocked. "How will you laugh with your blood all over London?"

"Fuck you and all your mothers."

Omar's eyes narrowed to slits. "Maybe we take turns with your girlfriend first."

Monica's slamming heart threatened to rip open her chest and bounce across the room. Why was Colin poking at them? How could he act so calm in the face of what was about to happen? She knew better than to count on Nasser stopping it if the two evil Freaks decided to rape her—she was amazed they hadn't already. Thank God Omar's threat had shut Colin up.

After filling the pockets with explosives, Bashir duct-taped a long wire from Colin's chest down his arm and around his wrist. He put the detonator in his hand. "We give you earbud. You keep thumb on the button. When it is armed, don't let it go until you hear instruction."

"Don't let it go," Omar repeated with a cruel chuckle. "You let go—and *Boom!*" He threw his hands in the air, demonstrating.

"We put you out of the van near the target. Someone will be watching all the time. Any tricks, we shoot you. You and the girl hold hands together, nobody notice you. You get it?"

"Nice young British lovers, out for walk together," Omar added. "Who will suspect they carry death with them?"

"Let her go," Colin implored, no longer mocking. "She can't hurt you."

Bashir shook his head. "She should not have attacked my brother Omar. Now, you both pay for it."

"She's a kid. You don't have to do this."

Monica could smell his desperation. With a sense of finality, she knew he had done everything he could to save her and it wasn't going to be enough. As if an angel had wrapped her in its wings, her pulse slowed to normal and she stopped trembling. She accepted her fate.

The terrorists gave each other congratulatory slaps on the back. Omar raised his fist and shouted, *"Allahu akbar!"*

"Allahu akbar," Bashir and Nasser echoed together. "God is great!"

37

CLAUDIA

Elliott begged her to slow down as they dashed the short half-mile from her hotel to the Tower of London. Claudia allowed a few impatient seconds to catch up.

"You don't s'pose Wyatt told you it was going to be the Tower to throw you off the scent, do you?" Elliott panted, struggling to catch his breath.

"What are you talking about?" Claudia snapped.

"Well, he didn't want you poking your nose in. What if it's one of the other monuments and he sent us here to keep you out of the way?"

"For God's sake, Elliott, are you *trying* to drive me crazy? Because right now, that's a very short drive."

She kept walking, considering what he had said. Unthinkable that Neil Wyatt might be so devious as to deliberately throw her off the scent, although he must have known she would head straight to the Tower.

"You don't have to go with me," she told Elliott. "But there's no reason for me not to. They haven't cleared the area. It's not like I'm crawling under a barrier. If Wyatt lied to me, I'll find out. And if he did, I *will* have to kill him." When Elliott's eyes snapped open wide, Claudia gave him a small push. "Don't be ridiculous, not literally."

"Well, that's good. And I *am* going with you."

"Suit yourself," Claudia said, but she was glad not to be going to the Tower alone.

THE CHILL after the morning rain was no deterrent to stalwart Londoners ready to take advantage of the weak sun poking through the clouds. Walkers and joggers were out in droves. Bypassing the Tower of London Welcome Center, Claudia and Elliott crossed the road and entered the gates that led to the grounds. Long lines of tourists were waiting to buy tickets.

With her coppery hair a dead giveaway, Claudia had covered it with the knit hat again. Elliott's head was bare and he carried a large black umbrella. "Makes a jolly good weapon," he said, showing her its pointy tip, which he told her was called a ferrule.

"Do you have it sharpened?" Claudia asked suspiciously, not wanting to touch it and find out. Elliott gave her a mysterious look and said nothing.

"Okay, fine, don't tell me. Shall we sit at one of those tables?" She indicated the outdoor seating area that belonged to the Tower café, conveniently located next to the ticket windows. "We can watch the people buying tickets and anyone who might be going to the river."

"Yeah, okay. You want a coffee?"

"Yes, please. Black. I'll wait for you out here."

Claudia handed him some money and claimed a table, taking a chair that let her sit with her back to the wall. While she waited for Elliott, she phoned Joel, then Pete. Neither answered and both voicemail boxes were full. She texted the latest news, annoyed that she couldn't get through that way, either. No surprise; everything annoyed her today. She was more on edge than she could ever remember being. She sent a quick text to Annabelle and asked her to keep trying the guys.

Elliott returned with two steaming cardboard cups. "Don't go and drink so much that you need a wee. If you do, though, there's toilets inside."

Claudia rolled her eyes. "Thanks for the information." Not that she would dare leave her post. That's when something would go down, she had no doubt.

The Tower of London stood on the far side of what had been a moat until the mid-nineteenth century and today was a grassy lawn. The Union Jack was flying full mast. If all went well, it would still be there at the end of the day.

Their table was on a terrace with a view of the four turrets of the White Tower, which allowed Claudia to scan the faces of people strolling past, many in tour groups buying tickets. Trying to listen to Elliott talk about his terrorism podcast, she soon lost the thread.

"...William the Conqueror—" Elliott stopped talking and glared at her until she realized he was waiting for a response and she didn't know to what.

"I'm sorry, what did you say?"

"Yeah, I knew you wasn't listening."

"I was. Something about William the Conqueror."

"Right. That was a test to see if your mind was wandering as far as I thought it was, and it was, too," said Elliott, patently satisfied that he was right.

"Well, what about him?" Claudia retorted. "William the Conquerer..."

"All I was saying was, our William built the White Tower close to a thousand years ago. They used to torture prisoners in the basement, like when Guy Fawkes tried to blow up parliament."

"I'd put those terrorists in there," said Claudia. "A few twists on the rack ought to make them see things differently."

"I never knew you were so bloodthirsty," said Elliott admiringly.

"Neither did I, until my niece's life was at stake," Claudia said. "I wonder where Wyatt's people are."

"You know we're never going to see them."

"I know. I'm actually glad they're here, somewhere. Assuming your theory is wrong and we are at the right place."

"I'd bet they have people at all the sites."

The sun went behind a bank of dark clouds and a wintry breeze sprang up. "Is it going to rain?" Claudia asked, worried. "They might not show up."

Looking up at the sky, Elliott shrugged. "It might. Nothing we can do if it does, is there?"

"As long as it's not an omen. It's been an hour since Wyatt said they were on the move. I should have asked him where they're coming from."

"What are you on about?" Elliott said with a cheeky snort. "You don't think he would've told you, do you?"

Claudia gave him the side eye and said nothing.

"Haven't we sat here long enough?" Elliott said five minutes later. "My bum's flat."

"Fine; let's walk around a bit. Not too far, though. We need to stay close to the ticket booth, where we can watch everyone going in."

"What if they come in from the Thames side 'round the back side of the Tower?"

"I walked back there the other day, it's all foot traffic. Wyatt said they're in a van."

"They can't get close enough to drive into people like they did before, but the driver could drop them at Tower Bridge and let them walk in."

"That broadens the possibilities," said Claudia. "How wide do you suppose Wyatt's people are spread out?"

"You can bet there are loads of them. Maybe we should go to the way in and hang about there."

"The way in what?"

Elliott looked at her as if she were daft. "The Tower."

"Oh, the entrance. Okay, let's do that. If the bad guys plan to do something inside the Tower, they'll have to go through that way. Try to look casual."

That earned her another incredulous look. Claudia binned their used cups and the two of them strolled towards the entrance, where a large group waited their turn to go onto the grounds—people they had seen first at the ticket window.

They had been watching the tide of people ebb and flow for about a half-hour, when a scruffy looking man in a dirty overcoat slouched over.

"Whatchu doin' here? You oughtn't be 'angin about. Someone might fink you was up to summink."

"None of yours what we're doing," said Elliott sharply. "Shove off, mate."

For all his dirty-looking clothes, the man didn't have the rancid smell Claudia would have expected from someone sleeping rough.

"Thanks for the tip, we're going now." She took hold of Elliott's arm, ignoring his protests, and dragged him away.

"He's undercover," she hissed. "He must be one of—"

Her eyes had fallen on a young couple, instinct screaming at her that something was wrong. They were holding hands like lovers, but walking like a pair of robots, past the ticket office, moving towards the entrance to the Tower. Claudia got out her phone and trained the camera app on the girl, enlarging her face, which was pasty white. Her brown hair was badly cut in a boyish style and she wore a grey sweat-shirt with a pink heart and the lettering, 'Be Kind.'

Monica's aunt knew that shirt, and she knew the face of the girl who wore it as well as she knew her own. "It's them," she said quietly. "What do we do now?"

"Where?" Elliott answered in an undertone. "Don't be conspicuous about it."

"The tall guy in the hat and the girl with short brown hair coming this way. Her best friend gave her that shirt. Elliott, it's them. It's really them. We have to do something. Look at her face; she's scared shitless."

"It's just the two of them? The terrorists will be somewhere close, monitoring them. That's what they do. Look, he's wearing an earbud. They'll be using it to give him orders."

Claudia clutched at his sleeve. "Something's wrong with his coat. At Piccadilly it was hanging loose. Look at it. It's all bulky and—"

Elliott gripped her arm hard enough to hurt. "I'd swear on my mother's grave there's a suicide vest under that coat."

She had considered the possibility. Hearing it from him had the impact of hitting a brick wall head-on. Like a stop-action film, one frame advancing at a time, everything slowed down. Colin's jacket hung like Joel's when he wore a bulletproof vest underneath his clothes.

Elliott was right.

Claudia's mind turned to mush. She could see nothing but Monica and her sweatshirt, and the utter terror on her face. They were twenty feet away.

Ten feet.

Five.

"Now!" Elliott hissed. "Grab her."

38

MONICA

"MONICA!"

Monica faltered. She must have imagined that familiar voice calling her name. Her head twisted in the direction of the voice, and there she was, like something out of a movie—her aunt, barely an arm's length away, reaching out to her. She had dreamt so many times of seeing Claudia again. And now it was too late.

"You have to go, Aunty C," she cried shrilly. "You'll get killed." She tried pull Colin along, to move away from her aunt, but Colin halted his stride.

"Wait, this is your aunt? The amazing Aunt Claudia?"

As if she had been drugged again, Monica's mind was fuzzy and confused. "How is she here? She can't be here."

Claudia was moving toward her as slowly and cautiously as if she were a feral cat that would run away if she tried to touch it. "Come with me, baby. I'm going to take you home."

"No, I'm staying with Colin."

Monica kept tugging at him, but he wouldn't budge and she stamped her foot like a small child demanding her way. "We have to get away from her."

"There's help close by, sweetheart. I need you to come with me."

Colin pressed Monica's hand in his. "Listen to Aunty. You're going to be all right, little Mo. You've been so brave." He brought her hand to his mouth and brushed her knuckles with his lips. "As brave as Hatshepsut." His eyes were glistening as his gaze swung from Monica to Claudia, who was rooted where she stood, watching the exchange.

He spoke to her aunt. "You've got to hurry. Get her as far away as you can, quickly."

Reaching up, he tore the earbud from his ear and dropped it to the ground, crushing it under his boot heel. "Go with Aunty, Mo, and *don't look back.*"

"Colin, no, you can't. We can get help; she said so."

Monica was too intent on clinging to Colin's hand to hear what Claudia was saying. If she let go and he took his thumb off the trigger, they would all die, and everyone around them, as the Freaks had planned. Her eyes swung around wildly like a bird caught in a trap, desperate to find a way out.

"Let go, Monica," Colin said.

She looked up into his face, chilled to her core by the determination she saw. "No!" she screamed. "There has to be another way."

He looked down at his thumb, bloodless from the pressure of holding it on the detonator button, and without warning, wrenched his right hand loose from hers.

Monica gasped a ragged breath. If they had been Siamese twins, the shock of separation could not have been any greater. She didn't bother to wipe away the tears that streamed in a torrent down her face.

"Please, Colin, please, you don't have to—"

He shook his head sadly. "See, Mo, I told you we'd find a miracle—a way for you to escape. I'm sorry, luv. I'm so sorry for everything."

"No—the miracle is for both of us. Please don't—"

Colin gave her a wistful smile and dropped a kiss on her cheek. Then he spun around and began to run, sprinting in the direction of the Millennium Wharf.

Something hit the ground near Monica's feet with a stinging crack. Particles of concrete and dust flew. The man with Claudia bellowed, "Gun! He's got a gun!"

Monica turned. Bashir was aiming a handgun at Colin's running figure.

Before she could react, a volley of loud pops sounded from all around them and Bashir dropped to the ground.

People were screaming, stampeding towards the gate. Hysterical mothers with strollers rushing screaming babies out of harm's way. Old people struggling with canes and walkers. Selfless heroes running in to help. A flood of men in tactical gear from out of nowhere, shouting commands.

"Come on," Claudia called to her friend above the din. "We have to get her away from here."

Throwing their arms protectively around Monica's shoulders, they rushed her along with the crowd racing away from the Tower. But she wasn't having it. After all she and Colin had been through together, she would not leave him to face his horrible fate alone.

Monica ducked out of their grasp and charged after him. And came up against a wall of uniformed bobbies setting up barricades around the Tower. Over the loud noise all around, she could hear Claudia's voice yelling her name. She tried to shoulder through the bobbies. One of them yanked her back.

"Oy! Where'd you think you're—"

"Let me go!" Monica screamed, clawing at his face, kicking his shins. With the same single-minded resolve she had used on Omar that morning, she twisted out of the cop's grasp and started running after Colin. She had made it twenty yards when the cop caught up with her. It was a fight she could never win, but she fought him anyway.

He made to slam her to the ground, when over his shoulder she saw Colin reach the wharf railing.

"*No!* Colin, no, no, no—"

Without a second's hesitation, he vaulted over the side and disappeared into the Thames.

Monica's anguished shriek was lost in a tremendous explosion.

A cloud of dense gray-black smoke rose from the river and a geyser of bloody water fell on them like rain.

39

TEN DAYS LATER

"He was a hero," Claudia said. "Even considering how you ended up where you did. Those terrorists would have come up with another way to do their evil. We'll never know how many lives Colin saved."

"Yes, he was," Monica agreed in the subdued manner Claudia had become accustomed to. They were an hour out of Los Angeles on a Virgin Atlantic flight. Claudia's father had insisted on purchasing their first-class seats to keep his two girls away from the media storm. The flight attendants, aware of Monica's story, had made sure to give her extra-special attention and care throughout the long trip from Heathrow.

Knowing the fasten seatbelt sign would soon come on in preparation for landing, Claudia went to tidy up in the lav. She was headed back to her seat when one of the flight attendants from the economy cabin peeped through the curtain and beckoned her over.

"I wanted to say, I'm so happy your niece was rescued. Her boyfriend saved a lot of lives, jumping in the Thames like that. I read it in the Guardian how the water spread the shock of the blast and there wasn't as much damage as there might have been. What a brave lad."

And without his sacrifice, Monica would be dead, too.

Claudia thanked her with a grateful smile. "Thank you. And thank heavens the police were able to round up the rest of the terrorist cell. They'll be locked up for a long, long time."

The flight attendant shuddered. "Yes, thank heavens indeed. You don't know these days, do you? Well, luv, I wanted you to know we're all happy to have you on our flight."

CLAUDIA REACHED over to squeeze her niece's hand. Monica, who had been staring out the window, produced a wan smile. After several days of debriefing, both by British authorities and the US State Department LEGAT—the legal attaché—she had nothing left. Her eyes, red and swollen, held a deep grief that would not easily be erased. She had known Colin for a matter of weeks; their experiences bound them together forever.

While they were in London, Claudia, wanting to give Monica something of her old self back, had nagged Neil Wyatt into arranging enough of a break from all the interviews with government officials for a visit to a hairdresser.

A local friend recommended the stylist, who worked his magic on the cheap shampoo-in color the terrorists had supplied. He snipped the chopped-off locks into a professional pixie cut that suited her. Leaving the salon, Monica looked, not like her old self, but less like a girl who had been kidnapped, drugged, and terrorized, and who had lost her lover to a horrendous death.

New clothes helped, too. The jeans and underwear she had worn for endless days—even the sweatshirt Annabelle had given her— went into the nearest rubbish tip. Monica knew that her best friend, who had once been kidnapped too, would understand. Shedding those physical reminders of her ordeal had helped lighten her mood a little.

AFTER THE ELEVEN-HOUR FLIGHT, they were first off the plane, met at LAX by airlines officials who gave them VIP treatment and hurried them through the lines and out to a waiting Uber. Monica's rescue and Colin's act of heroism continued to be splashed across the front pages of every major newspaper at home and abroad. She had refused dozens of requests for interviews from all the news shows.

Since deplaning, Monica had become increasingly tense. silently twisting her hands in her lap, throughout the short drive. When they drove away from the airport, Claudia texted Joel to let him know their short ETA. As the Uber turned the corner onto the street where Monica and Pete lived, she could see her brother and her husband on the porch, watching for them.

Monica saw them, too, and grabbed Claudia's hand. She had refused to talk to her father or FaceTime with him since her rescue.

"I don't know how to do this, Aunty C. I'm not the same person I was when I left."

Claudia looked into her young niece's anxious eyes and held them with her own. "All you need to know is this: we love you—your dad loves you—no matter who you are."

"How can he love me after—"

"There's *nothing* you could do to stop him from loving you, Monica. I know you feel guilty for what he—we—went through. None of us care about that now. All we care is that you're home, safe. See." She pointed out the window. "Does that look like someone who doesn't love you?"

Pete was running toward the car. Joel, an uncommonly big smile splitting his face, followed. Their longest separation was over.

Claudia squeezed her niece's hand and opened the car door. "Come on, kiddo; you can do this. Colin was right. You *are* as brave as Hatshepsut. You can do anything."

Monica climbed out. The pinched face and pixie haircut made her look like a stranger, and she stared awkwardly at the ground as if she had never met these people, didn't live in this house.

Pete had told his sister that he intended to let his daughter take the lead, but those intentions flew out the window and he pulled her into an embrace tight enough that Monica cried out, "Dad!"

And they all started sobbing and laughing.

. . .

Claudia, praying for the return of her niece's sunny, happy self, saw a shadow pretending to be a whole person; putting on a smile at appropriate times, saying the appropriate things. When she thought no one was looking, her shoulders drooped and her eyes went distant.

The news of the murder charge against her father was one more blow for Monica to absorb. She spent a lot of time with Zebediah Gold, Claudia's psychologist friend, whose oath of confidentiality prevented him from sharing anything they discussed. He counseled Pete and Claudia to 'give her as long as she needs.' No pressure to start college.

"I'm trying not to be a clingy dad," Pete confided to his sister when they were sharing a beer at Cowboys, the neighborhood bar one afternoon. "After nearly losing my daughter, it's not easy."

"How do you feel she's doing?" Claudia asked.

Pete released a gusty sigh. "A lot better now she's convinced that I'm not 'mad' about her going off on that weekend with Colin. Am I so harsh that she was afraid to tell me about him?"

Claudia smiled. "Not harsh, Pete; a little restrictive maybe."

"Well, we know how that turned out. I'm trying my best to let her be an adult who gets to make her own choices." He gave a joyless chuckle. "The irony is, she doesn't want to let me out of her sight. I'm only here right now because she has a session with Zebediah."

40

TWO MONTHS LATER

ROBIN CROSS' LAW OFFICE WAS IN A RESTORED 1950S HOTEL NEAR THE Tucson Courthouse. She had called a meeting with her client to discuss the findings of her investigator, Tim Brody, in the case of the State of Arizona v. Peter James Bennett. Claudia and Monica were there to give Pete moral support.

They sat around the table in the conference room Robin shared with three other attorneys. The eyes of Pete, Claudia, and Monica were on Tim as he enumerated the results of his investigation to date. "Here's who I've interviewed so far. The five friends who were with Pete the night of the—" his eyes flicked to Monica. "The night of the fight. I spoke with them all independently and everyone described it the same way: Mitch started it. Mitch threw the first punch. Mitch was always a—jerk. So, at the very least, you have self-defense."

"I didn't—" Pete interrupted hotly.

"Cool your jets, Pete," Robin interrupted. "Let the man finish."

"Okay, sorry. It's just my life, you know?"

"Yes, we know."

"I talked to the general manager at the bar, and he concurred," said Tim. "So, that's six good witnesses if this goes to trial."

"What does that mean, 'if'?" Claudia asked.

Robin gave them all a significant look. "We've had some interesting developments."

A half-smile curved Tim's mouth. "One of the other people I interviewed was Mitch and Ellie Graham's housekeeper, one Zola Villalba, after I spoke with Mrs. Graham—a real piece of work. She had nothing to say to me, and she said it with condescending, holier-than-thou attitude. Let me add, her 'grieving widow' act was less than convincing.

"Anyway, when Zola showed me to the door, she slipped me a scrap of paper with her phone number. She's not too happy working for the Grahams. She's undocumented, from South America, and they've been working her like a navvy; holding it over her that if she doesn't do everything they say, they'll see she's deported. Getting out for an hour to talk to me was a major deal."

"How'd you do it?" asked Pete.

"We arranged to meet when she went to pick up groceries. I walked around the Whole Foods with her. She told me the Missus had been having an affair with Mitch's law partner, a guy named Beckham Blaine." Tim checked in with his audience, who were listening, riveted, to his story.

"Is this leading to '*Ellie* killed Mitch'?" Pete asked, the anticipation in his voice out in the open for all to hear.

"Not quite." Tim suspended his narrative as the office aide came in with a tray of cold drinks. He waited while she arranged them on the credenza and exited the room. "Zola claims that on several occasions, Blaine has been over at the house lately to er, 'console' Ellie. In her bedroom. And she was sure they'd been seeing each other for quite a while.

"A few days before Mitch's death, Zola overheard a big to-do between the Grahams. Mitch was drunk, which apparently was SoP for him. He was telling Ellie that no other man was gonna get his money, and he had arranged things so that if she divorced him, she got nothing."

Silence fell over the conference room as each listener grasped the information in his or her own way. Pete was first to speak. "If she *divorced* him, she got nothing. What about if he died?"

"Had he filed a will with the court?" Claudia asked.

"Wills aren't filed in Arizona," said Robin. "Once a will is made, whoever has the original keeps it somewhere safe, and when the person dies, an estate attorney would file for probate. In Arizona, the assets of someone who dies without a will pass by intestate succession."

"What does that mean?" asked Monica.

"It means the estate goes to the spouse. In other words, Ellie gets everything."

"Mitch was an estate attorney," said Pete, incredulous.

Claudia thought that was interesting. "Was his estate significant?"

Robin pointed a gun finger at her. "A lot more significant than his law practice. We've had a forensic accountant looking at their books under court order, and they're in a financial bind. From what our expert has uncovered, Mitch was siphoning money from the practice into his personal accounts."

Pete's mouth dropped open. "His partner is screwing his wife, and he's cooking the books? They deserve each other. All of 'em."

"If this can be proved, it gives *Blaine* a good motive to kill Mitch," said Claudia. "Is that what we think happened?"

Robin nodded. "Yes. And since the evidence against Pete is all circumstantial, if we can convince the county attorney, there's a small chance she might drop the charges. Unless we can produce very strong evidence, though, it's likely we will go to trial. In that case, we have to convince the jury that there's a good chance somebody else committed the murder. This new scenario gives a better motive than Pete's twenty-year old grudge against Mitch. I have a good relationship with the prosecutor on our case. I'll call her and have a chat."

"Erm, I'm not quite finished," said Tim.

Robin broke out into a smile. "The Perry Mason moment. Go for it."

Tim nodded. "Robert 'Geronimo' Lester." He looked around the table at each of them in turn.

"Who's that?" Pete asked, since it was obvious Tim was waiting for the question.

"Snitch; a druggie who'll do anything for a high. He's currently in jail for trying to hold up a 7-11 with a butter knife. He was going to use the money to buy meth."

"Oh, a real genius." Claudia rolled her eyes. "And this 'Geronimo' affects Pete's case somehow?"

"Robin has received discovery from the county attorney's office. Do you want to tell it, Rob?"

The attorney opened a folder on the table in front of her. "Let me first say, from what I can tell, the county attorney hasn't seen the significance of this evidence. Or, she's ignoring it. So. Two days after Mitch's death, a stolen car was recovered around the block from Dirt-bags. When the crime lab went over it, there was a pocket notebook under the seat; a log that detailed Mitch's movements over the week prior to the murder."

"You're kidding." They'd said it simultaneously, Pete, Monica, and Claudia.

"Someone was following Mitch?" said Claudia. "How does this tie to the Geronimo dude?"

"His fingerprints were all over the stolen car. And the notebook. We can get a court order to compel him to produce a handwriting exemplar to compare to the writing in the notebook."

Claudia started to speak. Robin stopped her. "There's one other thing. In the back of the notebook where he logged his surveillance of Mitch, there was a paper with Mitch's home and work addresses written on it. I'm going to show you photocopies of the notebook and the paper. I'd like you to tell me whether they were written by the same hand."

She passed several sheets of paper across the table. The first three were images of small lined notebook paper with a list of times and places, conveniently titled "Mitch."

The handwriting was childish printing, emotionally undeveloped and uneducated. "This guy has a learning disorder," said Claudia.

The fourth was a torn-off page of legal pad with no name and two handwritten addresses.

She stared at Robin, mounting excitement making her tingle all over. "You don't have to be an expert to see this is written by a different person than the others. This one's intelligent, and a real bastard. If you can get a sample of Beckham Blaine's handwriting and it's consistent with this one, we can tie him to Geronimo, who was following Mitch, and who can be placed near the crime scene with the stolen car."

"Hold on," said Pete. "Tim, you said Geronimo is locked up. You must have asked him about Mitch. Assuming you think he's the killer, could he get a deal by identifying who hired him?"

Tim Brody nodded. "We have asked him. He says it's not worth his life to put the finger on who hired him to follow Mitch. Amazingly, he wasn't dumb enough to admit to the killing."

Claudia looked around at them all. "So, how do we get Beckham Blaine's handwriting?"

41

Wearing a designer suit and a pair of high-heeled shoes she had purchased at a local boutique for the occasion, Claudia strode to the reception desk in the offices of Blaine & Graham, Attorneys at Law. They were located on the second floor of a historic adobe home hidden behind a beautiful ornate arched gate that made Claudia think of Petrie House in Egypt. Did Monica ever think about her time there? If she did, she never mentioned it.

"Good afternoon," she said to the receptionist. "I have an appointment with Mr. Blaine. I'm Aileen Ellis."

She had opted to use their grandmother's name when Pete pointed out that while it was a long shot, Beckham Blaine might recognize her name from the media. Using a name that came effortlessly would be easier than an unfamiliar one she might forget to answer to.

The receptionist favored her with an impersonal smile and gestured to the three club chairs artfully placed around a coffee table, which looked out over a panoramic view of the desert. Across from the reception desk was a glass-walled conference room furnished with a long, polished table and eight chairs. If she ended up having to meet with Beckham Blaine in that fish bowl, it was going to be tricky to get what she needed.

"Please have a seat, Ms. Ellis. Mr. Blaine will be with you shortly. Can I get you something? Coffee? Water?"

Assured by Monica that she looked every inch the affluent prospective client she intended to project, and using her court demeanor—which meant not showing that she was nervous—Claudia declined with thanks.

In less than five minutes, a door opened, framing an attractive man in shirtsleeves neatly rolled to the elbows, and a tie. The expensively tailored trousers and tassel loafers didn't quite fit Tucson's casual style. He held out his hand. "Ms. Ellis? Beckham Blaine. Pleased to meet you."

In good shape, a gym rat, Claudia suspected. She rose and went to meet him with a firm handshake. "Thank you for seeing me on short notice."

"My pleasure. Let's go to my office."

Claudia followed, noting the dusting of light brown hair that covered the back of his head.

Beckham Blaine's private office design was as chic as its occupant, though there were as many stacks of file folders and books on the credenza, desk, and floor as Claudia had seen in every other attorney's office she had ever visited. She sat across from him, thankful that they were not in the conference room. She would be sweating over whether her mission to get a sample of his handwriting would succeed. The plan was loose and flexible, and the execution depended on how things progressed.

Blaine clasped his hands on his desk, giving her his full attention. "Tell me, Ms. Ellis, what can I do for you?"

The light blue eyes were sharp in a finely chiseled, clean-shaven face. Looking into them, Claudia imagined she could see behind them the ruthlessness of a man who would hire a killer to rid himself of his thieving partner, while at the same time sleeping with his partner's wife. None of that showed as she recited the lines she had rehearsed with Pete and Monica until they came naturally.

"I'm here on my father's behalf, Mr. Blaine. He's looking to have a will drawn up, or maybe a living trust; something that will help us avoid estate taxes. My mother passed on last year, so it's just my father and me."

Giving no indication that he suspected that anything was less than on the up-and-up, Blaine gave an easy nod. "That's what we specialize in. How did you happen to come to us?"

"A friend of mine told me she'd heard good things about you from a friend of hers, so, here I am."

"We're always grateful for referrals. If you could find out the name of the friend-of-a-friend, I'd love to send them a thank-you note."

Which was why she had put an extra person between them. A friend of a friend meant she didn't have to know the other person's name. "I'll find out and get back to you," she said.

"I'd appreciate it, thanks." Beckham Blaine switched to the subject at hand with a well-practiced smile. He had given this intro many times, and it showed. "Estate planning can get very complicated. It's not something people want to think about."

Claudia returned his smile, adding a dash of ruefulness to give it authenticity. "My father is getting older and he's not at all well. We don't have much choice. He'd prefer we avoid probate, so we want to make sure it's all done properly. I'll be the executrix."

"Of course. Let me begin by defining the differences between a will and a living trust."

"Oh, good. Um, would you mind writing down the key points for me? Dad won't trust me to remember everything."

He waved away the request. "I'll give you one of our brochures. It will tell you everything you need to know."

"Ah. Thank you," said Claudia with a sinking feeling. There went Plan A.

Beckham Blaine spent about ten minutes on his explanation while Claudia was on pins and needles over how she was going to get a handwriting sample out of him. From where she sat, the top page of the yellow legal pad on his desktop looked blank. He started asking about her father's supposed estate, and she was supplying the fictitious answers she and Pete had prepared when her phone dinged with a text message.

Right on time.

Apologizing, Claudia took her phone from her purse. "Would you excuse me? This might be about my father."

"No problem." Blaine was looking at his own phone while Claudia checked the text from Monica:

Need Plan B?

Claudia typed back:

ASAP.

She looked up at the attorney. "I'm so sorry about that. I'm always on call in case there's a problem. He's not feeling well today."

"Please don't worry about it." The perfunctory expression of sympathy failed to convince. "Now, where were we? Oh, yes. You said your father has a number of substantial investment accounts. Did you happen to bring the account numbers with—" The desk phone rang. Irritation flickered across his features.

"Now *I* have to apologize." He picked up the call. "Tina, you know I'm—what's that? You've got to be kidding. I'll be right out." He hung up with a sigh. "Ms. Ellis, would you mind excusing me? There's something I need to handle up front."

"No worries, Mr. Blaine. Please, take your time."

Claudia was up and out of her seat, rummaging through the trash can under his desk almost before the door had closed behind him. She stuffed one of several balled-up sheets of legal paper in her pocket, hoping it had what she needed.

The attorney's voice sounded in the hallway.

Claudia swung around to Beckham Blaine's surprised face—asking himself what she was doing on that side of his desk, no doubt.

"That's an amazing view you've got," she said, returning to her chair. "I just had to come back here and get a closer look. Is that okay?"

His eyes skimmed the desk as if checking to make sure there was nothing his prospective client should not have seen. He resumed his seat with a faint smile.

"Of course, it's fine. The view is the main reason I selected this office."

"Everything all right up front?" Claudia asked.

"Pardon me?" He looked puzzled, then his face cleared. "Oh, yes. An odd misunderstanding. A young woman was insisting on seeing someone I never heard of and who doesn't work for me. She was making enough of a fuss, threatening to barge in here, that my receptionist asked me to handle it. So, getting back to your—"

Claudia's phone rang. Putting a hint of annoyance into it, she heaved an exaggerated sigh. "I am so sorry, Mr. Blaine. Please, excuse me again."

Monica was giggling. "Did it work?"

"Yes, this is she. What happened?"

"See you on the corner."

Claudia bluffed listening, then groaned. "Thank you, I'm on my way." She slid the phone into her purse and rose. "Dad's being rushed to the hospital. I'll give you a call to reschedule once I know what's going on."

Blaine rose from his seat and came around the desk to show her to the door. "Do let me know if there's anything—"

"I will, thank you. We'll be in touch."

Monica's eyes were more alive than Claudia had seen them in a long time. She was practically jumping up and down with excitement. "That was so much fun. Maybe I'll go to work for a private detective."

Claudia chuckled. "You did a great job of getting him out of his office."

"I was afraid he wouldn't be gone long enough for you to find something. He pretty much shoved me out the front door. What did you get?"

"Something out of his trash; the best I could do in a hurry."

Pete pulled over in his rental. Riding shotgun, Claudia reached into her pocket for the paper. "I hope it's something comparable I can use."

Beckham Blaine had been making notes pertaining to the purchase of a Ferrari sports car.

Pete whistled. "That car is worth over two-hundred K. I bet he's planning on buying it with Mitch's money. His money, too, I guess, since Mitch was embezzling from the firm."

"The dealer's address is here. That gives me a direct comparison to the word 'Tucson,' which was on Geronimo's paper, and numbers." Claudia paged through the images on her phone, looking for the photos she had taken of the pages Tim and Robin had shared with them.

She could feel the grin spreading over her face. "He wrote it."

"WE CAN'T USE THIS," said Robin when they got to her office and told her what they had done. "You stole it out of his trash. What the hell were you thinking?"

Claudia's lips twitched. "What I was thinking was, if it was a match —and it is—you can compel him to produce a real exemplar. You'd need a local handwriting expert to do it, to avoid any appearance of conflict, as I'm sure his attorney would claim there was if I did it."

Robin let go of her pique. "I should have known you would have a plan. I'll call the county attorney and—" She broke off at a knock on the conference room door. Tim Brody poked his head around it.

"Sorry to crash the party, Rob, but you'll all want to hear this."

"Come on in."

In his plaid shirt and jeans with a big buckled belt and boots, Tim looked more cowboy than private investigator. Robin had told Claudia that she didn't care what he wore because he was very effective at his job. Besides, it was the local 'uniform.'

He entered the conference room and dropped into a chair. "I've been chattin' with someone I know at the crime lab. You'll be getting this in discovery anyway, Rob, but being as my friend owed me a favor, you're getting it early."

They all waited expectantly.

"That notebook the crime scene folks took out of Geronimo Lester's ride—it wasn't the only thing they found there."

Monica was the first to ask. "What else?"

Tim made room for a dramatic pause. When everyone's attention was on him, he announced, "The murder weapon."

The silence didn't last long. Pete jumped out of his chair. "Are you saying what I think you're saying?"

"That dumbshit's prints were there, right alongside Mitch Graham's blood. It was what the medical examiner said—a screw-driver, a goddamned big one. Geronimo is a big dude; bigger than Mitch was, which is in all likelihood why Blaine hired him. We knew he was stabbed several times. He was stabbed in the neck and the eye. That's what killed him."

Robin high-fived her investigator. "That's fantastic news. For us, not Mitch."

Claudia cringed at the thought of being stabbed in the eye. "It'll prove who the killer was; not who hired him. We can't let Blaine get away with it."

"If I can get the county attorney to dismiss the charges against Pete, which oughta be a cinch with what we now know, and I tell her about Beckham Blaine, her office will take over the investigation and his ass will be in a sling in a hot minute."

"So, their crime lab will get the exemplars and do the handwriting examination," said Claudia. "That sounds good to me. Who am I kidding? This whole thing sounds *fantastic.*"

Monica flung her arms around Pete, whose shoulders were shaking with emotion. Claudia grabbed both of them, hugging them tight until Pete decided he was being unmanly and gave her a gentle shove.

Claudia moved away with a huge smile. "Let's go celebrate. I'm buying."

42

As Robin Cross had predicted, the county attorney dismissed all charges against Pete.

"She was delighted to avoid the embarrassment of a major loss in court," the attorney informed them. Beckham Blaine was arrested afterwards and was refused bond as a flight risk. His big mistake had been hiring a druggie to put a hit on his partner. Robert 'Geronimo' Lester, upon learning of the evidence they had against Blaine, changed his mind and was willing to deal.

"Zola, the Graham's housekeeper, is out of a job," said Claudia to Joel. They were walking on the beach, enjoying the spring sunshine. "Robin's put her in touch with an immigration attorney who's going to help her get her legal status straightened out."

"And everyone lived happily ever after?" said Joel, making her pulse flutter with a deep kiss.

"*I'm* happy," said Claudia. "Pete's happy. Monica's getting there slowly. How about you, Columbo? Are you happy?"

"As long as you're with me, I'm as happy as Pavlov's dogs when the bell rings."

That made her laugh. "Are you saying I make you salivate?"

"Oh, yes, you do. How about we turn around and go home, and I'll show you salivate?"

"Sounds good to—"

Monica's ringtone cut off the rest of her sentence. Her niece still worried her, though Claudia sometimes thought it was her own response to all that had happened that was the problem. With an apprehensive glance at her husband, she answered the call.

"Hey, kiddo, what's up? Everything okay?"

"Everything's fine, Aunty C. I just wanted you to be the first to know. I'm going back to Egypt."

SHARE YOUR THOUGHTS

Did you enjoy *Dead Letters*? Please consider leaving a brief review on Goodreads, BookBub, Amazon or wherever you review books.

Get the latest on Claudia Rose and download "10 Things Handwriting Can Tell About Your Partner" when you sign-up for updates at sheilalowebooks.com.

facebook.com/SheilaLoweBooks
twitter.com/Sheila_Lowe
instagram.com/SheilaLoweBooks
bookbub.com/authors/sheila-lowe
goodreads.com/sheilalowe
linkedin.com/in/sheilalowe

THE CLAUDIA ROSE SERIES

FORENSIC HANDWRITING MYSTERIES

Read all the Claudia Rose Novels:

POISON PEN

WRITTEN IN BLOOD

DEAD WRITE

LAST WRITES

INKSLINGERS BALL

OUTSIDE THE LINES

WRITTEN OFF

DEAD LETTERS

BEYOND THE VEIL SERIES

#1 BESTSELLERS

WHAT SHE SAW: A PREQUEL (Book 1)

Imagine waking up on a train with no recollection of how you got there. You have no idea who you are--no name, no memories, no life. The only thing you know is, you cannot tell anyone, especially the police.

By chance or by fate, leaving the train in a beach town, this young woman runs into someone who knows her and gives her a ride home. There she finds two IDs, two sets of keys. One face, but two separate lives.

PROOF OF LIFE (Book 2)

Since recovering from amnesia five years ago, Jessica Mack has done her best to ignore the voices that plague her from the spirit world. But when FBI agent Zach Smith wants her to use her "gift" to find an abducted four-year-old, she is forced to listen. Time is running out as Jessica, and Sage Boles, a man with a mysterious past, are guided by the voices to a seance, where they hope to get clues to the child's whereabouts.

ABOUT THE AUTHOR

Photo by Kathy Cruts

Sheila Lowe writes stories of psychological suspense that put ordinary people into extraordinary circumstances. Like her fictional character Claudia Rose, Sheila is a certified forensic document examiner who testifies in court cases, and her analyses of handwritings are often seen in the media.

The books in Sheila's Forensic Handwriting series and her Beyond the Veil paranormal suspense series have all been #1 Amazon bestsellers. She also authored the internationally acclaimed *The Complete Idiot's Guide to Handwriting Analysis* and *Handwriting of the Famous & Infamous*. Additional non-fiction titles include *Reading Between the Lines, Advanced Studies in Handwriting Psychology, Personality & Anxiety Disorders, Succeeding in the Business of Handwriting Analysis,* and *Handwriting Analyzer* software used in law enforcement, governments, and business. Sheila has published with Capital Crimes, Penguin/Obsidian, Macmillan/Pearson Education, Suspense, and now Write Choice Ink.

Sheila holds a Master of Science degree in psychology. In addition to writing, Sheila teaches handwriting analysis to students around the world through her online course. She has also taught in the Crime Scene Investigation Certificate program at the University of California Riverside campus and has been a guest lecturer in the UC Santa

Barbara Discovery Program and at Ventura Community College. She has served as president of the American Handwriting Analysis Foundation for nearly a decade and is on the board of directors of the Scientific Association of Forensic Examiners. Sheila lives in Ventura, California.

Connect with her online at www.SheilaLoweBooks.com or linktr.ee/sheilaloweauthor. Sign-up for Sheila's occasional newsletter—she will never share your information.

- facebook.com/SheilaLoweBooks
- twitter.com/Sheila_Lowe
- instagram.com/SheilaLoweBooks
- bookbub.com/authors/sheila-lowe
- goodreads.com/sheilalowe
- linkedin.com/in/sheilalowe

CPSIA information can be obtained
at www.ICGtesting.com
Printed in the USA
FSHW022325150721
83271FS

9 781970 181159